PRAISE FOR REBEKAH CRANE

Postcards for a Songbird

"An earnest exploration of the demise of a family, this book captures the sense of disconnect a teen can feel when buffeted by changing winds . . . The characters are well-developed, complex, and intriguing. A finely crafted story of the healing that can happen when family secrets rise to the surface."

—*Kirkus Reviews*

"An enjoyable read. Wren's vulnerability and decision to no longer play it safe will engage readers."

—*School Library Journal*

The Infinite Pieces of Us

A *Seventeen* Best YA Book of 2018

"Crane has created an organic and dynamic friendship group. Esther's first-person narration, including her framing of existential questions as 'Complex Math Problems,' is honest and endearing. A compelling narrative about the power of friendship, faith, self-acceptance, and forgiveness."

—*Kirkus Reviews*

"Crane's latest is a breezy, voice-driven, and emotional read with a well-rounded cast of characters that walk that fine line between quirky and true to life . . . The novel stands out for its depiction of the American Southwest . . . Hand to fans of Jandy Nelson and Estelle Laure."

—*Booklist*

"[This] journey of self-discovery and new beginnings will resonate with readers seeking answers to life's big questions."

—*School Library Journal*

"*The Infinite Pieces of Us* tells a story of judgement, family, trust, identity, and new beginnings . . . a fresh take on teenage pregnancy . . . Crane creates relatable, diverse characters with varying socioeconomic backgrounds and sexualities that remind readers of the importance of getting to know people beyond the surface presentation."

—*VOYA*

The Upside of Falling Down

"[An] appealing love story that provides romantics with many swoon-worthy moments."

—*Publishers Weekly*

"Written with [an] unstoppable mix of sharp humor, detailed characters, and all-around charm, this story delivers a fresh and enticing take on first love—and one that will leave readers swooning."

—Jessica Park, author of *180 Seconds* and *Flat-Out Love*

"*The Upside of Falling Down* is a romantic new-adult celebration of all of the wild and amazing possibilities that open up when perfect plans go awry."

—*Foreword Magazine*

"Using the device of Clementine's amnesia, Crane explores themes of freedom and self-determination . . . Readers will respond to [Clementine's] testing of new waters. A light exploration of existential themes."

—*Kirkus Reviews*

"This quickly paced work will be enjoyed by teens interested in independence, love, self-discovery, and drama."

—*School Library Journal*

"First love, starting over, finding herself—the story is hopeful and romantic."

—*Denver Life*

The Odds of Loving Grover Cleveland

One of Bustle's Eight Best YA Books of December 2016

"Now that the title has captured our attention, I have even better news: No, this book isn't a history lesson about a president. Much more wonderfully, it centers on teenager Zander Osborne, who meets a boy named Grover Cleveland at a camp for at-risk youth. Together, the two and other kids who face bipolar disorder, anorexia, pathological lying, schizophrenia, and other obstacles use their group therapy sessions to break down and build themselves back up. And as Zander gets closer to Grover, she wonders if happiness is actually a possibility for her after all."

—Bustle

"The true beauty of Crane's book lies in the way she handles the ugly, painful details of real life, showing the glimmering humanity beneath the façades of even her most troubled characters . . . Crane shows, with enormous heart and wisdom, how even the unlikeliest of friendships can give us the strength we need to keep on fighting."

—RT Book Reviews

ONLY THE PRETTY LIES

ALSO BY REBEKAH CRANE

Postcards for a Songbird

The Infinite Pieces of Us

The Upside of Falling Down

The Odds of Loving Grover Cleveland

Aspen

Playing Nice

ONLY THE PRETTY LIES

REBEKAH CRANE

SKYSCAPE

▥ SKYSCAPE

Published by Skyscape, New York

www.apub.com

Amazon, the Amazon logo, and Skyscape are trademarks of Amazon.com, Inc., or its affiliates.

ISBN-13: 9781542019644 (hardcover)
ISBN-10: 1542019648 (hardcover)

ISBN-13: 9781542019668 (paperback)
ISBN-10: 1542019664 (paperback)

Cover design by Adil Dara

Cover illustration by Leah Goren

Printed in the United States of America

First edition

For Jason, who trusted me with this story.
And for Coco, who inspired it.

1

HOME

When my grandmother died, she left me a legacy. I never knew her, which has only increased her legendary status. A hippie, my mom calls her. A Woodstock-attending, protest-marching, Nixon-hating feminist who bucked the patriarchy and knew that the only way to live was raw and free. A woman who stood for something.

It's much easier to idolize the dead. The living constantly fail us. But in death, we remember a person as near perfect. Flaws are forgotten until one day, you're listening to Cat Stevens's "Peace Train," imagining a woman in bell-bottoms with flowers in her hair hanging out the side of a Volkswagen van with a "Make Love, Not War" bumper sticker, on her way out west, in search of herself. You're not sure if it's an image from a movie you once saw or a picture from an old photo album somewhere in your house. But does it even matter? All you know is that you like her.

My grandma's legacy is all around me—the house I live in, the café where I work, the crates of vinyl stacked in my room, filled with records alphabetized by band name, from America to ZZ Top.

Grandma is dead, but I've never known a time without her. She's always been here, like a birthmark.

"Use the records carefully," my mother, Rayne, said to me when I was younger.

Rayne would sit me down on the bed, slide a record out of its sleeve, and place it on the turntable gently. The collection is vinyl from the sixties and seventies, when rock stars weren't flashy, and jean shirts with bell-bottoms were the height of fashion. When all a person needed for the perfect album cover was a beat-up old truck in the middle of a field, or a couch sitting on the lawn in front of some abandoned house, to make the perfect statement. Slowly my mother would lower the needle. "If you scratch the record, it'll skip, and then it's ruined. Always be gentle, Amoris."

To Rayne, they weren't just records. They were the soundtrack of her memories. Of her life with a mother she could no longer see in the flesh. We'd sit on my bed, and she'd tell me story after story. How her mom hitchhiked from Michigan to Florida for spring break one year when she was in college. How she made her own clothes and refused to wear a bra. How she smoked weed out of her father's tobacco pipe and inadvertently helped his glaucoma. How she traveled all over the United States, living out of a van, in search of "home"—a place where the cosmic energy was just right, the scenery was awe inspiring, and the human connection was potent. That's how she found Alder Creek.

"She may have had a short life, but my mom knew what was important, and she didn't stop until she found it," Rayne told me, more than once.

Once Grandma found her utopia, she borrowed all the money her parents could afford and opened the very first coffee shop in Alder Creek. I work in that café now, though Rayne sold the business to a woman named Marnie after her mom died. Rayne isn't one for baking scones and making lattes. She knew Grandma would want the café passed on to the right hands, and Rayne's hands were built for other purposes.

Rayne is well known around our town for working magic. She is a bodyworker, a healer, a true kind of witch, before men took control of the word and made it ugly. A witch with long brown hair streaked with gray, and strong pale hands, and eyes the color of twilight, a mix of dark blue and brown. Rayne has an energy about her—a knowing that some people are just born with. People want to be around her, in her presence, because her energy simply makes them feel better. That's why I've never minded when she holds me captive in my room, playing vinyl and telling me stories. I watch her and imagine her as a child, sitting with her mom as she passed along her wisdom. If my grandma created Rayne, I would let Rayne mold me. Give her clay, and she'll sculpt something beautiful with her magical hands. Plus, I love the music.

I was five years old when my parents gave me my first guitar. My dad, Christopher Westmore, found it at a garage sale. It was small, perfect for a child. He placed it in my hands and said, "I got it for free 'cause it's so beat up. But I think there's still life in it. See if you can find it, Amoris."

I had that guitar tuned, shined, and singing within days. I taught myself how to play listening to the Beatles, Nina Simone, Simon and Garfunkel, Bob Dylan. With each note and each chord, I felt like I was learning the soundtrack of my life, becoming who I was meant to be.

When I turned twelve, Chris bought me a Martin D-28. "An upgrade," he called it, though the guitar was used, the wood worn down in places where players had plucked and strummed. By then, I could play, to some degree, nearly every album of my grandma's—within reason, I'm no Jimi Hendrix or B. B. King.

"Maybe it's time you start writing your own music," Chris offered.

Easy for him to say, he's an artist. He creates for a living. Chris surrounds himself with chaos and wild ideas. He doesn't mind a mess, which his art studio confirms. Somehow he sifts through it all until a concrete painting emerges. But the idea of writing music petrified me. Whatever song I wrote, whatever notes and chords and riffs I put together, could never equal the genius of the albums I'd grown to love, and to play. My own ideas and thoughts were incoherent most days, so far from brilliant they verged on ridiculous. Embarrassing, really. No, it was much easier to play someone else's genius. There's beauty in imitation, and every once in a while, a cover song can even rival the original.

That was my life—a cover song. It still is. But I'm OK with that. Better than OK. I prefer it. Aren't we all cover songs, in a way? I was sculpted from Rayne, who was sculpted from her mom. Breaking from that tradition sounds lonely. Imitation may lack in creative genius, but it's a lot more inclusive. And let's be honest, I'm no John Lennon. Who would want to be? Murdered at forty, shot by a lunatic? I'll take the safety of another person's genius over the danger of creating something my own. Plus, I like my life as it is. It's a good life. It would take a lot of convincing to give that up for the uncertainty of a pencil in my hand and a blank piece of paper.

~

Alder Creek is busy today. Cars with out-of-state license plates, mostly from Texas and California, line the streets of our quaint downtown. People are in a hurry to grab the last Zen of the summer in our mountain oasis. But despite the crowd, a week's worth of my tension eases as we approach the two gray-and-white duplexes of the only home I've ever known. Its overgrown garden, creaky screen door, chipped paint, and basketball hoop with a net hanging on by a thread—it might not sound idyllic, but trust me, it is. I can practically smell the palo santo burning in Rayne's bedroom, cleansing the air of any bad energy that might have seeped in through the cracks. My trip to New York was only a week long, but I'm desperate to get out of this car and run up to my bedroom, or sit under twinkle lights in the Zen fairy garden in the backyard.

My grandmother nicknamed our house Shangri-La when she bought it. Back in 1975, Alder Creek wasn't much of a tourist destination, more a hideaway from traditional society—a place where counterculture thrived.

Shangri-La comes into view. Mr. and Mrs. Hillsborough pull into the driveway, and I thank them for taking me along on their trip. For buying my plane ticket. For the Manhattan dinners and lunches and sightseeing that must have cost them a small fortune. All so I could properly say goodbye to my boyfriend, Zach, their son, who's now officially a freshman at Columbia University.

"Don't be a stranger," Mr. Hillsborough says as he brings the car to a stop.

"I won't."

Mrs. Hillsborough reaches back and places her hand on my shoulder. "Thank you," she says, catching me off guard.

"For what?"

"For being so good to our Zach. He cares about you a lot."

I smile, but I hate to admit that it feels forced. I blame fatigue brought on by unfamiliar travel. "He makes it easy to be good."

At that, I scoot out of the back seat. I don't want to be too hasty, but I'm exhausted, and the smell of Rayne's pecan pie is wafting out of the kitchen window, making my mouth water and my heart melt. It's her mom's recipe. Rayne may not be a natural baker, but she can make a mean pecan pie. It must be a homecoming surprise. I didn't think I could love my mom any more, but at this moment, I do.

Zach's mom rolls down the window of their Volvo. "Think about Thanksgiving, Amoris. I know Zach will be anxious to see you. And don't be put off by the expense. Our treat." She winks at me, her light sandy-brown hair the same color as her son's. I can't think about Thanksgiving. School hasn't even started. It's eighty degrees and the leaves on the trees are still green. I give the Hillsboroughs a nod and a smile, and they finally pull away.

After a busy week in New York City, followed by a long flight home, I've never been happier to see Shangri-La. The light is on in my dad's art studio next door, the hum of music vibrating out the open windows. After her mom died, Rayne built a matching house right next to Shangri-La, with an art studio for Chris on the first floor and a rental apartment on the second. I contemplate knocking on the studio door, but the pecan pie is too tempting. My dad isn't very social when he's deep in his art anyway. That's why Rayne built the second house, that and the income they get from the apartment. I can see Chris later, when the weed has worn off.

When I walk in the door of Shangri-La, Rayne stands at the kitchen sink, washing dishes. Her long salt-and-pepper hair is pulled into a loose braid down her back. I've always envied her straight, manageable hair. The less I touch my curly hair, the better.

My mom turns, slinging the dish towel over her shoulder.

"So. Did you see the Statue of Liberty?" she asks.

"Check."

"Go to the top of the Empire State Building?"

"Check."

"The Met?"

"They had a Matisse exhibit that was amazing. I brought Dad a pamphlet."

"He'll be jealous." I can tell she wants to ask me about the most important part of the trip, but she pauses, leaning back on the sink. "Did you . . ."

"Brought a daisy and everything. Just like you said. Laid it right on the ground next to the memorial. Zach took a picture on my phone." I show Rayne, and her eyes fill with tears.

"Grandma would have loved that."

My usually lenient, carefree mom had one very specific condition when she agreed to let me accompany my longtime boyfriend and his family on a trip to New York City. I had to visit Strawberry Fields, Central Park's circular memorial to John Lennon, and put a daisy right next to the word IMAGINE in the center.

Rayne hugs me, her familiar earthy scent mixing with the smell of pecan pie. I feel overwhelming relief at being home.

"Do you want to move to New York City now?" she asks.

"Never," I say.

"Never say never," Rayne chides.

"I think it's safe to say never in this case. It's a cool city, but it's not for me. Every day seems to be garbage day there."

"And how is Zach?"

"Nervous, mostly."

"That's to be expected," Rayne says. "And how are you?"

"Exhausted."

Rayne examines me, gently caressing my long, curly blond hair, a trait I can thank Chris for. My brother, River, has Rayne's straight hair. All he has to do is wash and go, whereas I have to use special products to give my hair the finished look I want. "Is that all? You know you can talk to me. This must have been a tough week."

For a moment, I have no idea what she's referring to. And then it hits me. I just left the only boyfriend I've ever had on the other side of the country. I should be devastated. A pile of tears. Heartbroken, missing him already. But all I really want is my bed and my guitar and my records. I attempt to muster some sadness, but only find guilt. I'm happy to be home, not devastated. What does that say about me?

"Yeah . . . goodbyes are hard," I say. "But we have plans to FaceTime later. And I was already texting him when we landed so . . . it's not too bad."

Rayne touches my cheek. "Thank goodness for modern technology."

The oven timer rings. Rayne pulls out the pie and sets it on the counter to cool.

"You know, you didn't have to do that," I say, eyeing my favorite dessert and knowing that Rayne only bakes when pressured. "I'm fine, really. Zach and I will figure it out. It's all good. Not that I'm complaining you made a pie for me."

Rayne pivots toward me, looking guilty.

"Oh . . ." I say, feeling slightly stupid. "The pie's not for me."

"You know the pie is always for you, sweetheart."

"But . . ."

Rayne takes off her oven mitts and clasps her hands in front of her. "I have a surprise for you," she says. "We have new tenants moving into the apartment next door, and I think you're going to be happy about these ones."

"Let me guess. Deadheads? Crystal healers? Gypsies?"

Rayne holds her finger up. "My favorite healing blogger just wrote an article about the word 'gypsy.' We shouldn't use it. The correct term is 'Roma people.'"

"Stick to the topic, Mom," I state. "Not Grandma and Grandpa Westmore."

"No. You know they don't like coming this far west. But you're getting closer."

My brain isn't firing through the exhaustion. I have no idea who Rayne could be talking about. Who would be worthy of an afternoon of baking indoors when Rayne could be spending this sunny day in the garden, giving the flowers pep talks or coaching the growing vegetables?

"I give up," I say.

Rayne examines me from across the room. "I can't believe in a year from now, you'll be graduated. Off to new adventures."

She's delaying. Rayne knows damn well I'm bound for the local community college. I have no desire to leave Alder Creek.

"Who is it?"

Rayne crosses the kitchen and spins me around, her hands massaging my back, kneading into the knots that have formed. "You're so tense, Amoris. Are you sure New York was OK?"

Sometimes it's a disadvantage to have a bodyworker for a mom. I swear she can read my emotions simply by touching me.

"It was fine. Long flight. Dirty city."

Rayne continues kneading my back like it's bread, pressing and rubbing until a bit of the tension is gone.

"That's better," she says. "A bath with some Epsom salt and you'll be all relaxed."

"A bath does sound kind of dreamy," I say.

"Put some rose oil in it."

"Anything else?"

"And wash your hair."

I snap out of her magical massage trance. Rayne still hasn't answered my question. "Mom, who is moving in next door?"

She pulls plates from the cupboard, six in total. We're a family of four.

"Kaydene and Jamison should be here in about an hour," she says.

"Jamison." That name hasn't crossed my lips in years. Saying it now feels almost foreign. My back and shoulders tense up worse than before.

"Don't forget about Kaydene. She'll be living there, too."

"In *our* rental apartment."

"That's the one," Rayne says with enthusiasm, buzzing around the kitchen now. I don't move. My words are gone. "You used to *beg* to live next door to Jamison when you were little. You two were so cute."

The entire flight back from New York, I was looking forward to home. Going to work tomorrow at the café. Seeing my friends. Sleeping in my comfortable bed. Holding my guitar. Being back where I belong. In New York City, you can barely see the sky between all the buildings. Night and day mesh together in a blur of artificial light. In Alder Creek, we're illuminated by a blanket of stars almost every night.

But I haven't come home to the same place.

"How about that bath?" Rayne says, patting me on the butt.

I drag myself to the bathroom. But as I sit on the edge of the tub, waiting for it to fill, adding Epsom salt and rose oil, my shoulders are tense again, and I know that the bath won't help. I wish it was that easy.

Last night as Zach and I sat in his dorm room, searching for the right words for whatever comes next between us, I didn't think my life could get any more complicated. But all that mess was supposed to disappear when I got home. My life fits together when I'm in Alder Creek. Nothing feels irreparable. But I wasn't expecting this. I wasn't expecting . . . Jamison Rush.

I submerge myself in the bath as a deluge of memories washes over me. But I better not linger.

The Rushes will be here in an hour.

2

LET IT BE

More than one hundred bottles line the walls of Rayne's massage studio, which is at the back of our house and has a separate entrance for clients. Each is filled with a scent—wet leaves, tulips, Christmas cookies, thunderstorms, motor oil, report cards, spaghetti . . .

Rayne has spent years developing the smells, mixing essential oils and other fragrances to re-create them perfectly. It's a system she's developed over time. When a client comes for a session, she has them pick a scent off the wall.

"A memory in or a memory out," she says. "Whatever they need."

To Rayne, humans are living scrapbooks. Memories are coded in our skin and fascia and muscles. Even memories we don't remember. Ancient memories. And the best way to access and heal them is through the nose.

I understand the theory. I can't smell pencil shavings without thinking of my friend Sam, feverishly drawing, trying to catch a moment in his sketchbook before it's gone. His boyfriend, Tucker, is Aspercreme. His muscles are always sore from playing sports, and he uses at least a tube a week. Sometimes I think Tucker just likes the tingling sensation.

Zach is laundry detergent. I can't walk past our mudroom and not remember our first kiss.

My best friend, Ellis, is lavender.

I can find all of these scents on Rayne's wall, even the pencil shavings, though it took her awhile to get that one perfect. Some days, I'll go into her studio and open specific bottles, just to live in my memories, because it feels good.

Jamison Rush doesn't have a smell. His scent would be impossible to capture. What he is to me isn't easily replicated and bottled.

After the bath, I still haven't found my words. Even as Jamison sits before me at the dinner table, almost three years to the day since I last saw him.

My brother, River, smells like a sweaty locker room. His football stench is all over the house. It's completely unsavory. He is the reason my dinner sits practically untouched. Not because Jamison is sitting directly across from me.

River eats and smacks his lips as he talks. He's gotten more Neanderthal now that he's the starting quarterback on the varsity football team. He's the only sophomore on varsity, a fact he relishes like an Olympic gold medal.

"What about football?" River says. "You play?"

Jamison shakes his head. "Not really my thing."

I could have told River that.

My brother sits back, shaking his unkempt brown hair from his face. It's unfair he got Rayne's hair and I didn't. Neither of us has her eyes, though. We are squarely Chris's when it comes to our round faces and brown eyes.

"Basketball?" River asks.

"Nah." Jamison's attention is solely on his plate of food. He isn't eating much either.

"What sports *do* you play?" my brother asks. It's like he doesn't know Jamison at all. Like we didn't spend thirteen summers at his house in Kansas City, running through sprinklers and chasing each other with water balloons.

"I'm not here to play sports," Jamison says.

"But you're huge." River shovels in another mouthful of food. "You'd be a great running back."

"Is that defense or offense?" Jamison asks, goading River.

"You're fucking with me, right?"

"River." Rayne coughs his name. Rayne and Chris aren't sticklers for language most of the time, believing that if you forbid something, it only makes kids want it more. But my brother has been taking advantage of that more and more lately.

River asks, "Why *are* you here? We haven't seen you in like . . . three years."

The room goes silent.

"Just because we don't see people in person doesn't mean we're not strongly connected," Rayne says. I swear she glances at me for a microsecond.

Jamison's mom, Kaydene, offers a more concrete answer.

"We're here because of the creative writing program at Western University," Kaydene says. She goes on to explain the difference between in-state and out-of-state tuition at Western. Missouri is squarely out of state.

"So you're playing the system," River says.

"I like to think we're giving Jamison the best shot at acquiring his dream," Kaydene says.

"But why here?" River asks. "Alder Creek is so . . . boring. Why not move to a bigger city like Denver or Boulder?"

"River, are you aware how much it costs to live in a city like that?" Rayne asks.

"It's true," Kaydene says. "The rental price here was too good to turn down." She smiles at Rayne. Based on their body language, I'm guessing the Rushes aren't paying rent. Rayne wouldn't do that to friends, especially ones saving for college. We don't live on the income from the rental property. It's just a nice bonus when Chris's art isn't selling well. "Your mom can be pretty convincing when she wants to be. I was also a little worried I'd drive Jamison crazy, the two of us shoved into a tiny rental in the city. Out here, there's more space. And with you all next door, hopefully we won't kill each other."

"So you're staying the whole school year?" River asks.

"That's the plan," Kaydene confirms.

"Shit." River turns to Jamison. "But it's your *senior* year. That's like . . . the best year. Why would you want to leave your school in Kansas City?"

"There's more to life than high school," Jamison says.

"It doesn't feel that way. You must really want to go to that college."

"I do," Jamison says.

"Seriously, dude, you should try out for the football team. If you're spending a year in this hellhole, you might as well hang out with the right people."

At that, I can't help but laugh. Jamison and I look at each other quickly, but I immediately focus back on my plate. Not only is the idea of River knowing the "right people" outrageous, but Jamison would hate hanging around a bunch of jocks. He's a book nerd. Always has been.

But River is right about one thing. Jamison has gotten bigger. Not fat. Taller and broad. He has a similar build to River, a total gym rat who should spend more time showering and less time weightlifting. Unlike Chris, River is tall, well over six feet, a trait he got from Rayne's side of the family. If I put them back to back, River and Jamison would almost be the same height. But that's where the similarities end. River is pale white with brown hair. Jamison is dark brown, his near-black hair buzzed clean. Neat. His hair has always been that way. When we were younger, I used to run my hand over his head, feeling the tight curls, so different from my own long blond frizz. My hair drove me crazy, falling in my face all the time. One time when we were six, I told Jamison I wanted a hairstyle like his, short and buzzed. He offered to cut it for me.

"Trust me. I've seen the barber do it a million times," he said, scissors in hand. "We can be twins."

"Jay, I'm a girl."

"So? We *were* born on the same exact day at the same exact time. And boys and girls can be twins. It happens."

I loved the idea of being related to Jamison. It's all I wanted—to live in the same house, share the same room, be together all the time. Twins sounded like a great idea. His home felt like my home after all.

Rayne and Kaydene found us in the Rushes' bathroom, my hair covering the floor, Jamison snipping his way around my head. Luckily, he hadn't gotten to the clippers yet. I'll never forget the horror on Kaydene's face.

"What the hell are you doing?" she screamed, surveying the blond tufts scattered all around us. "Have you lost your mind?"

Jamison stepped in front of me, like a shield. "It was my idea."

"Leave each other's hair alone," Kaydene said. "Got it?"

"Yes, ma'am," Jamison said in a small voice. Kaydene made Jamison use the birthday money he'd saved for an entire year to pay for a proper haircut for me, but that night, when we were supposed to be sleeping, I heard Kaydene and Rayne howling with laughter over it.

"Did you hear what they said?" Kaydene giggled. "They wanted to be twins. Twins! Those sweet babies . . ."

"The beauty of being young," Rayne said.

"I fear the day they realize how different they really are," Kaydene said.

"Maybe it won't happen, Kay. Maybe the world will change for them."

"Oh," Kaydene said. "It'll happen. It always happens."

Without realizing it, I've gotten lost in the past again, twisting a long strand of my hair around my finger. When Jamison catches me staring, he looks at my finger in my curls, and for just a second, I wonder if he's thinking of the same memory I am. His brown eyes settle on mine, so familiar, before I tear my gaze away, drop my hair, and poke at the peas on my plate.

The mind is the worst kind of a tease, playing with memories at will.

"What I really need is an after-school job," Jamison says.

"Amoris works at my mom's old café," Rayne says. "I'm sure Marnie, the woman who owns it now, would be happy to give you a job. Amoris could introduce you to her. Couldn't you, Amoris?"

I don't make eye contact again. "Sure."

"Great," Kaydene says.

"Amoris, why don't you take Jamison with you tomorrow?" Rayne presses. "Aren't you going shopping with your friends? I bet Ellis will be glad to see him." *Thanks, Mom.* Like I need reminding. "You could introduce him around, so he knows some people on the first day. I bet he and Sam would get along great."

"I'm working tomorrow," I say quickly.

"That's OK," Jamison says at almost the exact same time. "Shopping's not my thing."

Rayne and Kaydene exchange confused glances.

"Who wants dessert? We have pecan pie!" Chris offers. Chris is rarely punctual, but when he is, it's magic. "It's a beautiful night to sit on the deck. The stars should be out in full effect."

"I'll pass on dessert," I say, standing from the table, plate in hand.

"But it's pecan pie," Chris says. "It's your favorite." One moment my dad saves me, the next he tosses me back out to sea.

"I'm on East Coast time. I'm tired."

"Before you race off to bed," Rayne says, holding her plate out for me, "the dishes need to be cleared and loaded into the dishwasher."

"Jamison will help," Kaydene says. "Don't worry, Jay. I'll save you some pie."

"Yes, ma'am," Jamison says, pushing back from the table.

"I'm out," River says, bounding out of his chair, phone already in hand. "Coach wants us watching our carb intake this close to the start of the season."

"Why doesn't River have to do dishes?" I ask like a petulant child, my tone annoying even to me.

"He did them while you were gone for a week," Rayne says.

And just like that, Jamison and I are alone in the kitchen. He clears the table, stacking plates before setting them down on the counter next to me.

"You rinse. I'll load," he says. My measly five-foot-three frame feels small next to him.

Kaydene was right. At some point, we realized we could never be twins.

You rinse. I'll load. His first words to me in three years, and it's a command. I want to push back and say, *No, I'll load, and you rinse.* But I don't.

"Sounds good," I say.

I scrub the first plate and set it down on the counter in front of him.

"You were in New York," Jamison says.

I nod, not adding anything because it wasn't a question.

"You still dating Mack?"

"Zach," I say.

"Right. Zach." Jamison and I haven't kept up, but Kaydene and Rayne have had a regular calling cadence for years. They sit on the phone for hours, talking about who knows what, but every time Rayne hangs up, it's as if she's lighter. I suspect it's the same for Kaydene. That's what good friendship is, I suppose—a place to unload the clutter of the mind.

I stack another plate, and immediately Jamison loads it into the dishwasher.

"So . . ." he says.

"So . . ."

"You're into shopping now."

"I didn't say I was into shopping."

"Rayne said you're going shopping tomorrow."

"That doesn't mean I like it," I say. "It's Ellis's idea."

"Ellis . . ." His tone doesn't give away any emotion, but I can fill in the blanks well enough. I shouldn't have mentioned her name.

"I'm sure you're tired from the long drive," I say. "Go unpack or whatever."

"It's fine. I was given a job to do, and I'll stay till it's done."

His responsible answer is infuriating. Jamison has always been focused and goal oriented, which explains his sudden appearance in Alder Creek. If he wants to get into the creative writing program at Western, he'll sacrifice what he has to. Whereas I move with emotion, like the wind, deciding daily which way to go depending on how stubborn I feel. Tonight, I feel moody and stagnant.

"I don't need your help with this," I say.

"Who said anything about help," Jamison states. He arranges the glasses in a tidy fashion in the dishwasher. "I'm following an order."

"Well, I relieve you of your duty. I can do the dishes on my own."

I go back to rinsing and stacking. Jamison sets down the glass in his hand. "Amoris, it's been three years . . ."

One of the biggest fallacies about life is this: Most people think that by telling the truth, their lives can go back to the way they were. But that's a lie. What was can never be again. The truth creates a whole new reality. And until someone is ready to confront the truth, it's better to just keep your mouth shut.

Even now, Jamison smells the same. Like skin warmed by sunshine. Like wet clothes hung out to dry. Like fresh summer air. Like playing hide-and-seek and sleeping in a tent in the backyard. Like lightning bugs and mosquitoes.

He loads the rest of the plates, checking the sink for any remaining dishes before walking out of the kitchen without another word. But his smell remains, etched in my skin.

~

"Did you hate New York? Tell me you hated New York," my dad says, joint between his fingers. Chris Westmore is a pothead. He says weed is the only way he can stand this planet.

"I hated New York." Hate's not really the right word, but it's the one my dad wants to hear, so it's good enough. My dad doesn't like "the East Coasters." They remind him too much of his parents.

He takes a pull of the joint. "Too many phonies."

"OK, Holden Caulfield."

"He had a point, you know. People will feed you a lot of bullshit, Amoris, but don't eat it. You know why?" A coarseness sometimes outlines Chris's voice, but it isn't there tonight. The weed must have kicked in.

"Why?"

"Because it's shit."

I can't help but laugh.

We stand on the second-floor bridge that connects Shangri-La and the house next door. It was Rayne's idea when they built the second house. A connector. So even when Chris is in his studio, he's always joined to us. My dad turns his face up toward the sky and exhales a long stream of smoke.

"Which one do you think I'm from?" He points skyward, joint nestled between his fingers. Chris has always contended that he's an alien. Most of the time he just doesn't get humans. That's why he paints—to find the beauty of us.

"Don't distract from the subject at hand," I say. "Start explaining, Dad."

"There's nothing to explain. You heard Kay. Jamison wants to go to Western University next year. Apparently, they have one of the best creative writing programs in the country. It's hard to get into, but they think he's got a real shot. The only way they can afford it is to get in-state tuition. And the only way to do that is to live in state. Rayne insisted they live here. So here they are. You know how expensive college is. If you want someone to blame for this, blame capitalism."

"I don't want to blame anyone. I just feel . . . blindsided. Why didn't you tell me? You must have known they were coming for a while."

"Actually, it all happened last week. Originally, when Rayne proposed the idea to Kaydene a few months ago, Jamison didn't want to come, but at the last minute, he changed his mind. Did you really want me to call you while you were bashing around New York with your boyfriend?"

"I just can't get over that it happened so quickly."

"Well, honey, I hate to break it to you, but all it takes is a week for life to change." Chris pats my back.

"Thanks, Dad. Real sympathetic."

He chuckles. "You gotta sway with it, Amoris. Don't be so rigid." He grabs my arms and gently shakes my body. "You know what your mom would say."

"Holding on tight only leads to more tightness."

"Exactly," Chris says.

"What about Victor and Talia?" I ask. Jamison's dad and sister. "Where are they?"

"They're staying in Kansas City," Chris says. "Victor can't leave his teaching job. He's got seniority and a pension. It's too hard to start over at another school. And Talia's only a sophomore. She didn't want to leave. Kaydene got a teaching job at one of those online schools, so she can work from anywhere."

Chris exhales the last hit of his joint before turning to face me.

"I'm feeling the Beatles tonight," he says. "What do you think?"

"Smooth change of subject, Dad."

"I'm not known for my social graces. You know that."

"Any specific album?"

"How about . . . *Let It Be.* I love that one." Then Chris Westmore looks at me with stars in his eyes. Some days, I think he might truly be an alien. "Let's create something together, shall we?"

Chris didn't always live next door in his art studio. He used to share a bedroom with Rayne, and make pancakes on Saturday mornings. Not that I'm complaining. I don't even like pancakes much anymore. Slowly over the years, Chris moved into his studio. Piece by piece so no one would notice. Rayne would find things missing. A coffee cup. A blanket. Shampoo. A fork. A plate. When she found them next door, instead of bringing them home, she left them there. Maybe she wanted to see if Chris would come back on his own. But he didn't. He just kept collecting. A chair. An air mattress. His bathrobe. Until one day he was gone from our house. Rayne told me to not take it personally.

"You've listened to enough of Grandma's music to know your dad's a rolling stone," she said. "Stop him and you'll end up crushed."

At these moments, it doesn't matter. It doesn't matter that my dad's a pothead who can't stay in one place for more than three months without verging on insanity, who looks at the sky to find his home when one is waiting for him right next door.

Back in my room, I sit by the open window, guitar in hand. The light is on in his studio, window open. Tonight, music will flow out my second-floor window and fall downward into his, filling his room while he works.

I play as the night turns extra dark, the lights around Alder Creek turning off one by one, the town quieting, until my dad's lights and mine seem to be the only two left.

When my fingers hurt and my arms are tired, I set my guitar to the side. I check my phone. It's after eleven. I'll pay for the late night tomorrow at work, but I've missed my guitar. I found myself playing chords on subway seats and restaurant tables and benches in Central Park last week.

Zach sent me a text a few hours ago.

The city seems to know you've left. It's quieter tonight. FaceTime?

He's one of those utterly annoying people who writes in complete sentences and uses correct punctuation in every text.

"It's the principle of it," he told me once. "If I cut corners with my text messages, I'll start cutting corners in my life."

It's past one in the morning on the East Coast. I don't want to wake Zach up by messaging him back. I'll respond tomorrow.

I'm ready to call goodnight to Chris when I see Jamison standing on the second-floor bridge. He turns from looking at the stars to looking directly at my window.

I quickly turn off the light, painting myself against the wall so Jamison can't see me, my phone clutched to my chest. I text Zach, forgetting that a moment earlier I decided not to.

Miss you.

It's a bullshit text, but it makes me feel steadier. When I look to find Jamison again, he's gone.

3

CRIME AND PUNISHMENT

Namaste, bitches!" Ellis Osmond shouts as she and Sam Pennington walk through the door of Get Sconed Café. It's Saturday afternoon, and the postyoga rush is finally dying down. In some towns, people get together at church on Sunday, followed by barbecues and football games. In Alder Creek, people flock to Jenna Finnigan's Saturday morning vinyasa yoga class. Religiously. They cram into her studio, mat to mat, the smell of incense permeating the room, the collective *om* ringing out through the open windows in summer. People leave blissed out and in desperate need of coffee. Most come to the café for their caffeine fix.

Ellis cuts the line at the register and grabs my hands. "Oh my God, Amoris, we missed you. Never leave again. At least, not without me. This town is dismal without you."

"You're such a drama queen, Elle." Sam apologizes to the customers in line for cutting, then turns to me. "Not to say we didn't totally miss you, Amoris. We did." He leans on the counter and smiles. "So . . . tell us everything. Is New York as fabulous as Carrie, Samantha, Miranda, and Charlotte make it out to be?"

Sam likes to binge old TV series. He's obviously started on *Sex and the City*.

"Who would I be?" Ellis asks. "Please say Carrie."

"You wish, Samantha."

Ellis balks. "Whatever, Miranda."

"How could you?" Sam says, aghast. "I'm totally Charlotte."

"While this conversation is existential and life changing on many levels, can we talk about this later?" I ask. "I've got customers."

"Whatever, you practically own this place," Ellis says. "They can wait."

"No, I don't own it. And no, they can't wait," I say.

Ellis dramatically rolls her eyes. "We can argue about this in the car. Come on, let's go." She tugs on my T-shirt.

I didn't text her this morning because I knew she'd try to convince me to ditch work, but Ellis can see the truth on my face right now, and she's not happy about my decision. "No, Amoris. You can't bail on us."

"I told Marnie I'd pick up a shift this afternoon. Eddie called in sick. You know how busy the town is right now. I couldn't leave her hanging." I attempt to sound disappointed.

"Fast Eddie isn't sick," Ellis scoffs. "He's too stoned to come to work."

That's probably true. Ellis's nickname is an oxymoron. Eddie has never done anything fast. He's too high all the time.

"You know what I'd do?" she asks.

Sam chimes in. "Murder?"

"Too messy," Ellis says. "You know I hate cleaning up. That's what our housekeeper is for."

"Snob much?" Sam says sarcastically. "Do you even know her name?"

"Of course I do. It's Lucía. And I'm just stating a fact. It's her job to clean, just like it's Amoris's job to make coffee. And my dad pays Lucía well. Better than most people in this town pay their cleaning people."

Ellis turns back to me. "You're just enabling Fast Eddie, Amoris. You've covered for him, like, a million times this summer. And he's an adult. Like an old adult."

"He's only forty-five," I say.

"Don't get me started on the fact that a forty-five-year-old, grown-ass man works at a coffee shop," Ellis states. "He needs a real job."

"He also works at the dispensary," I offer.

"Fast Eddie is *really* going places," she jokes.

"I haven't covered for him *that* much."

"Yes, you have. But when has he ever covered for you?" Ellis waits for my answer, and when I give her none, she knows she's won on some level. "My point exactly. Screw Fast Eddie. You're too nice. I'd make Marnie fire him. Why should you suffer because he's incompetent? He's taking advantage of you."

It's true that Eddie loves weed. It's also true that he calls in "sick" more that he should. But Eddie's the longest employee to have ever worked at the café. He was the last person my grandma hired before she died. He knew her. He tells stories of what the café was like back then. I would never want him fired. He's been working here for as long as I've been alive. If I lost him, it would feel like losing a piece of my grandma.

"I'm sorry, Ellis."

"Sorry isn't good enough, Amoris. You promised."

"I'll make it up to you," I say. "Whatever you want."

Ellis perks up. "Whatever I want?"

I probably shouldn't have said that, but it's out there now.

"Fine," she says. "I forgive you. But you owe me."

Before I can put any parameters on my impending payment, a middle-aged customer chimes in behind Ellis. "Excuse me, but you're really holding up the line."

"I'm not done placing my order," she says.

"But you cut in front of all of us," the man says.

Ellis turns on him, her dark-brown hair whipping around and cascading over her shoulder. "You know, caffeine shrinks your balls. You might want to think about that before you order another latte."

The man appears completely confused. "What?"

A woman behind him groans. I can feel the customers' eyes pressed on me.

"Either come with us now, or suffer the consequence," Ellis says to me.

I'm not going to win this battle. "Suffer the consequence," I say. "Now move out of the way so people can order."

Ellis steps aside then. "See you tonight at Sam's," she says. "And tell Fast Eddie to get his life together. He's ruining mine." She turns to leave. Death stares follow her out. Ellis ignores them all. Sam lingers at the counter, watching me.

"What?" I ask. "Not you, too. I said I'm sorry."

"You don't owe me anything," Sam says. "I love that you protect Eddie." But he's still glaring at me like he's got a secret he's dying to tell me. Or maybe he thinks I have a secret that I'm desperate to tell him. Either way, it's not the look I like to see on Sam. He's too perceptive. "You're acting . . . different."

Some days I hate that he's an artist, like Chris—an alien, analyzing human specimens.

"Did anything happen in New York?" he asks. "You didn't break up with Zach, did you?"

"No." I state the truth, but a lie is quick to follow. "Nothing's happened."

Sam doesn't press me. It's one of the things I love best about him. He knows when to accelerate and when to hit the brakes. Ellis, on the other hand, drives however she damn well pleases.

"Well," Sam says, "I can't wait to hear all about New York, *Carrie.*"

I shove my hands into my pockets. "Carrie would never wear dirty overalls."

"Yes, she would," Sam says. "And she wouldn't care what people thought about it."

~

At the end of my shift, I head straight to Black and Read Records and Books. The listening booth at the back of the store has been a therapist to me since I was little. Designed like a British phone booth—tall and red, but slightly wider to accommodate a bench and a turntable—the listening booth is completely soundproof. Anything you say or play is locked inside. It knows more of my secrets than Rayne does.

I grab an album from the store's vast collection and close the door. The record crackles as it comes to life. I sit down and practically melt into the bench.

The truth is, I offered to work the extra shift for Eddie. The moment Marnie announced that he called in sick, I was quick to cover. Working sounded drastically better than shopping. And I was hoping I might have extra time to come here after, to lock myself away and think. Or even better, not think, and just let the music make noise in my head for a while.

Ellis has never worked a day in her life and thinks I'm crazy for having a job when I "should be having fun," but Get Sconed Café is so much more than just a job. It's a part of my family. Like Shangri-La, its bones are my grandmother's. And if I'm ever lucky enough to be able to, I want to buy it back. That's one of the reasons I took the job in the first place. I've been working there since freshman year, saving paycheck after paycheck. I don't blame Rayne for selling it. It was the right thing for her to do. But the older I get, the more I know it's meant to be mine. I can't help but think Grandma would want it back in my hands.

The music plays on, and I try to relax and let the past twenty-four hours melt away. I've been tense ever since Rayne said the name Jamison Rush. And no massage could get rid of it. Jamison is in my bones. I thought I was over it. I've done my best to ignore him for the past three years. And when there were hundreds of miles of distance between us, it wasn't that hard. Life moved on. But now that our bedrooms are mere feet from each other, it's as if everything I pushed away has come back in a tidal wave.

Music isn't working like it normally does. I exchange one album for another, but my mind chews on memories that are too strong, even for the sound booth's usual tonic effect.

Black and Read is where I met Zach Hillsborough. I was in this very listening booth when I saw him. I watched him for a while, wandering like a lost puppy and looking like a young Republican.

"The books are in the back," I said.

"Who said I'm looking for a book?" Zach asked.

"You just look like the type."

"And what type is that?"

I gestured to his buttoned-up exterior. "A snobbish intellectual who wants to write the next great American novel."

"Actually," Zach said. "I hate reading. It's a total bore. Can't keep my eyes open. But life is all about looking the part, right?"

"Well, you're doing a good job."

He smiled at me in this gleaming, endearing way before confessing that he had never been in the store before and just wanted to check it out.

"This might sound crazy," Zach said, "but I think I came in here so I could meet you."

"Either that's a load of total bullshit, or you *are* crazy."

"Do you want to get coffee with a lunatic?" he asked. "There's this place just down the street. Best scones you'll ever have."

That's how it started. It was so easy and natural that it seemed like Zach was right—like we were meant to meet that day. But it doesn't feel that simple anymore.

The listening booth feels more claustrophobic the more I think about Zach.

I leave the booth and put the album back in its proper location. Terry Fredericks, the owner of Black and Read, is very particular about organizing records correctly, in case of a music emergency, he reasons. In a moment of helplessness, no one wants to dig for relief in a messy record bin. But the records are the only thing organized about Terry.

The store's front door chimes as a new customer enters, and I realize that I'm due at Sam's house. He and Ellis should be done shopping by now, and there's no bailing on tonight. Not after I already disappointed Ellis. She's become more sentimental now that we're seniors, declaring some events "mandatory" under the pretense that next year "we all scatter to the wind" and "we'll never get to do this again." Ellis and Sam may scatter, but I'm not going anywhere.

I turn to go. I stop short at the sight of Jamison.

Neither of us moves.

"The books are in the back," I say finally. Vinyl isn't Jamison's thing. Books are, and always have been. He doesn't go anywhere without one. Right now, I know he has at least one in his backpack or tucked into the back pocket of his jeans—jeans that fit perfectly, I realize. Since he was little, he's been a good dresser. Nothing flashy or over the top, but clean. Classic. Jeans and sneakers. Even his T-shirts look ironed. You won't find a stain on anything he owns. Jamison takes care of his appearance. Whereas I'm presently dusted in flour and wearing an old pair of ratty overalls. My hair is pulled into a messy bun, held back by a purple bandana. I look sloppy and disheveled next to Jamison.

"I thought you were shopping with Ellis today," he says.

"Change of plans. I decided to work an extra shift instead. Marnie needed the help. And actually, I'm running late."

"Where to now?"

"My friend Sam's house." I move toward the door.

But Jamison stops me. "Sam? Does Mack know about Sam?"

"Not that it's any of your business, but yes, Zach knows Sam."

"Are you avoiding me?"

"No."

"Really?" Jamison asks.

"Really." It's a lie, and by the disappointed look he gives me, I'm pretty sure Jamison knows it.

Terry walks out of the back of the store then. I step aside to put some space between me and Jamison. Terry eyes Jamison, and I wonder if Terry can feel the tension between us.

"Welcome to Black and Read," Terry says to Jamison. "Can I help you find something?" He walks up behind me, almost protectively, which is a joke considering Terry has lived on cereal and weed for the past forty years. He's skinnier than me.

Jamison gives me this expression that seems to say, *Are you going to tell him, or should I?* But tell him what? That we're friends? That Jamison's living next door? That I spent a month of every summer throughout my childhood at Jamison's house in Kansas City? That when we left, I'd cry nearly the whole way home?

"You visiting for the weekend?" Terry says, still acting overly protective. "I hate to break it to you, but I probably don't have what you're looking for. I don't carry any of that rap music or whatever it is kids listen to nowadays."

Jamison nods. "Right. I must be looking for rap music."

I should introduce Jamison and correct Terry. Tell him that while Jamison might listen to rap, like we all do, he's here for the books. He's a bona fide book nerd. He might become Terry's best customer.

"Have fun at Sam's house, Amoris," Jamison says, but as he turns to leave, Terry stops him.

"Whatcha got there in your backpack?" he asks.

"A book and a laptop," Jamison says. As I suspected.

"Can I see your book?"

Jamison pulls it out and shows Terry the cover. I don't recognize it, but that's not saying much. I've never been a big reader. "Have you read Colson Whitehead?" Jamison asks.

"Can't say I have," Terry says.

The exchange feels tense, awkward. Jamison shoves the book back into his pack. "I'll be going now. See you later, Amoris."

He exits, the bell ringing in his wake.

"You know him?" Terry asks, more relaxed.

"I used to."

4

THE PRETTY LIES

Ellis's clothing bags are strewn around Sam's bedroom. She is nothing if not goal oriented. There isn't an AP class she can't ace or a wardrobe she can't overhaul, and by the looks of it, she has bought herself a closet's worth of new clothes.

Tucker lies on Sam's bed, tossing a tennis ball at the ceiling rhythmically. Thud. Pause. Thud. Pause. Thud. The bedroom smells like a mix of Aspercreme and lavender, not a pleasant combination. I open one of Sam's windows to let in the cool night air.

We're being subjected to Ellis's personal fashion show, all the new items she's purchased today. She's currently in the closet, changing. Not because she is modest, but because she likes a dramatic entrance.

Sam is nestled in a chair in the corner of his room, observing one moment, drawing the next. Sam likes to say he has busy hands. He's the kid in elementary school who drew all over his folders and scribbled on papers and doodled in his notebook, who couldn't sit still for the life of him, who was constantly behind on the task at hand, who missed homework assignments and often seemed lost in another world. Sam was pegged as a failure and troublemaker in elementary school. Then he was diagnosed with ADHD and put on meds. "It's a classic cautionary tale of the dangers of labeling," he said once, explaining why he rejects labels now. "There's always more to the story."

"Tucker, look at me," Sam says now.

The repetitive sound of the tennis ball stops, and Tucker turns his face toward Sam. "What?"

"Just checking." Sam smiles and goes back to drawing. They're opposites in so many ways—Tucker has strawberry-blond hair, blue-green eyes, and a stocky, athletic build. He looks like he comes from a long line of ranchers—Carhartts and all—which he does. But Sam is lean. He can pull off skinny jeans better than I can. And his looks favor his Chinese mom over his White American dad. She's petite with straight black hair, just like Sam. And they both have softness in their nature. You just want to be around Sam. He's one of the most comforting people I know. Almost as much as Rayne.

"You're so weird," Tucker says.

"And proud of it. We're all weird." Sam scribbles, smiling at Tucker over the top of his sketchbook. "And may I remind you that you like this weirdo."

"Maybe I do . . ." Tucker admits, before throwing the tennis ball at the ceiling again.

They met on Instagram. Tucker lives in Eaton Falls, a small ranching town about twenty miles from Alder Creek, though the two places couldn't be more different. Unlike Alder Creek, Eaton Falls isn't so friendly to kids who are out. Tucker only ever comes here to be with Sam, but Sam has never been to Tucker's house. Which is to say, Tucker isn't out. He's so far from out, he's *in*, hanging with the popular crowd at his school, playing sports, commenting on hot girls, and hitting on cheerleaders. It's like a bad episode of *Friday Night Lights*, which happens to be Tucker's favorite show.

I asked Sam if it bothered him, knowing that Tucker lives a completely different life in Eaton Falls. But he said no. That barely anyone shows outwardly who they are on the inside. That high school is survival of the best façade, and he would rather have Tucker alive than have him come out and lose him forever.

Ellis dramatically emerges from the closet, startling us.

"At least one of us is coming out of the closet tonight," Sam says.

"Ha. Ha," Tucker mocks. "Very funny."

"Give me your honest opinion," Ellis says, twirling, demonstrating just how built for high school and its clichés she really is. Football games, pep rallies, Senior Skip Day, prom—Ellis eats it up. They're all events where she can be on display.

"Honestly?" Tucker says, perking up on the bed. "I hate it when you call me a hick."

"Honestly?" Ellis counters. "Then stop acting and dressing like one, hick."

"You do own multiple pairs of cowboy boots," Sam says.

"That's because I work with cows. My family owns a ranch, for fuck's sake." Tucker resumes throwing the ball at the ceiling. Sam intercepts a toss, crawling onto the bed with him.

"I'm not complaining," Sam says. "The look is very Tim Riggins."

"Don't butter me up with *Friday Night Lights*," Tucker says. "You know that show is my weakness."

"We can watch it tonight if you want," Sam says, nuzzling into Tucker.

Ellis examines her butt in Sam's mirror. Her long dark-brown hair reaches down her back. She has her mom's curves and her dad's height, a lethal combination. When she's satisfied with the view, Ellis plops down onto the floor next to me, a devious expression on her face.

"What?" I ask.

"I know how you're going to pay me back for today."

"How?"

"I'm throwing you a party," she says. "A back-to-school party. My house. Next weekend. Matt's going out of town to some bullshit woo-woo silent retreat in Joshua Tree, so I have the house all to myself. Invite anyone you want." Ellis takes lavender oil from her pocket. She inhales deeply and dabs some on her wrists.

"Your dad's leaving again?" I ask.

"Whatever. Fuck him. We can use this to our advantage. I haven't thrown a party all summer. It's perfect."

"Can I come?" Tucker chimes in.

"Only if you leave the bro-tanks at home and actually wear a shirt with sleeves," Ellis says.

"I can't help it if my biceps need to breathe," Tucker says, flexing his muscles.

"Personally, I prefer your biceps exposed," Sam says, grabbing Tucker's arms and gently squeezing.

"Personally, I prefer not seeing your gross, deodorant-flecked armpit hair all the time," Ellis says. "If modern beauty demands that women make themselves practically hairless, why not men, too?"

"Elle, you know this country doesn't like women making their own rules about their own bodies," Sam says. "If we give you control of your bodies, what's next?"

"God, men are such cowards," she says.

"Powerful cowards," Tucker adds. The men telling women to be hairless are the same men telling Tucker not to be gay.

"This conversation is utterly depressing," Ellis says. She turns to me. "Back to happier topics. It's our senior year. This might be the last party I ever throw."

"Not likely," Sam says.

"OK, that's probably true," Ellis amends. "So, are you in?"

"There's more to this party," I say. "Spill it, Elle."

"Remember, Amoris. We made a deal."

"What is it?" I ask, more emphatically.

"You have to agree to kiss someone by the end of the night. That's your payment for missing today."

"I have a boyfriend!"

"Whatever," Ellis states. "A boyfriend at *college*. That so doesn't count."

"I'm pretty sure Zach would see it as counting."

"Look, I'm doing this for you. I don't want you wasting your senior year pining over some guy who's probably banging half of Columbia University. College guys never stay faithful to their high school girlfriends."

"I'm not pining," I say.

"You know what I mean. I can see it in your face." Ellis points at me. "It's been too long since you've been single. You need to be reminded of how good it feels. How much fun it is. You need to make out with new lips. Boy, girl, I don't care. You have years to be locked in a boring marriage with one penis for the rest of your life. But not this year."

"I'm not single, Elle. Zach and I are still together."

"Stop acting like I'm asking you to go to the gynecologist," she says. "This isn't stirrups and speculums. It's a party."

"Some days I'm so glad I'm a man," Tucker says.

"Men would never survive the gynecologist," Sam adds. "We're too weak."

"Let's face it," Ellis says, staring directly at me. "How together can you really be if Zach's all the way on the East Coast, and you're here?"

It's a good question. I thought I knew the answer, until last night. Spatially, Ellis is right. Zach and I are not together. We're farther apart than we've ever been. I thought the distance would be no big deal, but I wasn't expecting Jamison, who *was* far away, to move in next door. Jamison's proximity makes Zach's distance feel like an untraversable abyss.

"It's just an innocent kiss," Ellis says. "It won't mean anything. You don't even need to tell Zach. It's only cheating when it actually means something."

"Is that true?" Sam asks.

"I've kissed a lot of girls in the name of survival," Tucker says.

"Have you kissed any girls lately?" Sam asks, a slight panic to his voice.

"No," Tucker says.

Sam relaxes, and no one presses the topic further. Ellis takes her new clothes off and changes into pajamas. We turn on *Friday Night Lights* and all cram into Sam's bed to watch. But I don't pay attention. I'm fixated on the question: *Is any kiss ever innocent?*

From my experience, the answer is no. There are always repercussions, even when we think no one is looking. This I know for a fact.

~

Sam and Tucker are asleep in the bed, Tucker curled around Sam like a spoon. Ling and Pat, Sam's parents, are OK with Tucker sleeping over as long as Ellis and I are here, too. We're on a blow-up mattress tonight. I stare at the ceiling, wide awake and yet exhausted.

I can't stop replaying my encounter with Jamison this afternoon. It was awful and awkward. I can't believe this is the state of our relationship. How can he feel like barely an acquaintance, when I know that he's had poison ivy? That he has a scar on his knee from a bad rug burn? That he fell off his bike and broke a toe? That his house smells like fresh air, chlorine, and flowers in the summer? Kaydene used to hang our bathing suits out to dry on the back porch, letting the hot and humid Midwestern sunshine do its work. Our month-long visits, planned by Rayne, were meant to be spent having quality time with my grandparents, who live next door to the Rushes. But they turned into sleepovers and campouts and long days at the local pool with Jamison. Every night I had to spend at my grandparents' was torture. Rayne eventually gave up and just let me stay next door most nights. My grandparents would rather play golf than play with me and River anyway. The month at their house was more symbolic of family ties than any actual bonding. Chris said it was better than listening to Grandma Westmore complain about never seeing us, though he always seemed to have an art show pop up during that month, calling him off on an adventure and leaving us to weather his parents without him. Not that it mattered to me. I had Jamison.

We would sit on the couch after an afternoon at the pool, Jamison's nose in a book and me pestering him to stop reading, my blond hair a mass of frizz. I constantly annoyed him at the good parts, pestering him about sleeping outside or roasting marshmallows. But I could tell when he wasn't listening. One time, I grabbed his book—*Harry Potter and the Sorcerer's Stone*—and complained that reading was boring.

"It's not boring." He tried to take it back.

"Well, I hate this stupid book." I tossed it across the room carelessly. Looking back and knowing how much he loved that series, I'm appalled at my actions. Jamison would never do that to one of my records. But he calmly collected it from the floor.

"You haven't even read it," he said.

"So? I've heard about it and it sounds dumb."

"You don't know what you're talking about. Why don't you try reading it?" He handed me the book.

"No."

"What's wrong?"

"I can't read it, OK? I'm a terrible reader."

"No, you're not," he said.

"Yes, I am. I'm stupid."

"Who told you that?"

"My teacher."

"Really?"

"No . . ." I admitted. "But I can just tell."

"Well, both of my parents are teachers, and they don't think you're stupid," he said. "In fact, they don't think anyone's stupid. They just say you need to try, do your best, and work really hard for what you want."

All I wanted was to be around Jamison.

"Maybe you could read it to me," I said. And without hesitation Jamison turned to the first page and started reading.

At one point, he stopped. "You know what else my parents told me?"

"What?" I asked.

"That some teachers are going to believe in you, and some are only going to believe in what they see, so you can't always trust their judgment. I'm telling you, Amoris, you're not stupid."

I believed him, because back then there was no one I trusted more than Jamison. "Do you like reading more than you like me?"

And Jamison said, "I don't like anything more than I like you."

"OK, continue, please."

And he did.

Of all my summer memories from Jamison's house, my favorites are from when we were squished next to each other on his couch, him reading aloud to me. Space didn't matter back then. We could get as close as we wanted. But now . . .

Ellis shifts in bed, pulling me from the memory. "Amoris? Are you awake?"

"Yeah."

Ellis rolls onto her side. "You OK?"

I know the moment I lost faith in what Jamison and I had. The moment I stopped believing in us, and how he felt about me. It all withered away when I saw Jamison's lips on hers. The memory of my two best friends kissing still hurts, like a burn that stings long after the skin begins to heal. Neither of them knows I saw. And neither of them ever confessed it. I don't know what hurts more—the kiss, or the secret they still share.

"Jamison is here," I say quietly.

Ellis sits up quickly. "What?"

"He's going to go to Alder Creek High."

"What? Why?"

I explain that Jamison wants to go to Western University, and about in-state tuition.

"Jamison . . ." Ellis's tone has a reminiscent, undefined quality to it. Like I can't tell if she's upset or excited for a new challenging conquest. "God, I haven't heard that name in a long time. You used to talk about him incessantly."

"Not incessantly," I whisper to myself.

"Why didn't you tell me?"

"I had no idea until yesterday."

"Jamison . . ." Again, Ellis's tone is unreadable. "You know what this means. He needs to come to the party. We can introduce him to people. Show him a good time."

I don't like her tone. I don't like her enthusiasm. The last time Jamison was in Alder Creek, Ellis gave me no indication that she liked him. Their relationship was more like frenemies, like opponents facing off, arguing over who was right, who was fastest, who knew more than the other—until I found them secretly lip-locked. I should have seen the tension for what it was: foreplay. Then maybe catching them wouldn't have been such a surprise.

"I hope you told Zach you have a hot guy living next door to you now," Ellis says. "Not that he has any room to complain. He's living in a coed dorm with communal showers."

Telling Zach about Jamison never crossed my mind. For some reason, revealing the situation feels more like a confession than the simple statement of fact.

"You'll tell Jamison about the party?" Ellis asks. "Or do you want me to?"

"I'll do it," I answer quickly.

Ellis reaches to the side of the bed and grabs the bottle of lavender oil. "This year is going to be the best one yet. I can feel it."

"Yeah. It's gonna be great."

But she can read my tone. Ellis knows me as well as I know her. "Are you sure you're OK?"

"I'm fine."

It's a pretty lie—the kind of lie meant to keep the peace, to keep life comfortable. I prefer it that way. What's the point of creating drama now? I can't change the past. What's done is done. I just wish I could forget that kiss.

And with that pretty lie to soothe us, we both drift off to sleep.

5

THINGS ARE NOT AS THEY SEEM

A few days later, the night before school starts, Rayne requests a family dinner. It's not that uncommon, but I fear Jamison and Kaydene will be attending as well. Rayne better not make another pecan pie. But she sets the table for four and says she has ice cream for dessert.

The occasion for dinner is the announcement that Chris is leaving for an art show in Las Vegas in two days. After that, it's on to Santa Fe, and then San Antonio. He'll be gone for a month, traveling in our old Airstream van and selling his art. I can tell by the grin on his face that he can't wait to get out of town. It's hard not to be bothered by his enthusiasm. I knew this was coming. It's unfair to be upset at the news, but I am. Wanting Chris not to leave is like wishing for the sun not to rise. He has been a traveling artist since before I was born. And while I know it's good money for the family, there are days when I wish he would just open a gallery in Alder Creek and stay home with us full-time.

River is immediately pissed because Chris will miss his whole first month of football games.

"I'm starting, Dad. As a sophomore. It's kind of a big deal."

"I saw you play last year," Chris says. "How much has changed?"

"Are you serious?"

"You're only a sophomore. I have two more years to see you play."

This tactic doesn't ease River's angst. He gets up from the table, shoving his chair back. "I'm going for a run."

If Chris is fazed, he doesn't show it. Instead, he takes the opportunity to initiate his own exit. "Well, I've got a few pieces to finish before I leave. Better get cracking." He kisses Rayne on the forehead, clears his plate, and heads back to his studio.

With family dinner officially dissolved, Rayne quietly gets up from the table, carrying plates and cups to the sink.

"Do you wish you could go with him?" I ask her. Sometimes I catch her gazing longingly at the Airstream. Bumper stickers plaster its back, a collage of all the places she and Chris traveled together. Zion National Park, Yellowstone, Graceland, the Everglades. Before Grandma got sick and Rayne got pregnant with me, that was their life for the first years of their marriage—a traveling artist and his wife, living out of an Airstream. There are so many bumper stickers they overlap, cities upon national parks that Rayne and Chris have adventured to as a couple.

"The only reason moments smell better after they're gone is because we can't go back," Rayne answers. "Even the bad ones tend to smell sweeter than the pain most of the time."

"I don't know," I say, piling my dishes next to the sink. "How is the memory of your mom's death sweet?"

"Because I survived it." Rayne winks at me.

She finds a playlist to accompany dish duty. When we finish, Rayne gets the ice cream out of the freezer.

"I miss him when he's gone," I say.

"I know."

I want to put words to my thoughts, to say that at times I wonder whether if he was forced to choose between us and his wandering nature, Chris would pick himself. But Rayne is distracted by a noise outside. "What is that?"

It sounds like someone playing basketball.

When I check to see who it is, I expect to see River. "It's actually Jamison," I say to Rayne.

I sit back at the table. The ice cream isn't making me feel any better.

"You know what my mom always said?" Rayne asks.

"What?"

"Anger is the thief of time. Sometimes I wonder if deep down she knew her years on earth were limited." Rayne shrugs and picks up her phone, scrolling through music options. "Have you heard the new Avett Brothers album? It's so fresh."

"Nice, Mom."

"Just trying to stay relevant."

Bounce. Bounce. Bounce. The basketball echoes through the kitchen window.

"I think I need some fresh air," I say.

And Rayne says, "I think that's a great idea, Amoris."

~

Jamison stops dribbling when I walk out the front door. The sun is setting, the sky painted in violet and magenta and orange. We stare at each other, a string of tension between us.

He bounces the ball to me. "H-O-R-S-E?"

The evening breeze still carries the warm scent of summer. "You sure? If I remember correctly, you kind of suck at this game."

Jamison gives me a familiar smile. It pulls me closer to him, the setting sun on his face. "You know me, I'm better with words than with a basketball."

"I do know you," I say quietly. I want to tell him that I miss him reading to me. I miss his different voices for different characters. How he reads with emotion, like books aren't just meant to be read, but felt.

At least, that's how he used to do it. I don't know what his favorite book is anymore.

"You gonna shoot or what? It's getting dark," Jamison says.

River would say I shoot like a girl, to which I'm quick to point out the obvious sexism. My technique may not be refined, but the ball sinks through the hoop with ease, and I grin as Jamison rebounds.

"Right here," I say, pointing down.

Jamison dribbles over to me. "I know the rules."

"Just making sure."

We haven't been this close since the first night he arrived. I was so rude to him while we washed dishes. It's only just hitting me tonight that Jamison left everything he knows—his friends, family, school.

He shoots, the ball hits the backboard, and for a moment, I think it will topple through the net, but at the last second it falls the other way, out of the hoop.

"I believe that earns you an H," I say.

"I believe it does."

Jamison passes me the ball. I dribble to another part of the key. "Don't worry. I'll take it easy on you."

Jamison smiles. "Don't. I've always liked a challenge."

~

The sun has set, and the backyard is blanketed in twilight. The basketball rests at my feet. Jamison and I sit in Adirondack chairs, the scent of full-bloom flowers in the night air. Twinkle lights hang over the fairy garden Rayne created years ago, giving the yard a magical, wild feel. The lights illuminate his face as he tosses raspberries from the garden high into the air and catches them in his mouth.

"That guy at the bookstore . . ." Jamison says.

"You mean record store?"

"That guy at the *book*store. Do you know him well?"

"Terry? Yeah, I've known him for like . . . ever. He's a good guy."

"A good guy. Really?"

"What?" I ask.

"Nothing." The more H-O-R-S-E we played, the more we seemed to settle back into our old comfort. But now . . . he's closing himself off?

"Are you nervous for school tomorrow?" I ask.

Jamison rolls a raspberry between his fingers. "A little." He throws the berry into the air. It lands perfectly in his mouth.

I laugh. "You'll be fine."

"What makes you say that?"

I gesture at him. "You're just . . ." I fumble for the right word.

"What?"

"Things come easy to you," I say.

"That's not true. Basketball doesn't."

It was a close game, but in the end, I beat him on a three-point shot.

"Most things," I amend. "When was the last time you got anything below an A?"

Jamison inspects the raspberry in his hand. "I got a C in art."

"Seriously?"

He smiles at my surprise. "Nah. You've seen me draw. I would never take art. I'd fail." I shove him playfully. "There's a lot more to high school than just academics, Amoris."

"I doubt you've ever had a problem with the ladies."

We both freeze. It came out before I could think better of it.

"I appreciate the compliment, but that's not what I mean," he says finally.

"Then what?"

"I'm different than most of the people in this town."

"Different how?"

"I'm Black."

I laugh. "You are? I thought that was a summer tan."

"I'm serious, Amoris. No one here looks like me."

"That's not true."

"Really? How many Black kids go to Alder Creek High?"

"A few," I counter, feeling slightly defensive of my town. On some level, Jamison is right. We don't have the most diverse population of students, but it doesn't matter. It's not the number that matters, but how they're treated, right? And I've never heard of anything bad happening to the kids of color at school.

"A few," he repeats flatly. "Well, at my old school, you would have been the minority."

"No one here cares that you're Black, Jay." I state it with confidence. "This is Alder Creek we're talking about, not Boondocks, Mississippi. It doesn't get any more liberal than this town."

"Sure," he says. "No liberal was ever racist, and people don't see color."

"Look, when my friend Sam came out, it was no big deal. No one cared. In fact, I think it only made him more popular."

"So, Sam is gay." Jamison throws me a quick glance. "You failed to mention that."

"Technically, Sam isn't into labels. They're limiting. He's into attraction. Feelings. Love. Right now, he's dating a man. And might I remind you that you were being a butthead at the *record* store."

"A butthead?" Jamison asks skeptically.

"Yeah, a butthead."

"I can't believe you just used that word."

"What's wrong with butthead?" I ask.

"Nothing," he says, "if we were still in third grade."

"You're just mad I kicked your ass tonight."

"You did not kick my ass. You beat me by one shot."

"Turns out that's all you need to be a winner, loser," I say dramatically. I pick up the basketball and chuck it at Jamison—harder than I intended. It hits his shoulder with a thud.

"I think you owe me an apology," Jamison says. "First you call me a loser, and then you throw a ball at me. I know your mother raised you better than that."

I keep my lips sealed, but I'm dying to laugh.

"Apologize, Amoris."

I shake my head.

"I'll give you one more chance," Jamison says. "Apologize."

"Or what?"

"That's it." Jamison is out of his seat and coming toward me. I yelp and bolt down the driveway. Speed is not on my side, though. Jamison's long legs give him an advantage. Always have. Every game we played as kids—tag, ghost in the graveyard, manhunt—he would catch me, every time.

Jamison grabs me around the waist, holding me to him. He's too strong for me to break away. He hoists me up, wiggling, over his shoulder, carrying me like a fireman would.

"Who's winning now?" he taunts. "You never were very fast."

"Put me down, Jay!"

But he doesn't. He starts to spin, his arms wrapped tightly around my legs. It's a move he's done more times than I can count. My curls fly everywhere, and I can't stop laughing as I spin. God, I've missed this feeling, like a little girl playing with her best friend again, hoping our parents don't call us in for the night.

"Apologize!" he hollers.

But I'm stubborn, and he knows it. "Never!"

He spins faster. I can hardly breathe, partly from laughing and partly from being squished against him. It feels too good.

"What the hell is going on?"

Jamison stops. I move my tangled hair from my face, still propped on his shoulder.

River stands sweating in the driveway, just as annoyed as when he left the dinner table.

"Get a room," he groans before disappearing inside.

Jamison sets me down, his breath labored. "Shit, you got heavy."

I slap his arm. "I am *not* heavy."

"You know what I mean. You're not a little girl anymore."

"Yeah, but you're still a butthead."

Jamison laughs deeply, his voice more mature than it was three years ago. He sounds confident, like a grown man. "Are we cool now, Amoris?"

There's so much more to say. I owe him an explanation for the distance I put between us, but I can't bring myself to confess why I've been withdrawn, the kiss I saw, the damage it did.

My phone rings in my pocket.

"Shit." I yank it free. Zach attempting to FaceTime me.

"Need to get that?" Jamison asks.

Annoyed, I silence the phone. "No. It's nothing important."

"Does he know that?" Jamison's question isn't judgmental.

"Let me know if you ever want a rematch," I joke. "I'm happy to kick your ass twice."

Jamison smiles wryly. "I guess I'll see you in school tomorrow."

And with that, we go back to our respective houses. I don't call Zach back. Instead, I sleep peacefully for the first time in days.

6

AM I MISSING SOMETHING?

I'm called down to the guidance office during my third-period
Spanish class on the first day of school. I've never actually been to see
the guidance counselor before. Never had the need. Ellis was required
to meet with Ms. Collins our freshman year. She bitched about it incessantly. "The school thinks I have dead mommy issues," she said. "No
shit. But I don't need a state-issued grief counselor who probably works
at Chili's on the weekends. If I wanted therapy, I'd hire a real shrink."

On first inspection, Ms. Collins's office is a bit of a mess. Papers
and files are stacked on her desk. Her laptop is open, and she's typing
furiously as I enter. I take a seat in the chair opposite her desk. Pictures
hang on the walls, along with framed degrees. I notice she has a doctorate in psychology, which is counter to how Ellis described her. She
seems like a real shrink to me, but that still doesn't answer the question
of why I'm here. I don't think I need . . . shrinking.

"Amoris Westmore . . ." Ms. Collins says.

"Yes."

"Amoris Westmore . . ." Her face is still stuffed behind the computer. The longer she avoids eye contact, the more nervous I get. "Westmore . . ."

"Yes. That's my last name."

She finally looks at me, her blue eyes bright behind a pair of thick-framed black glasses. "You know, I have this theory about kids with last names at the end of the alphabet."

"Really?"

Her brown hair is cut short and tucked behind her ears. She's young, with a disregard for fashion, which actually makes her quite fashionable in an oddly hip way.

"You have to wait your turn while the whole alphabet goes before you," she says. "You're so used to being last all the time, you think it's OK for people not to pay attention to you. You let others shine. Wait your turn. Let others take the lead, because you've always stood at the back of the line, while Allison Arnold never had to stare at the back of someone's head or try not to step on someone's heels. But you've been cautious about stepping on people your whole life, simply because teachers like alphabetical order. But alphabetical order is bullshit. And you deserve the front of the line as much as any other student. Am I right?"

What do you say after a speech like that? I just sit still, stunned.

"It's just a stupid theory." She waves it off. "What do I know?"

Judging by that doctorate, she knows a lot.

"Is that why I'm here? Because of my last name?"

"No," she chuckles. "That's my way of telling you that I like to start at the end of the alphabet when meeting with students. It's just my little way of fucking with the system. So, Amoris Westmore, have you thought about your future after high school?"

"A little."

"Really?" Ms. Collins sounds surprised. "Care to tell me more? What do you want to be when you grow up? Actually, I hate that question. At what point are you considered 'grown up'? My last date played more video games than my ten-year-old nephew. He also lived in his mom's basement and wanted to be a YouTube star. Needless to say, we only went out once."

"So, you're saying I shouldn't complain about high school guys?"

She laughs. "Oh no, you can complain. I'm just saying, if you've ever considered experimenting with your sexuality, now is a great time. Women are taking over the world. Men will have no one to blame but themselves when they go extinct."

"I'll keep that in mind, Ms. Collins."

"Lori," she says. "You can call me Lori. But back to more important topics, what do you want to do? College? Get a job? Travel?"

"My plan is to go to community college and keep working."

"So you work right now?"

"At the café on Main Street."

"And you plan to stick around Alder Creek?"

"Yeah," I say.

"Well . . ." Lori shuffles some papers around on her desk. "Your grades aren't terrible. You lack some extracurricular activities, but if you write a tight, clean essay, I'm sure we can find plenty of universities that would be happy to have you. Some out-of-state colleges even offer tuition reciprocity, so the cost isn't exorbitant. And there's plenty of financial aid and scholarships we can look at."

"I appreciate that, but I don't want to go away to college."

"OK, I get it. Some kids who don't feel ready for college are taking a gap year and traveling. Seeing what the world has to offer. Have you thought about that option?"

The more Lori talks, the more my palms get sweaty.

"I know it's easy to feel stuck when you grow up in a small town, but there's a big world out there, and you should take advantage of it. You never really know what you're missing until you finally see it for yourself," Lori says. "Just think about it."

Lori has me pegged all wrong. I don't feel stuck here. I feel comfortable here. What's so wrong with feeling comfortable?

The bell rings for fourth period, startling us both. Lori checks the clock on her wall. "Shit. I've kept you here too long." She grabs a handful of college brochures and offers them to me. "I've put together a few schools that might interest you. In state. Out of state. We can talk about it at our next meeting."

Next meeting?

"It was nice to finally meet you, Amoris."

"Same," I say, though in truth, I'm not sure I mean it.

~

I drag myself down the hallway, distracted. What happened to easing into the school year? One day at a time? *Carpe diem* and all that?

In my haze, the warning bell sounds. The hallways start to empty in a rush. I attempt to pick up my speed, though my legs feel filled with lead as I move up the stairs to the second floor. With eyes down, arms full, I turn on the landing and run straight into someone. I'm jostled backward, and the brochures fly out of my hands. I'm about to fall when Jamison grabs my arms to steady me.

"Whoa. Careful on those sharp turns."

"Shit." I fall to my hands and knees, collecting the mess on the stairs. Jamison squats down to help and inspects the brochures.

"This looks promising." He holds up a pamphlet for local goat yoga classes. It must have gotten mixed in with Lori's pile.

I snatch it from him. "It's supposed to be calming."

"Until a goat shits on you during Savasana."

"Do you even know what Savasana is?"

"I know all about White trends," he says. "Yoga. Reiki. Chakra cleansings. Veganism."

I snatch the pamphlet. "If you ever need your chakras cleaned, I bet my mom would do it at no cost."

He laughs. "Are you saying I'm dirty?"

It's the way he says it—all sexy and flirtatious. The hallway gets eerily quiet. Neither of us moves. I go back to picking up the brochures.

"What is it?" Jamison asks.

"Nothing."

"Come on. I've known you our whole lives. I can tell when you're off. Spill it."

Where to start? "How long have you known you want to go to Western?" I ask.

"A while."

"What if you don't get in?"

"I'll go to one of my backup schools, I guess."

Zach was the same way. He was determined to go to Columbia. Zach wore this old, beat-up Columbia hoodie, handed down to him from his dad's college days. Like a legacy. Kind of like my records. Columbia was all Zach talked about last year. But even he had backup plans that didn't include staying in Alder Creek. It's starting to hit me that everyone has plans to leave, except me. I've known this, and yet it's only now becoming real. But what's so wrong with staying put? I love living here. The idea of leaving has my stomach in knots.

"How's your first day going?" I ask, diverting from the subject.

"It's . . . interesting."

"How so?"

"You have some very odd art here at Alder Creek High." Jamison points to a mural on the wall, leading up the staircase. I've never paid attention to it. Leave it to Jamison to notice the fine details. Next he'll do an in-depth inspection of the library's collection of books, making sure they're up to his standard.

"Do you see anything weird about this mural?" he asks.

America threw up on the wall. There's an eagle, a space shuttle, a waving American flag that looks like the sea below an old-fashioned ship. There's the Statue of Liberty, Mount Rushmore, famous Americans like Helen Keller and Sally Ride.

"I notice that it's ugly," I joke.

"Yeah. It's pretty damn ugly." But I get the feeling that's not what Jamison is talking about.

"What is it, Jay?" I ask. "Am I missing something?"

"It's just an odd painting to have in a school." He readjusts the backpack on his shoulder. It's partially open, and I see a taped-up laptop inside.

"I can't believe you still have that." But as I reach out to touch it, Jamison pulls away. The laptop was a gift for his thirteenth birthday. He wouldn't shut up about it the entire time we texted that day. "I was just looking," I pout. "Is that duct tape?"

He wags his finger at me. What I wouldn't give to read what Jamison has written on that laptop.

"It's amazing what duct tape can hold together," he says. "If I ever make it as a writer, I'm sending that company a thank-you note and a check."

"*When* you make it," I correct him. "Anyone who carries around that piece of shit for five years is clearly dedicated to his craft."

Jamison zips up his backpack. "Mind how you talk about my girl."

I chuckle. "By the way, Ellis is throwing a party on Saturday. She wants you to come."

"Well, you can tell Ellis she might be able to boss everyone else around, but I'm not so easily persuaded." That stings. Is he including me in that judgment? Ellis has a strong personality, for sure. And I've never been a fighter, raised as I was by an artist alien and a witchy pacifist. Fighting isn't my strong suit, but Jamison always pulls out my stubborn side.

"I'll let her know." I make my way up the stairs.

Jamison touches my arm to stop me. "I'm sorry. That came out wrong. I'm just a little on edge today. Getting used to a new school and all."

"It's fine," I say, though it's not really.

"Are you going to the party?" he asks.

"Of course I'm going."

"Then tell Ellis I'll be there."

The rest of the day, I lug around the brochures Lori gave me. I can't bring myself to throw them out. When I get home, I set them on my dresser to collect dust. This school year has not started as I expected. And I have a feeling there are more surprises to come.

7

AMERICAN MYTHOLOGY

In the late afternoon, Sam and I sit on the sun-soaked patio at Get Sconed Café. I'm on break, and I play guitar while Sam gets his caffeine fix. Right now, he's busy sketching, his hands flitting around the page. To apply to art programs at universities, he has to submit a portfolio. He's been working on it all summer, as diligent with his art as Jamison is with his writing. I examine my coffee-stained overalls and apron. I'm diligent with making lattes, and sure, I have the guitar, but I'm only proficient at playing other people's music. Even Ellis has been working on her college applications for basically her whole life, joining every club she can, playing on sports teams. And last year, she achieved her ultimate goal when she won a coveted seat on the Senior Senate, the governing body at Alder Creek High. It's a traditional popularity contest, and Ellis desperately wanted to win.

"So Chris left yesterday?" Sam asks, his focus on his sketchbook.

The Airstream was gone when I got home from school. Rayne gave me and River his goodbyes. River called Chris an asshole, and Rayne reminded my brother how much our dad loves us. To which River proclaimed that Chris only loves himself.

"Why do you stay married to him?" he asked Rayne.

She was taken aback by the question and said that marriage is complicated. But River said we were better without him. That Chris is never here anyway, that he doesn't even really live with us. I wanted to punch River in the mouth to shut him up—he was hurting Rayne—but he stormed off before I could get a good swing at him.

And I hate to admit it, but River had a point. Chris leaves Rayne alone when he travels. Chris moved next door. Yet he's free of dealing with what he leaves behind. I didn't feel better laying the blame on Chris. That's not how blame works. I only resented Chris *and* River more.

What I wouldn't give for an hour in the listening booth at Black and Read. My brain can't work anything out. It would be nice to just disappear with my guitar and music. Instead, Marnie is short-staffed, and I'm picking up extra after-school shifts at the café. It's never bothered me before, but today it's grating on my patience.

And as if that wasn't enough, Zach won't stop texting and calling. I silence yet another one of his FaceTime attempts.

"Trouble in paradise?" Sam asks.

"I'm working. He knows that. I'll call him later."

Sam cocks his head at me, an all-knowing expression on his face.

"Don't bullshit a former bullshitter," Sam says. "May I remind you, I pretended to be straight for fourteen years. I know a lie when I see one." He points at me with his pencil. "It's in your eyes."

"It's not a lie. I *will* call him later." Maybe. If I have the energy. Lately, I haven't. Zach is just another thing I can't deal with right now.

"You know, it's not just gay people who live in closets," Sam says, casually going back to his sketch. "Why don't you just come out with it? I promise you'll feel better."

What Sam conveniently left out of that statement is the word *eventually*. Eventually, I'll feel better, but I can't wait for eventually right now. Zach is at least consistent. Solid. With Chris gone, River acting like an ass, Jamison living next door, college brochures collecting dust, nothing feels like it used to. But Zach . . . he does. And I need that right now.

"Is that what you say to Tucker?" I ask.

"Tucker is different."

"How?"

"Because when Tucker comes out, he becomes prey," Sam says. "He goes from being at the top of the social food chain to the bottom. He's playing the part of a straight White man. No lion ever wants to become an insect."

"You did."

"First of all, I was never a lion. Maybe *half* lion, on my dad's side. Second, I don't give a shit about society and its bogus patriarchal hierarchy. Lions don't create lasting art. But they did create everything Tucker loves. Have you seen that guy watch football? He practically salivates. Giving up lion status isn't easy."

"Well, I'm not a lion either. Women get eaten in this patriarchal hierarchy, too."

"That's not the point." Sam sets his sketchbook down and squares himself to me. "Just tell me, Amoris. Sometimes saying it takes the pressure off. Silence is heavy."

Sam might be right, but what exactly to say? Where to start? And what's the point? If I say out loud everything that's in my head, will anything change for the better? Or will it only disrupt my life more?

When I catch sight of Jamison walking up to the café, I take it as a sign and keep my mouth shut. Sam seems disappointed.

"What are you doing here?" I set my guitar down as Jamison approaches us.

"Does this place not serve Black people?"

"Not funny, Jay. Don't joke about that."

Jamison gives me a small grin. "Who said I was joking?"

Sam extends a hand to Jamison. While they know of each other, they haven't properly met. "I'm Sam. You're in my AP American History class."

"You mean AP American Mythology?" Jamison says, shaking his hand and offering his name.

"Wise observation." Sam chuckles. "Just wait until winter. Every classroom will be littered with Martin Luther King Jr. quotes. White people *love* MLK."

"What's wrong with Martin Luther King Jr.?" I ask.

"Nothing," Jamison says.

"He's just been put through the White American history factory," Sam says. "Now he's palatable, mislabeled, and highly processed, but at least he tastes good to White people. They hate eating their vegetables."

"But they love taking credit for it when they do," Jamison says.

"Not all White people are bad," I say.

"I didn't say White people are bad," Jamison clarifies.

"Then what *are* you saying?"

"You wouldn't get it."

Jamison's avoidance irritates me, but then my coworker, Agnes, sticks her head out the café door, interrupting us. "Time's up, Amoris. I need you. The espresso machine is acting up again. You're the only one who knows how to fix it."

"Coming," I say. Jamison stops me before I can disappear back into the café. He holds out a piece of paper.

"What is this?" I ask.

"I'm applying for a job."

"Here?"

"Is there something wrong with here?"

"Well, a lot of White people work here. Are you sure you want to interact with us?" My tone is too snarky. I sound like Ellis. Immediately, I want to take it back.

"Don't do that, Amoris."

"Do what?"

"Minimize my perspective. It's not that simple and you know it."

Do I? Lately, it feels like I know nothing.

"And to be clear . . ." Jamison leans into me. "I'm not concerned with *all* White people. Just one in particular."

Our eyes meet. An intensity sparks.

"Look, college is expensive, and I need to help my parents out, but I can apply somewhere else," he says, reaching to take back the application. "I just thought, with this café being in your family . . ."

"And you get free food and coffee," Sam hollers.

"Just tell me if you don't want me working here," Jamison says softly.

Agnes pokes her head out the door again. "Amoris. The espresso machine. I'm dying in here."

I glance at the application. Jamison has listed Rayne as a reference. A smart move, not that I have any doubt that Marnie will hire him.

"I'll make sure Marnie gets your application," I say to him.

When I'm back behind the counter, espresso machine fixed, my feet aching again, Sam brings me my guitar. I can't believe I left it outside. I've never been that careless with it before.

"I get it now," he says.

"What?"

"What I saw in your eyes last week."

"Do I look *that* tired?"

"It was him," Sam says knowingly.

"I don't know what you're talking about," I insist. But Sam knows damn well I've just served him a pretty lie. He can smell bullshit from a mile away.

8

OUR SONG

On Friday night, Ellis stumbles into my room, drunk. Her hair is messier than she usually allows, and her makeup is smudged. Ellis's hazel eyes are glazed over with a look only booze gives her. I figured this would happen when she said Matt would be out of town all weekend. She strips off her clothes and digs in my drawers for a pair of pajamas.

"Where were you?" I whisper. As mad as her unplanned appearance makes me, I was waiting for her. She tried to get me to tag along with her after the football game, to whatever hidden fiesta she was planning to attend. Not everyone advertises their parties as widely as Ellis does, but I wasn't in the mood. This week has exhausted me. All I wanted to do after River's game was curl up in bed and watch TV alone.

"Beckett's," Ellis says, exhaling a wave of booze in my direction. Beckett Stranahan's family rivals Ellis's for the wealthiest in town. He's usually dressed head to toe in Patagonia, though his outdoor wear is more for the status than actual use. Ellis flops down onto my bed and giggles. "Ask me if we had sex."

"Did you have sex?"

"Totally."

"You did?"

"He asked me to homecoming afterward," Ellis says. "Like he's some kinda gentleman."

"What did you say?"

"I told him to stop being so sappy." She giggles. "And then I said yes."

Ellis shimmies across the bed, finding the part of the mattress that's practically molded to her body. Even on the nights she's not here, I leave space for her. It's a habit I can't seem to break.

"It could be you tomorrow night," she says, grinning. "It's about time you had sex with someone other than Zach. How boring to go through high school only having one penis."

"I'm not having sex with anyone tomorrow."

"But if you did, who would it be?"

"No one."

"You're lying."

"Ellis, I'm dating Zach."

"If you wanted to keep dating Zach, you wouldn't have agreed to kiss someone at the party."

"I didn't agree," I argue. "I was blackmailed. By you. Plus, you said it was no big deal. It doesn't count as cheating if it doesn't mean anything."

"Don't blame me," Ellis slurs. "This isn't my fault. I'm not the one pretending I still like Zach."

"I'm not pretending. I do like Zach."

"But admit it. You're kind of excited to kiss a new person tomorrow, right?"

I'm not answering that.

"I knew it," she says. "I know you better than you know yourself. I'm doing this for you, Amoris. I'm making your senior year interesting. You should be thanking me instead of pouting."

"So you're making me cheat on Zach to keep things interesting? That's messed up, Ellis."

"Blame it on Dead Mom Syndrome."

I don't know why I bother talking to Ellis when she's like this. Nothing sticks in her drunken state. I refrain from offering my psycho-analysis. It wouldn't help, and it's not my place. But on nights like this, it's hard not to be mad at her dad. River thinks Chris is bad, but at least we have Rayne. Ellis has . . . no one.

Ellis's mom died when we were in eighth grade. She was crushed by a rockslide. The hikers who saw it happen said she didn't even have time to scream, though I don't think that gave Ellis or her dad, Matt, any comfort. They dealt with it in their own ways. Ellis rebelled, numbing the pain with boys and mischief. Matt decided to search the world for enlightenment, dropping Ellis on our doorstep two months after her mom's death. When he finally came home, more than nine months later, decorated in mala beads, he stepped back into Ellis's life like nothing happened.

"The room's spinning," she says. "Get me some water."

I normally don't mind when Ellis turns up at my house late at night, wanting a place to sleep other than her lonely, empty house. I prefer she stay here. But tonight, her appearance is grating. Why do I constantly have to be the one protecting her?

"Don't boss me around, Ellis."

"I was just asking. No need to overreact. I'll get it myself."

She stumbles out of bed, but I stop her. "Just stay put and don't puke on my bed."

"Yes, sir." Ellis salutes me and laughs, flopping back on the bed.

I contemplate sleeping on the couch. I just need space. To breathe and think.

Ellis seems to be sleeping when I return with water. She looks so young and peaceful. Ellis stays perfectly still when she sleeps. It's the only time she doesn't wrestle with the world.

I crawl in next to her. She threads her fingers through mine, holding on to me like I'm a lifejacket.

Rayne warned me that grief is a tidal wave. Instinct tells us to run, but no matter how quick we are, the tidal wave eventually sweeps us off our feet and knocks us down so hard that survivors emerge drenched, bruised, and nearly unrecognizable.

"Whoever she was before this, Amoris, Ellis will never be that person again," Rayne said. "Grief rewires the body."

During eighth grade, Rayne waited for Ellis night after night, sitting at the kitchen table, a cup of tea in her hands, and when Ellis walked through the door from wherever she'd snuck out to, Rayne would calmly ask if she wanted some chamomile tea and lavender oil to help her sleep.

"If I use that oil, will it make my mom come back?" Ellis asked one night.

"No."

"Then it won't help."

"Never underestimate Mother Nature," Rayne said. "She created everything."

"Don't talk to me about mothers," Ellis said.

I would lie awake, waiting for Ellis to climb into bed. I was so angry with Matt for leaving her alone. I wanted to beg Ellis to stop sneaking out. I wanted her to cry and scream and grieve. But I knew the only thing that would make Ellis happy was having her mom back, and I couldn't give her that. So I played her a song—James Taylor's "You've Got a Friend." Every night.

And then one night, months into Ellis's living with us, months after her dad should have been home, she came to bed smelling of lavender.

She slept until the sun rose.

It wasn't until later that I realized Ellis always snuck out of the house, but not back in. She knew Rayne was waiting, and she never avoided her. If she hadn't wanted to get caught, she wouldn't have done that. Somehow Rayne knew, and she was there every night, waiting for Ellis.

"People want a witness to their pain," Rayne said. "Not a judge."

That's what I've tried to do for four years—not judge Ellis.

Now, from her side of the bed, Ellis whispers, "You know I love you, right? I can't imagine my life without you. I'd be miserable."

"I know."

"Will you play our song?" she asks. "It helps me sleep."

Our hands are interlaced. I whisper back, "Of course."

9

THE F-WORD

People are overflowing from Ellis's house, spilling out the doors and into the yard. Music plays loudly inside, where the air is warm with body heat. I'm in my usual spot in her kitchen, drink in hand.

Ellis's house—a big rustic home with exposed wood and large stones and decks off every room—sits on the top of a hill outside of Alder Creek. Unlike Shangri-La, which is practically in the center of town, Ellis's house is tucked into the foothills. The house is up high enough that it overlooks town. It's private, practically hidden, and perfect for high school parties.

Sam and Tucker lean on the counter, talking casually. Sam prefers not to drink. He said once that he doesn't want to be so uncreative that he has to resort to drugs and alcohol for entertainment. Maybe if I had his imaginative mind, I'd agree. Tucker has a bottle of beer in his hand, but it's a prop. Tucker hates beer. If he had his choice, he'd drink hard seltzer. He stands tall, chest out, looking extra male tonight—jeans, baseball cap, Eaton Falls High School Football T-shirt, and a pair of heavy-duty cowboy boots.

Ellis returns to the kitchen, Jamison next to her, Beckett following behind like a sex-deprived puppy, his blond hair peeking out from under a baseball cap. He has the expensive-yet-unkempt look nailed. Chris would call him a frat boy and warn me to stay away from Republicans.

Ellis has been dragging Jamison around the party, introducing him to everyone she thinks worthy of introduction. Jamison looks as though he's just been tortured by bees. Like he wants to swat at the air to get rid of all the buzzing.

Sam takes the untouched beer out of Tucker's hand and gives it to Jamison. "You probably need this more than he does."

"Thanks." Jamison takes a large gulp.

"Ellis has officially initiated you into Alder Creek High," Sam says. "I hope she didn't haze you too much."

"I'm saving that for later," Ellis says with a wink. She's already tipsy. No matter how in control Ellis wants to pretend she is, when she drinks, her eyes get lazy.

She woke up in my bed this morning, popped two aspirin, and gulped down a glass of water. When I left the house for my shift at the café, she was helping Rayne make pancakes. They were dancing around the kitchen, singing into spoons.

I swear I don't mind sharing Rayne . . . most days. But this morning, the whole scene felt wrong. Like Ellis was trying to move into my spot instead of sharing it with me. I felt protective of my mom in a way I haven't before. It's ridiculous, I know. I'm overreacting and being too sensitive.

"Did you find your prey yet, Amoris?" Ellis asks me as she refills her glass with more vodka.

"For what?" Jamison asks.

"Nothing," I clarify.

"A deal's a deal, Amoris," Ellis says, "and you agreed. It's happening."

"Did I agree, Ellis, or was I coerced?"

"Either way. If you're not going to step up, I'm taking matters into my own hands." When she takes the beer from Jamison, I see the idea spark almost instantly—Spin the Bottle. Ellis chugs the beer and then grabs me by the arm, dragging me toward the living room. Sam, Tucker, Jamison, and Beckett follow us. Ellis pushes back the couch and chairs, creating a large space on the floor. She sets the bottle down in the middle. "Who wants to play?" she announces.

"Spin the Bottle. How perfectly juvenile of you, Elle," Sam says.

"You can thank me later." She takes a seat on the floor.

Beckett sits. "I don't know why we ever stopped playing this game."

"Because we started having sex instead," Ellis states.

"Right." Beckett smiles.

"I'm in," Tucker says, taking a seat next to Beckett.

Hesitantly Sam takes a seat on the floor, pulling his knees into his chest. "Me, too."

"I'm not playing if I have to kiss dudes," Beckett says. "Sorry, Sam. It's just not my thing."

"Believe me, I don't want to kiss you either," Sam says.

"Spinner's choice," Ellis declares. "We don't discriminate around here. If you can't handle that, Beckett, don't play. Take your homophobia somewhere else. It doesn't belong in this circle."

"Don't worry, Becks," Sam says. "I wouldn't kiss you if you were the last man on earth."

Beckett stays put.

As people come into the living room and notice what's happening, the circle begins to fill up.

"Come on, Amoris." Ellis pats the seat next to her. "It's just a harmless game."

But I'm solely focused on the fact that Jamison just took a seat in the circle.

When I sit down next to Ellis, she whispers, "Good girl." Then she leans into the center and grabs the bottle. "I'll go first."

She spins it, and I swear I hold my breath until the bottle stops, pointing at Aiden Price.

Ellis and Aiden lean into the center of the circle and kiss. It's quick. People laugh. There's an innocent energy to the room, like we've all been transported back to junior high.

The game moves clockwise, leaving me for last. Beckett's spin lands on Michelle Hernández. He looks relieved as he leans in to kiss her.

Tucker spins next. The bottle stops on Ellis. She leans forward. "Glad to see you followed the rules and wore sleeves," she says.

Tucker counters, "Don't worry, I'll rip them off later."

They kiss in an oddly tense way, but at least Sam is happy with Tucker's spin. Jamison is next. I swear it takes a millennium for the bottle to stop. When it finally does, pointing at Michelle, I feel relief. It's a quick peck. Uneventful, though Michelle appears to have wanted more.

"Boring," Ellis says. "You call that a kiss? I know you can do better than that."

"That was just a warm-up," Jamison says.

Was that an allusion to their past kiss? And why can't I just get up and walk away right now?

Paisley Phillips gets Veronica Lamont. They kiss, and Beckett whistles. Sam lands on me. He sighs in relief when we lean in for a brief, friendly peck. Aiden, Michelle, Veronica, and a few others spin, the bottle appointing their kissing partners until finally it's passed to me.

"Your turn, Amoris," Ellis declares. I tell myself this is nothing. A stupid junior-high game. I shouldn't be nervous. I'll probably have to kiss Aiden or Beckett or Sam, and it'll be over. Ellis will be satisfied. I spin the damn bottle. Then I sit back, watching.

It slows to a stop, pointing directly in between Tucker and Jamison.

"Spinner's choice. Who will it be?" Ellis asks.

Why couldn't the bottle land decisively? Why does Ellis constantly have to meddle in my business? And why am I supposed to live up to her expectations, and not the other way around? But that's how it's always been with Ellis and me. Can I really fault her now, when she's the same as she's always been? And isn't this what I've been waiting for? But not like this.

"Tucker," I say. I feel out of my body. I can't look at Jamison for fear of what I might see on his face. Relief or pain—either would be brutal.

I can tell myself all day long that I'm doing this for Tucker and Sam. That I'm helping promote their charade. But that's a lie.

My heart hurts, and it's my own doing.

But the moment Tucker's lips are about to touch mine, a loud crash startles everyone.

"Shit!" Ellis stands quickly. Everyone moves to see what's happened. I follow, only to find River pushing himself off the floor, a vase shattered next to him. He's so intoxicated he can't stand up straight. Jamison and I are at his side immediately.

"I don't need your help." River manages to stand by gripping the wall.

"Fuck," Ellis says. "My dad got that vase in Bali."

"I'm sorry, Elle," I say, as I attempt to hold River still.

"Just leave me alone, Amoris." River wriggles out of my grip.

Ellis waves off my apology. "Don't worry about it. My dad has broken worse things. He deserves it. Just get River home before he breaks something else."

I look around at all the staring eyes.

"He could get kicked off the football team if this gets back to his coach," I whisper to Jamison. "As annoying as he is and as bad as he smells, I don't want that. He loves football. It might be the only thing that makes him happy right now."

Jamison hefts River up, holding him steady under the arms. "Time to go, River Westmore."

We carry him to Sam's car, where Jamison puts him in the back seat. Sam and Tucker climb in the front.

"Our little River is growing up," Sam says. "Just don't puke in my parents' car, kid."

As we pull away from the party, River moans between me and Jamison. I really hope he doesn't throw up. I'm not in the mood to clean up any more of my brother's mess.

~

Jamison and I make as little noise as possible dragging River up to his room. I don't want Rayne burdened with this.

In bed, River curls into a ball, clothes and shoes still on, and opens his eyes slightly.

"What the hell were you thinking, River?" I whisper.

"You were at the party, too," he says.

"That's different. Do you want to get kicked off the football team?"

"I'm not gonna get kicked off the team. I'm the best player they have. They can't lose me."

"You're an asshole." I turn to leave River.

"Did Amoris tell you about Sam?" River says to Jamison.

"What about Sam?" Jamison asks.

"He's a faggot."

I'm back in River's face, appalled. "What the hell is wrong with you?"

"Stop acting all high and mighty, Amoris," he says. "You're a hypocrite like the rest of us."

"And you're a bad drunk."

He laughs, but it carries only anger. "So I get drunk once and you're all mad at me, but Dad can get stoned every goddamn day of his life and you still love him." River turns away from me. "Get out of my room."

I'm at a loss as I close the bedroom door. River might have an attitude sometimes, but that? That was not the brother I know. What is happening?

"Maybe we should get him some water," Jamison says. "He's gonna need it in the morning."

Ever since Jamison showed up, nothing's been right. He tilted my world. And while it doesn't make any sense, at this moment, I blame him.

"Just go," I say, exhausted. "I can take care of River myself."

Jamison leaves without another word, and the house goes silent.

But after I've washed my face and brushed my teeth, I lie in bed, staring at the ceiling, unable to sleep. The angry, drunk person River was tonight doesn't resemble the brother I know. How can we live under the same roof for fifteen years, and suddenly he's unrecognizable? I know he's mad at Chris, but River is acting like a spoiled brat. And he said *I'm* the hypocrite?

I spin my phone around in my hands, thinking about texting Zach. He's what I need right now. Stability. Familiarity. I send a simple sentence.

I wish u were here

But when three dots pop up—Zach typing back, like he's been waiting for me—I feel even angrier. Why does he have to be so good? So loyal? So . . . present? And worse, I'm evading him.

As quickly as I started the conversation, I end it.

Exhausted, going to bed

He writes back: Can we FaceTime tomorrow?

This is exactly what I don't need, and I've done it to myself.

Through my open window, I hear the sound of an outside door open and close. Jamison sits in the garden, reading by the brightness of the twinkle lights. I was awful to him. None of this is his fault, and yet I treated him like the guilty person.

I set my phone down and grab a blanket. When Jamison sees me emerge from the back door, he closes the book.

"I can't sleep," I say.

"Me neither."

I should say I'm sorry. Admit that I was blaming him when I shouldn't have. Jamison didn't do anything wrong. River did. And I did. I'm the problem. I'm doing everything wrong.

"He didn't mean it, Jay. River would never say that about Sam if he was sober."

"Is that true?"

I can't answer Jamison's question honestly. I don't know, and it only pisses me off more. With one word, River has morphed into someone else. I don't know who he really is. And if my own brother can be a stranger to me, who or what's next?

"Do you want to share my blanket?" I ask. It's the best peace offering I have. I sit down next to Jamison and spread the blanket over us. "Whatcha reading?"

Jamison shows me. *Harry Potter and the Sorcerer's Stone.*

"Remember when I told you that book was stupid?"

"Yeah," Jamison says.

"I was just jealous."

"I know."

I should tell him that I made a mistake tonight. I picked the wrong person to kiss.

"Will you read it to me?" I ask.

Jamison opens the book to the first chapter, and sometime later, I drift off to the sound of a turning page.

10

HARMLESS

River stays in his room all of Sunday. I don't see him, not that I would know what to say. When we run into each other Monday morning in our shared bathroom, I attempt to bring up what happened, but he cuts me off quickly.

"Whatever, Amoris. I was drunk. Get over it."

I want to say more, but all I hear in my head is River calling me a hypocrite. On some twisted level, he might be right, and that only makes this whole situation worse. But it's true—Chris is a pothead and I have never judged him for it. And yet River gets drunk once, uses the word "faggot" in a plastered stupor, and I yell at him. He's a kid. He's supposed to make mistakes, but Chris is an adult. Why do I let my dad's behavior slide and not River's?

But as the day goes on, I reason that maybe it was better I didn't say anything. River is obviously upset and rebelling, or he wouldn't have gotten so drunk. Piling on isn't going to help. And neither will bringing the issue to Rayne. In fact, outing River might just make it worse. Rayne is balancing enough right now. It's not like River is spray painting

Sam's locker with hateful slurs, or beating him up in the hallway. In fact, Sam is completely ignorant.

Ellis picks me up early for school on Tuesday. She has a Senior Senate meeting. They're discussing homecoming and potential prom locations. She's already decided she wants prom to be held at this fancy resort in the mountains just outside of town, and she's determined to get her way. I apologize for the vase again, though it should be River apologizing, but Ellis is blasé about it. Apparently, Matt came home from Joshua Tree sunburned, dehydrated, and no closer to enlightenment. Ellis sees the broken vase as payback.

The hallways are quiet. I find myself drifting down toward the guidance office, where Lori's light is on. Even as I poke my head in the door, I'm not quite sure what I'm doing here.

"Amoris?" she asks. "Did you want to discuss the college packets I gave you?"

"No . . . I'm . . ." For whatever reason, Lori makes me comfortable. I like her. She lacks the arrogance of the other adults at school, which makes her easy to talk to. And I feel like I need to talk right now. Get out what's in my head. "I . . ."

Lori stands. "Are you pregnant?"

"What?"

"Because if you are, I can help. I know it can feel overwhelming, but there are options." She starts rummaging around the papers on her desk.

"I'm not pregnant." Being pregnant feels like it would be easier than my problems. At least it would be concrete. A problem with multiple possible solutions. What happens when there's no brochure for your problems?

"What is it? You can tell me," Lori says. "Everything that's said in this office is confidential . . . unless it's potentially harmful to you or others, then I'm a mandatory reporter. You should know that."

What constitutes "harmful"? Was what River said harmful if only Jamison and I heard him? Is Chris's weed smoking suddenly harmful, when it never bothered me before? Are all my preoccupations with Jamison harmful to Zach if Zach is none the wiser? It's tempting to just lay it all out there, spread my problems on Lori's desk along with the papers. But I've never been brave with my own words. I'm a cover song, not an original. Words are Jamison's talent.

"I'm thinking of taking goat yoga, but I lost the flyer. Do you have an extra one?"

Lori knows I'm lying. I can see it on her face. But she doesn't push me. Another reason to like her. She just hands me the paper and says, "I hear it's relaxing."

~

I never say another word to River. Days pass, and life slips into a routine. Jamison settles into school, his presence becoming familiar in the halls and at lunch. It's like he's always gone to Alder Creek. Seeing him daily, and the intensely warm feeling I get each time, makes me wonder how I ever went to school without him. My days are so much better with him here. I become used to his presence, and I like it. How did I survive all those years, waiting for that one glorious month every summer when we were together?

Jamison is well liked, which isn't a surprise. He's easy to like. Clever and good-looking is an intriguing combination. I'll hear him laugh sometimes in the hallways, this deep, manly chuckle, and instinctively, I smile. Other times, I find him tucked in the corner of the library, head down, typing on his laptop, a serious expression on his face. Most days I could stare at him and never get sick of the view. But he doesn't sit on display, purposely attracting attention like most guys do. He's too focused for that, which only makes him more attractive.

As expected, Jamison starts working at the café. Marnie puts me in charge of his training. We spend days going over the cash register and how to make different drinks. Jamison busses tables, wipes down counters, and cleans dishes. Time goes by swiftly when we're working together. Jamison brings a level of enjoyment to work that I've never felt before. Our shifts together are exciting. I'm better just by being in the same space as he is. Sometimes when a familiar song comes on the radio, Jamison and I look at each other, and I know we're reliving the same childhood memory. Today, it's one by the Black Eyed Peas.

"Remember River and the marshmallow?"

When Jamison smiles, I can't help but do the same. We both break into hysterical laughter. Before I know it, tears are streaming down my face as I remember River frantically running around Jamison's backyard with a flaming marshmallow stuck to his shorts. He was showing off around the campfire, claiming he could jump over it without touching the flame. It was a supremely dumb-ass venture to begin with, but then right as River was about to try it, Jamison's marshmallow caught on fire. He flicked his stick to put the fire out, but the marshmallow went flying. It landed on River, who panicked, the marshmallow too hot to touch and too sticky to get off his clothes. He ran around the backyard, screaming as Jamison chased him with a hose. The Black Eyed Peas played in the background.

By the time "I Gotta Feeling" ends, Jamison and I are laughing uncontrollably. Customers are staring. I can't believe I ever worked this job without him and enjoyed it. He makes it so much more fun.

Life at home settles down, too. I begin to feel much more grounded. River is busy with football, and when he's home, he's mostly silent at dinner or locked in his room. Rayne sees her usual stream of clients. Even Zach texts and calls less.

But the problem with getting too comfortable is that the moment life decides to shift, you're caught unawares.

In late September, I'm smacked off kilter. During my Saturday double, Eddie announces that this is his last shift. "I'm moving," he says casually as he cleans the espresso machine.

"What?" I ask. "Where?"

"Ohio," he says. "My mom's not really doing that well. She's, you know, old. And there's no one else to take care of her except me, so . . . I figure, she put up with my shit all her life. It's about time I pay her back for dealing with me. I'm just glad Marnie hired Jamison. I don't feel so bad about leaving. And let's face it. I probably slow this place down more than help it. Jamison's way more responsible than I am."

"But Jamison isn't . . . you," I say. "I'm going to miss you, Eddie."

"Oh, you'll be fine without me. Better than fine. You won't have to cover for my ass all the time."

"I don't mind covering for your ass. I like your ass."

Eddie chuckles. "I'll miss you, too, Amoris."

As the day goes on, I feel the weight of Eddie's departure more and more, not only from the café, but from Alder Creek. Eddie's leaving feels like the end of an era. My grandma's era. He's the only person left at the café who was here when this place was hers. Now that he's leaving, it's like the café is solely Marnie's. Like I really am just an employee of someone else's business. Eddie's leaving feels like abandonment. Like he's moving on from my grandma and, in some way, me.

By afternoon, the café has calmed. A few people sit with laptops and earbuds. A table of older men huddles together, talking quietly. Eddie's bluegrass station plays lightly in the background. What I wouldn't give for a Black Eyed Peas moment right now. Jamison came in to help with the afternoon shift, and he leans back on the counter, his apron messy with coffee and milk stains.

"You have . . ." He gestures to my cheek.

"What?"

He wipes away a fine dust of cocoa powder.

"Thanks," I say, watching his face for any hint that he feels as unhinged as I do in these moments of warm, skin-to-skin contact.

The café door chimes with the arrival of another customer. Both of us step back from each other and turn. Wendy Betterman approaches the counter. She owns the Knitting Circle, a yarn shop in town.

"I got this one," Jamison says, moving toward the register. Wendy says hello to me as she examines the menu, even though she always orders the same thing—a coconut milk latte, extra hot.

"Marnie finally hired more staff," she says to Jamison.

"Yes, ma'am," he says. "What can I get you?"

She orders a coconut milk latte, extra hot, and then says, "Are you new in town?"

"Yes, ma'am. Just moved here."

"From where?"

"Kansas City?"

"Kansas?" Wendy says. "You don't have an accent. I thought people from Kansas had accents."

"An accent to you is just speech to someone else," Jamison replies.

"Smart observation. Tell me, what's Kansas like?"

"Missouri, actually."

She smiles. "What's Missouri like?"

"Not as bad as you think."

Wendy laughs. "I bet you're happy to be out of there. People can be so backward in the Midwest. They need to get out and see the world a little more. Are you enjoying our little slice of paradise? There's something about mountains that makes a person more open-minded, don't you think?"

"Nowhere is perfect," Jamison says. "But the mountains are nice."

"Isn't that the truth. I bet the girls at the high school were happy to see you."

"I wouldn't know anything about that." Jamison shoots me a sideways glance.

Wendy grins and hands him her credit card. "Sure you don't. Well, I think Marnie is lucky to have you. You're so polite and well-spoken."

Jamison runs her card. "Thank you, ma'am."

But he puts almond milk in her latte, instead of coconut milk. It's the first time he's ever slipped on an order. It's not like him. Jamison is meticulous. And when she asks him to redo the drink, Jamison abruptly says he's going on break, and he'll have Eddie or me do it.

After Wendy's order is fixed, I find Jamison in the back room, laptop open, typing away.

"Sorry about that. I needed a break," Jamison says. "I'm just a little stressed. I have to submit a short story along with my application to be considered for the creative writing program at Western and I'm nowhere near done."

I lean on the table, attempting to snag a peek at the screen, but Jamison hovers too closely for me to see what he's written.

"I'm sure your story will be great, Jay."

"I'm glad *you* believe that." He continues typing, but then he groans and says, "Damn it." He picks up the laptop and shakes it.

"I don't think that'll help."

"It constantly does this. Just dies on me, and I have to reboot it." He plugs it into the wall outlet.

I sit on the table, my legs dangling toward the floor. "Maybe it's time for a new one."

"No way. I'm a loyal man. She's been with me forever. I can't just let her go. She just needs some extra love."

"Do you always reference your laptop with female pronouns?" I ask.

"She's the best and longest relationship I've ever had with a woman."

"You're so weird."

"And you're short." Jamison nudges my dangling feet.

"I prefer vertically challenged."

"Whatever, shorty."

I shove him playfully. "Yeah, well, I can still beat you in basketball."

"Don't get on your high horse. That's only one thing."

I scoff. "Did you have another challenge in mind?"

"Maybe. Unless you're scared I'll beat you."

"Scared? If I remember correctly, you were the one who needed the night-light until sixth grade."

"This from the girl who wouldn't set foot in our basement."

"There were big spiders and old Halloween masks down there," I contend. "And it smelled bad."

"I'm telling Kaydene you said that."

"Don't!" I would never want to insult Kaydene's house. But truly, the basement is scary and damp. I extend my hand toward Jamison. "Fine. Thumb war."

"Seriously?" he taunts. "My hands are, like, double the size of yours."

I jump off the counter and get in his face. "Size doesn't matter. It's all about skill. And I've got the skills."

Jamison takes my hand and leans down toward me. "Don't say I didn't warn you."

"Like I'm afraid of you."

I've been playing guitar for almost thirteen years. If there is one part of my body that's in exceptional shape, it's my hands.

We count together. One, two, three, four, we both declare a thumb war. Jamison goes right for me, twisting his hand to grab my thumb, but I dodge, spinning out of the way. I attempt to trap his thumb next, and I almost succeed before he pulls it out from underneath my grasp.

Back and forth, our entire bodies get into the game, but neither of us gets the edge. And then Jamison spins his whole body around me, hugging me to him, using his other arm to hold me in place so I can't fight, and he captures my thumb.

"That's cheating!" I yell.

"It's called winning! Don't be a sore loser, Amoris. Just admit defeat."

Jamison has me locked to him, my thumb buried under his. I try to wrestle away from him, but he won't let go.

"Come on. Say it," Jamison demands, but I keep my lips sealed. Then he starts to tickle me, and I instantly crumble into a pile of giggles. We tangle together.

"Unfair!" I howl at him as he needles my ribs. "You know all my weak spots!" I finally manage to wiggle out from his grasp, winded and giddy, my face sore from laughing.

"Cheater," I say, pointing at him. "You know I'm defenseless when tickled. I want a rematch."

"Anytime," Jamison says. "You know where I live."

"And work, for that matter," I say, adjusting my apron and fixing my hair. "Speaking of . . ." I gesture to the front of the store, where I left Eddie to manage on his own. I'd give anything to spend the rest of the day goofing around with Jamison, and judging by his disappointed look, Jamison isn't keen on the idea of working either.

"You know, it's totally normal to mess up an order." I nudge him playfully. "It was bound to happen. No one's perfect. Wendy won't hold it against you. She's harmless."

"Harmless," Jamison says, with a tone of sarcasm.

And with that, the pull between us shatters. All laughing evaporates in an instant.

"If only people were self-aware enough to know when they're inflicting harm," Jamison adds. He looks right at me. "But people in this town don't want anything to do with self-awareness."

"What the hell did *I* do?"

Jamison stares at me intently. "Did you ever talk to River?"

"What?" I'm utterly confused. What does this have to do with Wendy Betterman?

"Did you talk to River about what he said?" Jamison asks directly again.

"Why are you bringing this up now? That was weeks ago."

"Because it's important."

"He was drunk and angry, Jay," I say, brushing off his comment. "He didn't mean it."

"How do you know, Amoris?"

"River's just going through some stuff right now. If I called him out, it might make him more upset. And I don't want to do that."

"So you decided to protect River instead of Sam?" Jamison says. "You'd rather defend the guilty than the victim."

"I know my brother, Jay. River's not a bigot."

"Bigotry isn't a disease, Amoris. You don't just have it or not have it. It's something you participate in, whether you like it or not. Excusing people for bigotry only makes it worse."

"It's not that simple," I say, turning my back on him.

"What if it was me?" he asks. At that, I spin to face Jamison again. He holds my gaze. "What if River called me . . ."

"Don't say it, Jay."

"Amoris, listen to me. That woman, Wendy, felt free to comment on how 'polite and well-spoken' I am, which means nothing to you because you're White, and no one has ever belittled your humanity because of your skin color. But as a Black person, I know exactly what she means. It's a sugar-coated way of saying, 'Good job! You're not like all the other Black people out there, those uneducated thugs raised by single moms in the ghetto.' When it's White people who made those ghettos in the first place, who created and perpetuate the system that holds Black people down. Wendy may not have said the actual word, but that's what she meant. I'm not like all the other—"

"Don't say it, Jay!"

He steps closer. "You need to ask yourself, Amoris—is your comfort really more valuable than my humanity?"

It's a question that begs an answer. But this situation is more complicated than that. Jamison is making villains out of good people, making a villain out of . . . me.

Jamison moves to leave. I reach out to stop him, but he slips through my fingertips.

"I guess old habits die hard, as the saying goes," he says. "This has always been your way."

I don't want to let him walk away again, and yet I don't hold on tight enough to make him stay. "What's been my way?"

"Silence," Jamison says.

He leaves, and the word he didn't say rings loudly in my ears.

11

THE KISS

Ellis is sprawled on my bed as I dig through my closet. A record spins, playing music softly in the background. Ellis's homework is spread out on the bed, but she's preoccupied with her phone.

"Beckett won't stop texting me," she says, annoyed. "It's homecoming. Not an engagement."

I peek out from the closet as Ellis rolls onto her stomach, nose in her phone, texting furiously. Her hair is pulled into a high ponytail, and she's wearing my pajamas. Sometimes I think the only thing that changes over the years is that we get bigger.

"If you don't like him texting you, why are you responding?" I ask.

"I treat boys like I treat my clothes. You never know what you're going to feel like wearing," she says, snapping a picture of herself. "And I'm not afraid to throw something out when it gets old."

I go back to searching for a small wooden box Chris made me years ago. The lid has a lacquered painting of his on the top, an impressionist sunset over the mountains that surround Alder Creek.

I crawl back out of the closet. "Am I a racist?"

"What?" Ellis says. "That's the dumbest question I've ever heard. Of course you're not a racist."

I want to believe her, but a part of me doubts her answer. "Are you sure?"

"Where is this coming from?" Ellis asks.

"Just something Jay said . . ."

"Did he call you a racist?"

"No, not exactly. I wouldn't even let him use the N-word."

"Case in point," Ellis says. "Racists don't mind using that word. Do you have a secret Confederate flag lying around somewhere that I don't know about?"

"Of course not."

"Then stop being ridiculous. You're as much of a racist as I am. Do you think I'm a racist?"

"No," I say. "Not at all."

"Well, if I'm not, you're not. End of discussion," Ellis says. "What are you looking for anyway?"

"A box my dad gave me." I go back to digging in the closet. I leave out the detail that inside this box is a stack of letters from Jamison.

It started in third grade, after our annual summer trip to Kansas City. I got home and there in the mailbox was the first letter I'd ever received, not including holiday cards from my grandparents. Jamison had typed it. Most of the words were spelled correctly. He gave me a list of books to read, which I didn't. I sent him back a list of songs to listen to, which he confessed later that he didn't. He complained about his sister, Talia. I complained about River. We wrote about how anxious we were for the next summer, and lists of plans we already had for each other. Sometimes a few months would go by without a letter, but when the next one arrived, Jamison would always apologize for taking so long. Those letters would be extra lengthy, walking me through his days at school, or what he was learning on his own, or the ideas he had for my return to Kansas City in the summer. Sometimes he would just ramble for pages and pages. Nothing of importance, just thought after thought. Those were my favorite letters.

"What do you think about Scott Kean?" Ellis asks.

I poke my head out of the closet. "What?"

"As a homecoming date."

"I'm taking Tucker. For Sam." Zach offered to fly home, but I refused him on the grounds that it was ridiculous to fly across the country for a stupid high school dance. That, and other reasons I was unwilling to share.

"Sam can't expect us to be Tucker's beards forever," Ellis says. "I'm getting sick of it. And Scott wants to take you. Beckett told me. Tell Sam you changed your mind."

"I can't do that to Sam."

"Yes, you can," she insists. "You just won't because you're too nice and you like using Tucker as an excuse not to put yourself out there. What are you so afraid of?"

Not this again.

Ellis is focused on her phone, or else she might see how annoyed her question makes me. "Beckett just asked me to come over," she says. "God, he's desperate. It's kind of pathetic. He called me his girlfriend a few days ago."

"What did you say?" I ask.

"Nothing. He can call me his girlfriend if he wants."

"Are you his girlfriend?"

"I'm neither confirming nor denying."

"Well, you can go over to his house if you want," I offer.

"No way. Chicks before dicks. Beckett can play with himself tonight." Ellis climbs off the bed and stands in front of my mirror, adjusting her long dark hair so it cascades smoothly over one shoulder. She snaps another picture of herself. She really is beautiful in a way most teenagers aren't, not a bit of awkward to her. "Beckett just sent me emojis of two blue balls. Guys are so gross."

She throws her phone on the bed and rummages around in her purse, producing a bottle of lavender oil. She dabs some on her wrists and rubs them together, then looks out the window and asks, "So what has Jamison been up to? I hardly ever see him at school, and he never comes out on the weekends."

"It's been busy at the café. Eddie quit. He's leaving Alder Creek." I go back to digging in my closet.

"Did Fast Eddie finally realize he needs a real job? I'd say I'll miss him, but that would be lying," Ellis mocks, picking up her phone again. "We should invite Jamison over. Do you want me to text him?"

"No!" I shout, too quickly. Ellis freezes, phone in hand. "He's working on college stuff. Don't bother him."

I actually have no idea what he's doing. It's taken all my energy not to stare at the house next door, waiting to see him. Nothing has been right between us since our tense conversation at the café.

"Amoris, boys want you to bother them. They live for that shit. I'm sure he'd drop whatever he's working on if we asked." She tosses my phone at me. I don't pick it up. "Come on. What are you waiting for? He won't say no. I promise." When I don't move to pick up the phone, Ellis rolls her eyes. "See. You're hiding again. Why are you such a sissy?"

"Because I won't send a half-naked picture to a guy? Sorry, Elle. I'm not like you."

"OK, first," Ellis states, "spare me the hyperbole. I wasn't half-naked in that picture. I'm in your pajamas. And second, what's so wrong with being like me? So what if I'm headstrong? If I were a man, people would call me a leader, but because I'm a woman, I'm a bitch. Well, fuck that. Excuse me if I won't sit back and let other people tell me how to live."

"I didn't call you a bitch."

"You didn't have to. It was in your tone."

She might be right about that. But I hate when she talks about Jamison. My entire body reacts. I contract, like I need to protect myself. I'm trying to keep the past squarely where it belongs, and yet the idea of what might happen if those two were alone together again keeps creeping up on me like a recurring nightmare.

The worst part was that I didn't see the kiss coming. One minute we were playing an innocent game of ghost in the graveyard, and the next I found Jamison and Ellis kissing behind our garage. When the game was over, they acted like nothing happened. And the next day, the Rushes left to go home. It was the only summer they came to Alder Creek, a decision Rayne made because Ellis was living with us, and she didn't want to take us all to Kansas City in case Matt Osmond came home from his travels. I knew it was wrong to be mad at Ellis—I wasn't the one with a dead mom, an AWOL dad, and a broken heart—but I felt it anyway.

"Please don't text Jamison," I beg. I hate the sound of it.

"What's the big deal?" Ellis asks. She stands at my window. Can I really blame her for who she is? For that kiss when I never spoke a word about my feelings for Jamison? Never gave her any clue?

When Ellis was finally living back at her house, I should have missed her sleeping next to me every night. But a part of me, the ugliest, darkest part, was glad she was suffering. It was worse to be Ellis than me.

But Ellis didn't need that kiss. Not like I did.

"I just want to hang out with you tonight," I say. "No boys. Chicks before dicks, right?"

"I guess I did say that," Ellis says.

"And you're not a bitch, Elle."

"Yes, I am." She smiles. "But I know that."

I finally find the box I'm searching for. I open the lid, and Jamison's letters are stacked neatly, organized by date. I take the top one.

Ellis sticks her head in the closet. "I'm making tea. Want some?"

"No, thanks."

When Ellis is gone, I open the last letter Jamison sent me. When it was my turn to write him back, so many times I sat down at the computer and tried to type. But all I could picture was the kiss. His hands cradling her in the way I had only dreamed about. Weeks turned into months that turned into a year that turned into years. It wasn't until he showed up at dinner six weeks ago that we spoke again. Eventually, I stopped trying to find the words. Instead, like always, I hid, and let silence do the talking.

12

DEATH BY A MILLION PINPRICKS

Chris returns to Alder Creek in October with a newly cracked tooth. Rayne scolds him lovingly about dental bills and self-restraint, but Chris just wraps his arms around her waist, pulls her into an embarrassingly mushy embrace, and says, "Will you still love me when I'm toothless?"

Chris is a nail-biter. Always has been. He'll stand in front of a canvas, nails between his teeth, thinking. When it's his day to wash the dishes, he'll put his hands in the hot, soapy water and seethe in pain, his nails bitten so far down they're raw. "Creativity has its costs, and I've paid in nails," he'll announce.

He chipped his first tooth last year. The dentist told him nail-biting had worn his teeth down, and if he didn't stop, more would chip. Clearly, Chris didn't heed the warning.

I leave my parents alone and go to play guitar in my room. But one thought keeps distracting me—would Chris really risk losing his teeth just to keep up with the gross habit of biting his nails? Why is it so hard for humans to quit what they know is hurting them? Why is it so hard to admit we're doing it all wrong?

Eddie officially left Alder Creek. I went by his apartment before he left. I'll miss him. The café just isn't the same now. Marnie hired a girl named Louisa. She's German, traveling the world for a year. She's staying in Alder Creek until she's earned enough money for a plane ticket to Australia. No one seems to stay put, except me. And I still haven't looked at the college brochures Lori gave me. They sit on the dresser in my room, staring at me. Taunting me to imagine a different life. I'm sure the universities have amazing sports facilities, or top-rated organic, allergy-friendly dining halls, but none of that would tempt me anyway.

"Amoris," Chris calls up. "How about the Allman Brothers tonight?"

He's standing under my window, acting like nothing has changed. Like he can just come home to the same music, the same routine. I glance at Jamison's apartment. It should be easy just to cross the bridge and say I'm sorry for being a wimp with River. I'm sorry I let Jamison down. His opinion means a lot to me, and knowing I've tarnished that feels shitty.

"Amoris?"

"Any specific album?" I reply like I always do with my dad, because I'm weak and I don't know what else to say.

"*Brothers and Sisters.* Let's make something beautiful tonight."

I'm imagining it, but I swear I can see Chris's chipped teeth from up here.

The album Chris has requested spins on the turntable quietly as I play along. My fingers move methodically. A habit ingrained in my muscles and bones. But there's no comfort in playing tonight, especially when the smell of weed drifts into my room.

It's so familiar, almost comforting. If he was bottled in Rayne's studio, Chris's label would read "weed." It never occurred to me how messed up that is. Not aftershave or mint shampoo or even sweat socks. He smells like drugs. Should I really be surprised that River has come home almost every weekend night since Ellis's party stinking of alcohol or weed? He comes by it honestly.

I slam my window closed and stop the record. My heartbeat pounds in my ears. But the silence now filling the room only makes me angrier.

Silence is the worst kind of screaming.

But what to say? What if Chris never changes? What if he can't? I know why he bites his nails. Sometimes familiar pain is just more bearable than change.

~

I can't take it anymore. I can't stare at college brochures. I can't send the same text to Zach night after night. I can't make another latte. I can't play the same music over and over. I can't be in the same room with my dad and keep pretending nothing's changed. I can't keep rereading Jamison's letters, wishing I had just written him back all those years ago, explaining what I saw, asking for answers I desperately needed.

I'm sick of being a cover song, I'm thinking as I arrive at the library. Jamison and Sam are sitting together, Sam with a sketchbook in hand, Jamison with his laptop open. But neither of them is working. Their heads are angled toward each other, exchanging whispers.

"Are you going to tell anyone?" Sam asks.

"Who?" Jamison asks. "There isn't a single Black teacher in this school."

"Mr. O'Brien?" Sam offers. "He's White, but he's gay, which means he's seen his fair share of bullshit."

"The principal?" Jamison states. "No way."

"Why not?"

Why would Jamison need to go to the principal? I had assumed they were whispering out of obligation to the library rules, not because they share a secret. I duck behind a bookshelf, telling myself I don't want to interrupt, knowing full well that I really want to eavesdrop.

"I just need to put up with it," Jamison says. "It's not worth the hassle."

"Said every oppressed person while continually being oppressed. That attitude won't change the world."

"I don't want to change the world, Sam," Jamison says. "I just want to get through high school."

"Maybe you can do both. Look at Parkland. Black Lives Matter. Fucking Tiananmen Square! All led by teenagers!"

"Keep it down." Jamison glances around the library. I press myself against the shelves, hoping he can't see me. "Sam. This is different."

"How?"

"Those are big issues," Jamison says. "National news. Social media fodder. The moments hashtag creators dream of. White people love retweeting and posting shit like that because it's easy. It makes them feel like they've done something good for Black people, all the while staying properly removed. But this? It's in their backyard. It's personal. The worst kind of racist is the person who insists they're not racist. I'd rather live with this than deal with White denial. Either way, nothing changes, and I'll pay the price. I just need to ignore it and move on."

"Can you really live with seeing it every day?" Sam asks. "Take it from the resident artist—everything in a painting is deliberate. It has meaning. You and I both know what that ship represents. I get that the big issues pull a lot of attention, but that doesn't mean you should suffer death by a million pinpricks just because you're one of the only Black kids in this school and White people are afraid of the word 'racist.'"

Jamison looks from Sam to his laptop. "Seven months and I graduate. That's what I need to focus on. Getting into college. This is temporary."

"Well, at least you aren't counting down the days," Sam says. Jamison chuckles. "What about Amoris? Are you going to tell her about it?"

"No," Jamison says emphatically. "She doesn't see it."

"I get it," Sam says. "Half the time my dad doesn't see it either. Don't take it too personally. She's never had her perspective challenged.

It's only been reinforced by everything she's ever seen and everything she's ever learned."

"And yet I'm the one who suffers from that miseducation."

"Have you told her that?" Sam asks. "Amoris cares about you a lot."

"And I care about her," Jamison says. "That's what so difficult."

"If she knew she was hurting you . . ."

"I tried telling her."

"And . . ."

"The conversation didn't go anywhere," Jamison says. "I hate having to defend myself when I'm the one who's been wronged. It's exhausting, especially with a person you think will understand. It's better to keep her out of it. This is between you and me. I'm just glad *someone* gets it."

I lean back on the bookshelf, deflated. I'm too late. Jamison's shut me out. I grab myself around the waist, as if that will bandage the gaping hole I feel in my chest.

"Not to change the subject and all," Sam says, "but a little bird told me Michelle wants you to ask her to homecoming. And by 'little bird,' I mean Michelle told me herself. She's never been one for subtlety."

Jamison exhales slowly. "I'm not in the market for a date."

"Did you ask someone already?"

"No," Jamison says. "And I don't plan on it."

"But you're going to the dance. You have to. I won't let you stay home."

"I wasn't planning on it."

"I know homecoming is a little high school cliché for one as sophisticated as you," Sam says.

Jamison nudges him playfully. "Shut up, man. I'm not above a high school dance. It's just . . ."

"Worried you'll sit on the bleachers all night, just hoping someone will ask you to dance?"

"I'm not worried about dancing," Jamison says.

"Then you're coming. It's decided. Something utterly dramatic and gossipworthy always happens at the dance. It's a must-attend evening."

"Fine," Jamison says. "If you insist, I'll go."

"So, what should I tell Michelle?" Sam asks.

"Tell her I have my eye on someone else. It wouldn't be fair to string her along."

"Such a gentleman. Well, don't keep me in suspense. Who's the special person?"

Jamison shakes his head. "It's just an excuse. I'm not here for a girlfriend. I don't have time for that drama."

One more second of this and I'll burst into tears. Before I can hear another word, I slink out of the library, Sam and Jamison none the wiser.

13

SHE'S NOT A FARM ANIMAL

ori sits across from me, tucked behind her desk. Rain slides down her office window in long, depressing streaks. It rarely rains in Alder Creek, but every now and then, heavy clouds will descend over the mountains and settle on the valley, encasing the town in fog and rain. The present weather has brought a chill that I can't shake.

"So," she says.

"So . . ." I echo.

"Did you peruse the college information I gave you?"

"Not yet. I'm sorry."

"It's OK. You still have time. Most applications aren't due until mid-January."

"I guess it's a good thing it's only October, then," I say.

Homecoming is this weekend. River was nominated for the sopho-more homecoming court. As traditional high school popularity goes, River's at the top of his game, and yet he's still acting like a complete asshole. It's worse when he's hungover, which has been more frequent lately. He's starting to drink like Ellis. Like he's numbing pain with booze. But what pain? It can't all be because of Chris.

"What's on your mind, Amoris?" Lori asks, her black glasses propped on the top of her head.

"I've been thinking about your last-name theory."

"What specifically about it?"

It's what Sam said to Jamison that's really eating at me. *She's never had her perspective challenged. It's only been reinforced by everything she's ever seen and everything she's ever learned.* But I didn't think that what I was learning was hurtful. Rayne would never raise a child like that. My life has been a collage of peace, love, and happiness. How is that wrong? Aren't Rayne's footsteps the right kind to follow? And yet, I've always just accepted that perspective as right. I've accepted her path, instead of trusting myself to find my own way.

"I'm worried I've been a follower my whole life," I confess. "And I'm only now realizing maybe that's not such a good thing."

"Don't be too hard on yourself," Lori says. "You've been brainwashed since you were in kindergarten. Maybe even before that. We all have."

"So, I'm just a cog in some messed-up societal system?"

Lori laughs. "Yeah, kind of. Capitalism doesn't thrive on unique thinkers. It thrives on factory workers. In a way, our public educational system is rigged. It always has been."

"Why are you here if you don't believe in it?" I ask.

Lori leans across her desk and whispers, "To fuck with the system. Someone has to."

"So is that the answer? Just step out of line and start walking in a different direction. You make it sound easy."

Lori turns serious. "It's one of the hardest things you'll ever do, Amoris. People don't like deserters. Especially people who benefit from the system, because the more people who refuse to live by the rules, the more the system crumbles. You have to decide how you want to live. Lines are easy to follow. They're comforting. It's why most people stay where they are."

"But there's a cost," I say, thinking of Jamison. *A human cost.* "Some days, I wish I was more like you."

Lori smiles. "What you should wish is to be more like *you.*"

More like me? Who am I, if not a cog in the machine? It's all I've ever known.

"Who am I?" I ask.

"Keep looking. You'll find her."

"I hope you're right," I say. "I'll look at the college brochures, but I can't promise anything."

"You can come to my office anytime, Amoris," Lori says. "That's what I'm here for. But you don't have to promise *me* anything. Make that promise to yourself."

~

Ellis is already halfway to plastered when we get to the homecoming dance. Beckett hosted a preparty with booze and weed, because God forbid any of us go to the dance sober. Maybe we feel the inclination to get drunk because, without knowing it, we've been programmed, set on a path we're desperately searching for a way out of, an escape from the inevitable. Except the morning always comes around, and the hangover reminds us of the cost of stepping out of line.

The dance is a formality. A photo opportunity for parents to get pictures of their teenagers all dressed up. For us to look like innocent, untarnished adolescents with good morals and prude intentions. A parental Facebook moment. And it's all a lie. The dance is an intermission between pre- and postparties, unless you're a freshman. It's foreplay on a grand scale. The night will inevitably end messy, dresses and suits balled up on the floor of someone's bedroom, left to wrinkle.

Ellis dances into the gym, Beckett on her arm, the two of them a pristine couple to be envied. Tucker is with me. For a fake date, he plays the part well. He's attentive and complimentary. In truth, it feels quite nice to have a boy dote on me. He even brought me a corsage. And dressed in a blue collared shirt, khaki pants, and cowboy boots, Tucker looks handsome. I can tell Sam thinks the same by the way he's eyed Tucker like candy all night.

And while Tucker's appearance is nice to observe, I have to keep telling myself to focus on my date. My gaze just wouldn't stop drifting to Jamison at the preparty. Still dateless, he's dressed in fitted dark-gray pants, a white, crisp button-down, and a clean pair of black Vans. It's impossible not to notice him, and it's excruciating at the same time. But I've barely been able to gawk at him since we got to the school. He and Sam disappeared before we made it out on the dance floor.

"One hour," Ellis says. "And then we're out of here. I don't want my buzz wearing off."

She and Beckett disappear on the dance floor, swallowed by people. I gesture toward the bleachers.

"Oh, thank God," Tucker says. "I can't dance in front of these people."

"Are you that bad?"

"No, I'm that *gay*. One Justin Timberlake song and the whole place would know."

I laugh as we sit down on the bleachers. It's not three songs into the dance when Tucker looks at me and says, "Is Jamison gay?"

"What?"

"Just be honest with me, do I have competition? I swear all I hear about is Jamison this and Jamison that. I'm worried." There's real panic in Tucker's voice. I put my hand on his thigh.

"You don't need to worry. Jamison isn't gay."

"You're sure?"

"I'm sure."

Tucker relaxes, leaning forward and resting his elbows on his thighs. I can see the defined outline of his muscles through his shirt. The girls at his school must be all over him.

"I'm worried Sam is getting tired of this," he admits. "I don't blame him. Lying is exhausting."

"Is it really that bad?" I ask. "You can't come out?"

"I'd lose everything," Tucker sighs. "No sports. No friends. I don't even know what my parents would do. They'd probably move just to get away from the shame, which means I wouldn't just be ruining my life, but theirs, too. My family's lived in Eaton Falls for generations. Our land is everything to them. I couldn't do that. Not now. Not when I'm so exposed. I can wait. College isn't far off. Next year at this time, my life will be different. I'll be on my own. My parents can make up some story as to why I never come home. No one in town needs to know, and we'll all be safe."

"But in that scenario, you're still losing your home, your family. Doesn't that make you sad?"

"Is it really my home or family if I'm not accepted as I am?" he asks. "Home should be a place where you feel safe. Where you're accepted just as you are. I'm living in the illusion of home right now, but the truth is, Sam is my home."

Tucker may have just described love perfectly, or at least what I think love is meant to be. "That's beautiful," I say.

Tucker stands and holds out his hand. "Enough moping. Come on. Let's dance."

"What about your bodacious gay moves?"

"It's a slow song," Tucker says. "I'll grab your ass. No one will know."

Tucker spins me out onto the dance floor and then pulls me in close, his chest coming to rest against mine. It feels good to be in someone's arms again, even if it is my gay best friend's boyfriend.

"You're right. You are a good dancer," I say as Tucker leads me around the floor, his hand pressed to the small of my back. "Don't forget the ass grab. Make it look real."

"Or I could just kiss you and make it really obvious."

Tucker's lips are tempting, all pink and full. My body feels abandoned. I went from kissing Zach nearly every day to nothing. I'd be lying if I said I wasn't craving some intimacy.

"It's an interesting offer," I say. "But your boyfriend just walked back into the gym."

Jamison and Sam emerge through the crowd. When Tucker lets me go, I immediately miss the warm feeling of his body next to mine.

"Tuck," Sam says seriously when they reach us. "I want to show you something."

"This better be good," Tucker says. "I was dancing with a really hot chick. I think she's into me."

"Woman," Jamison corrects. "She's not a farm animal."

"Sorry. An intelligent, strong, hot *woman*."

"I'll accept that," I say.

"I'll keep an eye on your date," Jamison offers.

"I don't need a babysitter," I counter.

"As if you'd listen to me even if you did," Jamison says.

"I'll go, but only if you promise to dance with her," Tucker says.

Jamison nods. "I think I can manage that."

Tucker and Sam discreetly walk away, and I swear Tucker winks at me. Jamison and I stand awkwardly next to each other. How did this happen? I went from a kid who could finish Jamison's thoughts to a tongue-tied teenager.

"Where did you and Sam go?" I ask.

"Nowhere important. It's nothing." I want to strangle his vague answer. But when I move to return to the bleachers, Jamison stops me. "I promised Tucker I'd dance with you."

"Don't do me any favors, Jay. I don't want a pity dance."

"Who said anything about pity?"

The DJ puts on another slow song. Jamison wraps himself around me. I feel consumed by him, my head on his chest, his arms pulling me into his strong frame. The heat is back, but this time more intense. An all-encompassing blaze that reaches deep into my skin and bones. As much as I want to deny it, force it down, ignore it—I can't. The pull is there, ever present, no matter the awkwardness.

"What's going on?" Jamison asks. My heart pounds so heavily in my chest that I worry he can feel it drubbing against him.

I put some space between us. "Nothing."

"Are we really gonna keep doing this?" he asks.

"Doing what?" But I know what Jamison means. Silence can be so destructive. If I don't say something, he's going to leave me on the dance floor, walk away frustrated, and keep his secrets. And it will be my fault. I will have let it happen because I wasn't strong enough to stop it. Just like I wasn't strong enough three years ago.

"You were right," I blurt out. "I should have talked to River. I chose my brother over Sam, and it was wrong. I feel terrible about it. If it was you . . ." I step farther back, running my hands through my hair. "Just the thought makes me sick."

"People have said it before," Jamison says. "And they'll say it again."

"People are awful, and I hate them sometimes."

"Hate doesn't help, Amoris."

"Look, you don't need to do this. I know you're only here because Sam coerced you into coming." I attempt to step back again, but Jamison takes me in his arms.

"Do you live in my head?" Jamison asks rhetorically. "Then don't tell me what I'm thinking."

We dance quietly.

"So what does help?" I whisper. "If anger doesn't work?"

He whispers back, "Merciless honesty."

The song lingers on as those two words hang between us. Jamison has said it perfectly. It's the writer in him, the wordsmith, the observer. Because the honesty that creates the most change is always merciless. And that's exactly why I'm afraid of it.

When the song ends, Jamison takes my hand. "Come on."

"Where are we going?"

"I need to show you something."

~

He leads me down the dark, empty hallway and up the staircase to the second floor. In the quiet, it feels like we're trespassing. Snooping in a place we shouldn't.

"What are we doing?" I ask.

Jamison faces me toward the mural on the wall. "Tell me what you see."

I stare at the familiar mural, wondering if this is what Sam and Jamison were talking about in the library. But why? What's so threatening about this mural? There must be something or Jamison wouldn't have brought me here. With each passing second that I have no answer, I worry I'm disappointing him. He and Sam see this mural differently than I do. They see something important.

"Really look at it, Amoris," he whispers.

And then, like one of those magic-eye pictures where you stare at it so long that your eyes are blurred and hurting, suddenly the real figure appears.

Then it's all I can see.

"Holy shit, Jay."

"Yeah. Holy shit is right."

In the middle of the mural, painted over the waves of an American flag, is a slave ship.

14

ALMOST

Neither of us moves. We just stand there, facing the mural. "You've known this was here for months," I say. "Why didn't you tell me?"

"Because it's not about you, Amoris."

"But you told Sam."

Jamison doesn't deny it. "He understands."

"Because he's not White," I state flatly.

"Yes, but there's more to it than that. Sam's an artist. He sees the world . . ."

"Like you," I say. "Because you're an artist, too."

"Yeah . . . something like that."

What he won't say is that I don't see the world like they do. I just copy and play other people's songs. I don't create my own.

But that's not fair. He didn't give me a chance to understand.

"Maybe it's not what we think it is, Jay. Maybe it's just a ship. I mean, we didn't paint it. Who knows what the artist meant?" Jamison tenses, and I know I've made yet another mistake.

"I'm not concerned with what the artist intended, Amoris. When I look at this, I see a slave ship. A *celebrated* slave ship. Like we should be proud of this piece of American history. That's fucked up."

"OK, you're right. It's totally messed up," I say, thinking out loud. "Then we need to take action. Get the school to paint over it, maybe."

"It's not that simple."

"But maybe it is, Jay. You're so quick to doubt."

"See, Amoris, this is what I'm trying to explain to you. The difference between you and me. You feel safe reporting something like this. But there are always consequences for people who look like me. It's the same thing that just happened with Tucker. He felt safe calling you a chick. But do you like being called a chick?"

"You know that was meaningless."

"But let's say it was Beckett," Jamison asks. "Would you want Beckett calling you a chick?"

"No," I answer.

"Would you ever call him out on it?"

"Probably not, because he'd say he was trying to give me a compliment, and he'd call me an overly sensitive bitch."

"Right," Jamison says. "Being a woman makes you vulnerable in that situation. It's the same with being Black in this situation. And I can't afford that noise right now."

"But you're always separating people by race, Jay. I don't see how that helps anything. We're all human beings."

"That's bullshit, Amoris, and you know it. What if men said that to women? When people see me, they don't see a man. They see a Black man. And that perception shapes my entire life, just like being a woman shapes yours. Asking me to pretend otherwise only protects racists."

I hate that word. It's ugly. And Jamison says it like they're all around us. But I can't believe that. That's not the world I live in.

"What do you want to do, then?" I ask.

"Truthfully?"

"Yes, Jay."

"I want to walk down the street and not get looked at suspiciously. I want to use my body without worrying that someone will think I'm dangerous. I want to pretend that this piece-of-shit mural doesn't exist. That it hasn't sat on this wall for God knows how many fucking years and no one noticed. And I want to act like a teenager for once, instead of constantly being on guard. I want to have fun without worrying about the consequences."

"We can have fun," I say, taking his hand in mine. Even his skin feels tense. "What should we do? Go streaking? Toilet paper Beckett's house? Egg my brother?"

That at least makes Jamison smile, and the tension eases slightly. "Your suggestions are stereotypically juvenile."

"You said you want to act like a teenager. Technically, we're still juvenile for a few more months. We should take advantage of it. I bet we could steal some toilet paper from the bathrooms." I attempt to pull him toward the stairs, but Jamison resists.

"How about we start with something that won't potentially get us arrested." He takes me by the waist, right here, with only the faint sound of music echoing down the hallway. His hand slides up my back, pulling me to him.

"This isn't a slow song, Jay," I whisper.

"Who said I want to dance?"

Jamison lowers his face, his nose coming to my hair, and I wonder if he's memorizing my smell, like I've done with him. I squeeze my eyes closed, feeling the gloom that edges elation, knowing this can't last forever.

"Please, tell me you understand what I'm saying," Jamison whispers.

I pull back. He stares down at me with an intense look. How many times have I disappointed him? How many times did he go to the mailbox, hoping to see a letter from me that wasn't there? A text? A phone call? Anything to break the silence. How could I have done that to him? I'd give anything to change my actions. But I can't. I can only change now.

"I do," I say.

The air feels fragile. I move slowly, cautiously, reaching up on my tiptoes. It's a question in movement. *Is this OK? Can we really do this?* My mouth knows where it wants to be. I've played this moment in my imagination so many times.

It's only cheating when it actually means something. This means everything. But I decide, right now, it's worth the potential consequences.

"Amoris . . ." Jamison whispers, his mouth so close to mine. "Are you still with Zach?"

I fumble with a response, but I'm unable to lie. I am still technically with Zach. And Jamison knows it. But I was willing to forget the promise I made to Zach. The years of our relationship. The time we spent together, the secrets we shared, the trust we gave each other, just to get what I wanted. *Who* I wanted.

How could I do that?

I hear the sound of people running down the hallway, and Jamison steps back from me.

"We better go," he says.

And we walk back to the gym, in silence.

15

A LOVE SONG

Snow peppers the mountains around Alder Creek. Football season is over, and River is incessantly playing basketball now. The sound of him dribbling and shooting and dribbling again, over and over for hours, is the soundtrack of my house lately. It's better than silence.

Chris is gone again. He swore he'd be back by Thanksgiving, which happens to be tomorrow. My house is eerily silent. No more River yelling and slamming doors. Just the sound of a basketball on pavement, ticking like an irregular clock.

I managed to flip through the college material Lori gave me. After homecoming, I decided I want to get as far away from Alder Creek as an in-state tuition will allow me. Multiple college applications are permanently open on my computer, though I haven't filled in a single one. I can't seem to type my name, let alone an essay. I thought this would be the fix. College was my easy answer to life's complications. But it's just another step following in line. College feels like more brainwashing. The applications just sit there, staring at me, reminding me of my indecision.

Coward, they whisper.

"Turkey. Mashed potatoes. Peppermint. Evergreen. Eggnog. Wrapping paper." I read the labels on the bottles in Rayne's studio as she folds laundry. "Why are the holidays so hard for people?"

"People feel the pressure to rewrite personal history the way they wish it had been, instead of the way it really was," she says. "It puts a lot of stress on the body. The hardest thing to dig out of a muscle is honesty. Honesty requires change, and most people don't have time for that. They just want the pain to go away for a short time, so they can keep moving forward."

"That's depressing," I say. *And true.* Because honesty is merciless. And yet wishing away pain, without making any real change, is exactly what I've done. "Why keep treating people if they never change?"

"My mom used to say that hope is the only antidote to fear."

"Do you have a bottle of hope lying around?" I ask. "I need to borrow it."

Rayne laughs. "Unfortunately, hope never sticks around long enough."

"How rude of hope to keep disappearing on us." I pick up a bottle labeled "Sunshine" and dab some on my wrist.

"Wait long enough, and she'll come back." She winks. "She always does."

A train of people have come and gone from Rayne's studio lately. So many broken people in search of hope and a quick fix. Making appointment after appointment. And maybe that's how it goes—you fix the little things until one day you wake up and everything has changed. You look in the mirror and you don't recognize your old broken self anymore. Or . . . you keep fixing the little things, and suddenly you wake up one day and the little things still break down, and you're still in pain, and nothing has changed.

Waiting is suffocating.

"I'll be back later," I say.

"Where are you going?"

"I need a therapy session."

~

A stack of records sits next to me in the listening booth at Black and Read. I don't know how long I've been in here—minutes, hours. I'm counting the songs, not the seconds. Life is easier that way. My fingers hurt from playing. I lean back in the booth, guitar resting on my lap, and close my eyes. My hands won't move fast enough to keep up with the music. I keep tripping on the rhythms, and yet I've played these songs over a hundred times before. I'm too distracted. Too slow. Too . . . imperfect. Or maybe I'm just sick of playing them.

A new song starts and simultaneously the door of the booth opens, startling me. Jamison stands in front of me, dressed like he's going to church—crisp button-down shirt, jeans, and pristinely clean sneakers.

"I texted you, but you didn't respond," he says.

My phone is somewhere in my purse. Possibly dead. I don't want to look at it.

"You're all dressed up." But my tone doesn't sound pleased at seeing him so handsome.

"Kaydene insists I look presentable when we fly anywhere, even if it's just back to Kansas City. It's easier that way. People leave us alone."

"When do you leave?"

"Our flight's in a few hours."

"Give Talia a hug for me," I say. It's not what I really want to say. I want to apologize for being weak. I want to explain myself and my choices over the past month. I want to grab him and not let go. I want to tell him that *he's* what I'm thankful for. But all those things will only lead us to this exact same place. Right here. Nothing changed.

Jamison grips either side of the booth's frame and then without warning, steps inside and closes the door. I stand quickly, setting my guitar down. My heart hitches into my throat, Jamison's chest mere inches from mine. The booth is not really big enough for two people, and the air is instantly warm and smells of him. I get lightheaded at the suddenness of it all. He doesn't touch me but stands with a sliver of space between us. His presence is overwhelming, the sheer size of him. Overwhelming in the best way, like I could get swept up in him and never look back.

Jamison sets his copy of *Harry Potter and the Sorcerer's Stone* on the seat.

"In case you need it while I'm gone." The words come out flat. Emotionless.

I pick up the worn, familiar book. "I can't take it, Jay."

But what I really mean is, I don't deserve it.

"I don't mind," he says.

"You know I'm not a reader."

"You could try," he says.

I only love *Harry Potter* because Jay reads it to me. It's him, not the book, that I need. I place it back in his hands. "I can't."

"Fine," he says, disappointed yet again. "Happy Thanksgiving, Amoris."

And then he's gone. I collapse back on the seat. Tears sting my eyes. A love song plays in the background. I can't stand the sound of it, but I don't turn it off either. It's my punishment. I am such a disappointment.

I dig my phone out of my purse and see the text from Jamison, along with one from Zach.

Zach is why I was hoping my phone was secretly eaten by my purse, never to be found again. *Coward,* it says, louder this time.

Zach isn't coming home for Thanksgiving, and I declined his parents' offer to pay for my ticket to New York. I blamed it on Rayne. Said she needed me to help with the holiday since she's so busy with work.

Zach has sent a picture of his family at the top of the Empire State Building. He's been sending a lot of pictures lately. And texts. And Snapchats. And voice messages.

I wish you were here. I'm counting the days until I see you.

Zach's perfectly written texts piss me off. The correctness of them is infuriating.

I read Jamison's text.

No goodbye?

It reeks of frustration, and I deserve it.

I tried to dump Zach. I did. The day after homecoming. It's what a person should do when she almost cheats on her boyfriend. I sat in my bed, replaying the memory of Jamison's lips, inches from mine, how good it felt to be close to him. How it seemed everything in my life had led me there, *right then*, and how one word destroyed it.

Zach.

I hated him for ruining my perfect moment, though it wasn't his fault. It was mine. My relationship with Zach felt like something in another lifetime. Another body. Zach never made me feel the way Jamison does.

I phoned Zach the next day, to end it properly. Clean. He picked up right away.

"I'm so glad you called," he said. "I need to talk to you."

"I need to talk to you, too," I said, trying to remain soft and calm. And then he blurted out, "I can't lie to you anymore!"

"What?"

"I hate Columbia, Amoris. I hate New York City. I hate how noisy it is. I hate how bright it is, even at night. I hate how it smells like garbage and dog shit all the time. And don't get me started on the subway.

114

Yesterday I got flashed by a homeless man. At the Forty-Second Street stop. In the middle of the day. No one noticed but me! And the subway was packed! These people are crazy! Worse, they think crazy is normal!"

"It can't be that bad, Zach."

"It *is*." He was in a panic like I'd never heard. "Worse. I'm failing. I can't concentrate. It's like I'm a prisoner. I spend every day devising a plan on how to get the hell out of here."

The conversation deteriorated from there. Zach went into an all-out confession of everything that had gone wrong since he left Alder Creek. How he's been lying to me, to his family, because he didn't want to let everyone down.

"It's Columbia!" he said. "It's an Ivy League school! My dad went here! I should be happy. But I don't belong in New York."

"This happens to everyone their freshman year," I said. "It's completely normal. It'll get better. This is your dream."

"No," he said. "It's not my dream. It's what's *supposed* to be my dream. People like me go to Ivy League schools."

"People like you?" I asked.

"Do you know the strings my dad had to pull to get me in? A friend of his is on the admissions committee."

"Are you saying you shouldn't have gotten into Columbia?"

"No," Zach said. "I had the grades and test scores and stuff, but It's competitive, Amoris. I just had an edge. It's a hell of a lot easier to get in if you know someone. But now, I'm fucking it all up. My dad's gonna be so pissed."

This was about the time I decided college wasn't for me. Zach sounded like a privileged asshole. I'd never heard him talk like that before. Or maybe I'd just never noticed. I kept imagining whoever got rejected because Zach's dad "knows someone." Maybe Columbia was their dream school. Maybe they worked, like I have, saving money just to afford it. Did they cry when they got the rejection? Where did they go to college instead? And how is their life different because of one single decision? It made me want to end our relationship even more.

But then Zach started crying. Not just a few whimpers. Messy, snot-ridden tears that made him hiccup as he talked. "I need you, Amoris." Hiccup. Snort. Wipe. "You're the only thing that helps. Thinking about seeing you again. Being together."

Hiccup. Snort. Wipe. Over and over again.

And then he said the three words that broke my resolve completely. "I love you."

Hiccup. Snort. Wipe.

He said it once before, and it paralyzed me then. I didn't say it back. Never have.

"There's magic between us. Right, Amoris? We're magic together. And I know you're overwhelmed right now with what I'm telling you, but I needed you to know. I love you, and I want to come home so we can be together."

When I could finally get words out of my mouth, I asked, "What are you going to do?"

Zach composed himself. "I just need to wait it out here until Christmas. I'll tell my parents everything when I'm home for the holiday. I'm not going back. I have it all figured out. I'll go to college in Boulder. Start fresh with a new semester. It's only a few hours away. And we can see each other on the weekends."

I tried one last time to stop him, but he cut me off.

"I'm happy when I'm with you," he said. "I swear, you're the only thing that gets me through the day here. If I didn't have you, I don't know what I'd do. Probably jump into the Hudson and put myself out of my misery."

Was that a suicide threat?

After that, I said nothing.

"It was fate," he said. "That day in the record store. We're meant to be together. I can just feel it."

I had nothing to offer but silence. Cold. Dead. Silence.

You'd think I'd have learned my lesson, but I was caught. How could I break up with Zach now? He was acting like Romeo, offering love and suicide in one breath.

And a part of me knew he deserved better. *I* was the failure. Not him.

"I'm sorry," Zach said. "You called me and I unloaded on you. I'm an ass. What did you want to talk about?"

I stood at my window, staring at the house next door, and served Zach a pretty lie that almost choked me to death. "Nothing. It's not important right now."

He went on to tell me all the research he'd done on apartments in Boulder. He'd called the school about transferring. "I'll only be a semester behind, but if I take classes in the summer, I'll catch up quickly and still graduate in four years. I just know I'll be more comfortable in Boulder. People in New York City just aren't like me."

I uttered almost those same words to Rayne when I returned from New York last summer. Hearing Zach say them made me cringe. Is life really about surrounding yourself with familiarity? Backing out of uncomfortable situations? A safe life like that feels empty now.

The conversation with Zach was over a month ago. I promised myself I'd wait for Christmas to break up with him officially. When he's home. I owe him at least that. Zach didn't do anything wrong. He didn't fall for someone else behind my back. Zach factored me into all the changes he has planned. But me—I've eliminated him without his knowing.

And it hurts. Some days, I think I might drown in my own sadness, just to save Zach from actually doing exactly that.

The booth at Black and Read gets smaller and smaller the longer I sit. And as a love song continues to play, I close my eyes and cry.

16

ATTENTION, ATTENTION

River and Matt, Ellis's dad, are watching football in the living room, occasionally yelling at the television, as Ellis and Rayne, who are wearing matching aprons, flit around the kitchen. Rayne is mashing potatoes in a large pot on the stove. Ellis is setting the table. Rayne wipes her long hair from her face and exhales, arching her back, her spine cracking.

"Oh my God. That did not sound good," Ellis says.

"Effects of the job," Rayne says.

"So, in fixing other people's bodies, you allow yours to fall apart," Ellis says. "That's kind of messed up." She forces Rayne into a seat so she can massage her shoulders. It's a nice gesture. Why didn't I think of that?

Grayish circles hang under my mom's eyes. She was up early tending to the turkey and shopping for last-minute supplies at the grocery store. Thanksgiving is Rayne's favorite holiday because the only gift exchanged is love, and thus no one is disappointed when they unwrap it. But this year, she's less enthusiastic.

"Better?" Ellis asks.

"Much. Thank you, Ellis."

Another uproar comes from the living room. Yelling about a bad call and a bullshit penalty. Then River hollers, "When's the food gonna be ready? I'm starving!"

Rayne opens the oven door to check the turkey. "Shit!" she screams, grabbing her hand and slamming the door closed. "I forgot to put on an oven mitt!"

I race to the freezer for an icepack, but Ellis is there first. She grabs a kitchen towel and wraps it around Rayne's burned hand, sitting her back down at the table.

"Are you OK, Mom?" Ellis says.

We all hear the slip. The room falls silent.

River yells again, "Mom! The food! When's it gonna be ready?"

"If you want food, come in here and make it yourself!" I yell at him.

River storms into the kitchen. "What the hell is going on?" he asks in an ugly, selfish way. In an "I'm hungry and growing and I need to consume a lot of calories, where is my food?" way. Just as I'm about to unleash on him, Chris appears in the doorway, duffel bag in hand.

"Happy Thanksgiving!" He drops his bag onto the floor. "I had to drive through the night, but I made it, just like I said I would."

River claps exaggeratedly. "Well, now today officially fucking sucks."

"Good to see you, too, son," Chris counters.

River exits the kitchen for his bedroom.

"I can see he hasn't changed a bit since I left." Chris kisses Rayne on the forehead, and then scoops a spoonful of mashed potatoes from the pot, eating it. "It needs more salt," he says casually, with no regard to Rayne's burned hand or the other tension in the kitchen.

"I was getting to that," Rayne says.

Chris is stoned. I can see it in his eyes, the way they're glazed over, the way he can't concentrate. His flippant attitude. The way he's eyeing the food like a famished animal. He's blitzed, like the thought of being with us had him reaching for an escape before he ever even got here.

"I'm gonna take a quick nap," he says with a yawn. "Thirty minutes. Maybe an hour. I'll be right as rain. Get it? Right as my Rayne. My perfect, beautiful Rayne."

He isn't making any sense. And he still hasn't noticed that his perfect, beautiful Rayne is hurt. He heads for the studio next door, leaving the duffel bag behind him, full of dirty laundry, no doubt.

"Amoris, can you salt the potatoes?" Rayne asks, setting to her tasks again, as if this whole disastrous scene didn't just happen.

Ellis bandages Rayne's hand. The football game ends. After we eat, Matt sets the bakery pies on the table and does the dishes. I guess he's good for something. River doesn't make an appearance until after everything is cleaned up. Then he gets leftovers from the fridge and makes a mess all over again.

Chris sleeps through Thanksgiving dinner, missing it completely. Our house is anything but utopian today. Shangri-La might exist, but it sure as hell isn't here.

~

Ellis flops onto my bed like a dead fish. "I'm stuffed. I can't move."

I can't sit down, but pacing isn't helping with my anger. Chris missed dinner. I can't believe he missed dinner. Why does he love weed more than our family? And why am I just noticing this now? For years, I thought he wanted me to play guitar while he painted so we could be connected, but really, he just wants music to create by. He doesn't do it for me, he does it for him.

Ellis is too preoccupied with texting Beckett to see how livid I am.

She called Rayne *Mom*. I know it was a slip, but that's eating at me, too. Like Ellis is attempting to take her away from me.

"Beckett wants me to come over tonight," Ellis says. "I swear he's a sexaholic. Is that a word? Well, whatever you call people who want to have sex all the time. That's what he is."

"Nymphomaniac," I say.

"Yes! That's the word. Beckett is a nymphomaniac. He's got major problems."

"Then why are you with him?" I ask.

Ellis looks at me pointedly. "Because we all have problems. Hold the bitch-mode judgment, Amoris."

"I'm just sick of hearing about Beckett."

"So, let me get this straight—you and Zach have sex and I have to hear all the *boring* details, but now, you don't want to hear about me and Beckett. Jealous much?"

"I'm not jealous."

"Could have fooled me. You just hate that I'm the one getting the attention and you aren't."

"What?" I gape at her.

"Oh, don't play dumb, Amoris. You love attention. It's why you dated Zach in the first place. Because he paid attention to you."

"Me? What about *you*?"

"It's no secret I like attention," Ellis says matter-of-factly. "I'm pretty sure any psychologist would say that's common for girls with dead moms. But I'm not pretending I'm someone else. I own it." Ellis grabs her purse and marches toward the door. "You, on the other hand, are the worst kind of liar, because you've convinced yourself you're a good person, that whatever you do, you're doing it for the good of others. But it's really just to benefit yourself. It's *all* about you."

She leaves, and my room grows achingly silent. I might break down into unstoppable tears. This day has dissolved around me. I can't stay here.

Sam answers my SOS text almost immediately. On my way to meet him, I check the glovebox of the Airstream where Chris keeps his weed. A bunch of prescription pill containers are filled with perfectly wrapped joints. I take one.

"Where do you want to go?" Sam asks when I get into his car.

"Anywhere but Alder Creek," I say.

Even if it is just for a night, I need to get out of this town before it suffocates me.

17

IT'S A VERB

Tucker and I are blazed. I didn't feel high for a while, so I kept hitting the joint. Then it hit me like a bulldozer. My limbs are numb, and my brain is a mix of fog and complete awareness. Like nothing makes sense and yet everything makes sense, but when it actually comes to speaking the truth of the universe, it gets caught in my head and only gibberish comes out. If only a person could see into my brain, all the world's problems would be solved. But that's the irony of weed. Chris might be a genius, but he's the only one who knows it. To the rest of the world, he's just a pothead.

We're somewhere between Alder Creek and Eaton Falls, pulled off to the side of a country road, lying in a field on a blanket, stars above us.

"I can't move," I say.

"Me, neither," Tucker says.

"Don't worry," Sam says. "I'll protect you from the bears and mountain lions." He's lying next to us, completely sober.

"You're such a good friend, Sammy," I say.

"A good friend wouldn't have let you get stoned in the first place. I'm a great friend."

"I think the earth is eating me," I say. "Are we sinking?"

"Yes," Tucker says.

"No," Sam says.

"Will you save us, Sammy?" I ask.

"Always." He takes Tucker's hand.

When Sam picked me up, he said Tucker had called in a panic. He was hiding out at a gas station in Eaton Falls. One of his little cousins, who was over for Thanksgiving, found his phone and was looking through the pictures.

"There was one from homecoming," Sam said. "It was completely innocent, but we were shirtless."

"What did Tucker do?" I asked.

"Luckily, his cousin is too small to really know what she was looking at. He told her we were friends. It's not like Tucker isn't around a lot of shirtless guys playing sports, so it's a plausible story." And then Sam was quiet for a time, before he said, "But he deleted the picture."

Sam kept his eyes on the road. He didn't need to say out loud what he was thinking. No one wants to be deleted, especially by the person they love.

Now as we lie in the field, Tucker holds Sam's hand, and all feels right between them again. For now. And maybe now is all we ever get.

"I wish we could stay here forever," Tucker says. He rolls onto his side to look at Sam. "Maybe we should run away." He sounds too earnest.

"Stick to the plan," Sam says. "We'll wait."

"I don't know if I'll make it," Tucker says. "I might disappear by then."

Sam turns to Tucker. Eye to eye. "*I* see you," Sam says. He brings Tucker's hand to his lips and kisses it. "I won't let you disappear."

I peel myself off the ground, sensing that they need some time alone. "I left something in the car. I'll be back in like thirty minutes."

Sam requests an hour.

But the idea of sitting in the car alone is too pathetic. The fresh air feels good tonight, so I wander through the trees. There are no lights to pollute the sky out here. The stars look like countless tiny crystals hanging in the dark night.

It's freeing to be lost in open space. Like I could go wherever I desire. I never thought that was something I wanted. I'm still not sure it is. But lately I've had more thoughts about life outside of Alder Creek.

I sit down, leaning up against a tree. And without thought, because thought has failed me too many times, I text Jamison. The past month, every moment between us has felt tense. But not tonight.

I'm lost in the middle of the woods.

My phone rings almost immediately.

"What the hell is going on, Amoris? Where are you? Are you OK?"

I whisper into the phone. "I'm stoned. It's rendered me useless."

"Your text scared the shit out of me."

"Sorry," I say, but I think, *Not sorry.*

His voice changes something in me—an invisible thing, a feeling, an essence, a being. Jamison makes me want to be a better person. Talking with him over the phone, we're suddenly *us* again. Everything that's happened over the past few months is washed away.

"Remember that dog in your neighborhood, the one I was afraid of?" I ask.

He chuckles. "Cooper."

"*Yes*, Cooper. He barked a lot."

"Don't judge a dog by its bark."

"I was so afraid of that dog. I thought for sure he was gonna bite me."

"Nah. He was harmless. Cooper just looked tough."

I can still picture Cooper's muscular body, the bared fangs, the sound of his snapping bark.

"You made us ride bikes past his house," I say.

125

"It was the only way for you to conquer your fear."

The memory is so alive in my mind, Jamison holding my hands saying, *You can do it, Amoris. You can do it.*

And me professing that *I can't! He'll bite me!*

But Jamison promised to be with me. He promised Cooper wouldn't hurt me. All I had to do was trust him.

Cooper was sitting in his front yard when we rode our bikes past the house. I couldn't tell if he was on a leash or not, not that it mattered. If he wanted to get me, I thought, Cooper would find a way. He started barking immediately, and I almost turned around. Everything was shaking. I could barely control the handlebars.

Jamison doesn't know that I was ready to admit defeat. My streak of cowardice goes back a long way. But right when I was about to turn my bike around, Jamison zoomed past me on his, peddling like a maniac. My stubborn nature kicked in. I knew Jamison wouldn't leave me behind, but I wouldn't let him go on without me. I needed to be with him. I was so hell-bent on catching up, I didn't have time to be scared about the dog. I just couldn't lose Jamison. All I wanted was Jamison. Cooper be damned. When we made it, and Cooper was still sitting safely in his front yard, Jamison jumped off his bike, taking me in his arms and swinging me in a circle. I held on so tightly, I thought I might choke the breath out of him.

But I wasn't holding him so closely because I was afraid of Cooper. For the first time, I realized Jamison could leave me. He could take off, and I'd be left following the dust of his trail. And I would follow. That's how badly I wanted him.

"I'd still be afraid of that dog today," I say, "if it wasn't for you."

"Cooper actually died last year."

"He did? That's so sad."

"It was weird to hear the neighborhood so quiet. I kinda missed the barking."

"You know what I miss?" I say.

"What?" Jamison asks.

"Us." The answer comes out as more of a whisper, like my mind somehow slipped through the cracks and spoke before I could think better of it. We don't say a word, but I can feel Jamison thinking. Even through the phone, the pull between us is undeniable. What would happen if we both just gave in?

"So where are you tonight?" I finally ask. "I didn't interrupt a date or anything?"

"Just a party with friends."

"Are you having fun?"

"I was until I saw your text."

"Sorry," I say again, still not meaning it. Jamison is what I need after such a disastrous day.

"What the hell are you doing getting stoned, Amoris? That's not your thing."

I play with the grass between my fingers, feeling the earth and wishing Jamison was next to me.

"My dad missed Thanksgiving. He came home stoned and slept right through it."

"So, you decided to get stoned yourself."

"I just needed to . . . get out of my head."

"And back at Chris?" he asks.

"Maybe . . . a little. How do you know me so well?"

"I'm well acquainted with your self-destructive tendencies."

I scoff. "I'm not self-destructive."

Jamison chuckles. "Right . . ."

We both get quiet again. I could stay on the phone with him all night and be completely content.

"You sound different, Jay. Happier," I say. "Are you happier in Kansas City?" What I really want to ask is—*are you happier without me?*

"It's complicated, Amoris."

"Explain it to me."

"Now isn't the time."

"I'm not going anywhere," I say. "I'm lost in the middle of the woods, remember."

"Seriously, that makes me worried."

"Don't be worried. Sam will find me when he's ready."

"Sam's there? I'm texting him."

"Come on, Jay. Talk to me."

"I'm just different here," he says. "I *feel* different. Alder Creek isn't my home, Amoris."

"But it *could* be. Can't you just try?"

"It's not about *me* trying." Jamison's tone loses its lightness. "We can talk about this later, when you're not stoned."

"No," I say. "I want to talk about this now."

"Just drop it, Amoris."

"If you hate it so much, why move here?"

"I didn't say I hated it."

"Well, there are plenty of other towns in this state. You didn't have to choose Alder Creek."

"Haven't you figured out by now why I came?" Jamison yells. All my words disappear. "I'm texting Sam to come find you."

"Don't," I finally manage. "Not yet. Please."

"I have to go."

I want to keep talking, but my mind is in a fog. Damn this weed. Did Jamison just say he moved to Alder Creek for me?

"Don't move," Jamison says. "I'm texting Sam to come find you."

I want to beg him not to hang up, plead with him to just stay with me. *We can figure this out. Just don't leave. Don't let me go. Don't give up on me. I know I've made mistakes, but I'll do better.* Instead, I say, "Enjoy your party."

"Don't do that, Amoris."

"Do what?"

"Self-destruct. Tell me you'll stay put until Sam finds you."

I pause, out of petulance, before conceding. "I'll stay put until Sam finds me."

I'm sitting against the tree, phone in my hand, when Sam comes through the darkness. He picks me up off the ground, and we walk back to the car.

"Have you ever noticed that love is a verb?" I say to him.

"Profound."

"I need to do something, Sam. I need to show him."

"Who?"

"Jamison."

"What are you going to do?"

The next day, as I'm lying in bed, the brain fog finally starting to recede, an idea comes to me. Jamison told me what he needed, but he was afraid to do it himself.

The mural.

It needs to go, and I'm going to make that happen.

18

BACKMASKING

I remember the first time I heard the words "I buried Paul" at the end of the Beatles' "Strawberry Fields Forever." It's harder to hear on my grandmother's old vinyl than on the newer digital remasters of *Magical Mystery Tour*. You have to listen really closely, past the crackles and white noise. But after I heard it once, I could never listen to the song again without hearing it. It was like this thing that barely existed, a whisper you aren't sure you even heard, all of a sudden becomes a shout.

Right at the end of "Strawberry Fields Forever," when the music gets all psychedelic, with flutes and brass and drums, like the instruments are trying to distract you from what's really going on, a person speaks: *I buried Paul*. Your ear has to reach for it or you'll follow the twittering flute instead of the words.

But once you hear it, it's like being invited in on a secret.

After that, I was so intrigued, I got online and researched all the other messages I'd missed. "Strawberry Fields Forever" wasn't alone. The Beatles loved secret messages. They riddled their albums with them.

It was during my research that I first heard the term "backmasking," where a message is recorded in reverse, and the only way to hear it is if you play the vinyl backward. At the end of "I'm So Tired," it sounds like John Lennon is speaking gibberish, but played in reverse, the gibberish becomes words. Unless you know about backmasking, you'll always just hear gibberish.

For nearly eighteen years, I had been playing the record how it was meant to be played. The way my mom taught me, and her mom taught her. I'd forgotten a record could spin in a different direction, revealing a whole new message.

I go to school early to meet with Lori, having emailed her the night before, asking for an impromptu meeting but not divulging what about. She didn't ask. She simply said to come to her office.

I don't expect to see anyone, so when Ellis appears in the hallway as I'm walking to the guidance office, I'm startled. I hadn't noticed her black Jeep parked outside, but I have a lot on my mind this morning.

"What are you doing here?" she asks.

"What are *you* doing here?" I counter.

"Senior Senate meeting. We're voting on prom locations." Ellis states it so plainly that I feel foolish for avoiding her question. But I haven't had any communication with her since she called me an attention hog and stormed out of my room to go hook up with Beckett, and I don't particularly want to talk to her now. I have heavier things on my mind.

"Don't be late on account of me." I continue down the hall.

But Ellis hollers after me and runs to catch up, so I have no choice but to stop.

"I'm sorry," she says. "I was a bitch on Thanksgiving. It's just . . . you know how I get on holidays. Empty Chair Syndrome rears its ugly head."

That's what Ellis started calling it after her mom died. At random moments her mom's death would become so overwhelming, Ellis couldn't breathe. She'd notice that her dad still slept on the same side of the bed, or that he only drove his own car so her mom's was constantly

131

parked in the driveway, or that he'd set the table for three people, so there was this empty chair where her mom used to sit. Like they were just waiting for her to come home. Ellis said it was like every day she was taking roll call, and when she got to her mom's name, no one answered. And each day she couldn't help but ask again, even though the seat would always be empty.

"It's OK," I say to Ellis now. "I get it."

"So, we're cool? You forgive me for being a bitch?"

It's amazing how easily Ellis owns up to being herself. It's enviable, really. I give a nod, and Ellis seems relieved, though I can't say I feel the same. A slow-moving distance is creeping up on us.

"I gotta go," I say and gesture toward the guidance office. "I'm meeting with Lori."

"I can't believe that woman still has a job. Remember when the school made me go see her freshman year for dead mommy issues? She kept trying to get me to talk to her like she was my friend or something."

"I think that's the point of therapy."

"She's a high school guidance counselor, not a therapist. She should stick to scheduling problems and college applications, not deconstructing mommy issues using the Socratic method." Ellis checks her phone. "Shit, I'm gonna be late. Text me later."

I'm relieved to walk away.

Lori is sitting at her desk typing when I walk in and take a seat.

She leans forward, resting her forearms on the desk. "Seeing as most teenagers relish any opportunity to sleep an extra minute, but you've come in early—on a Monday morning no less—this must be a big deal. What's up?"

I start into it without hesitation. "Well . . . my dad showed up to Thanksgiving high, after being away for two weeks. I haven't told you this, but he's a complete pothead. He then proceeded to fall asleep and miss the dinner, which pissed off my brother, who's been a complete ass lately and drinking way too much, but I'm starting to think maybe River's right about our dad. Then I got into a fight with my best friend, who I'm not so sure is my best friend anymore, which oddly enough, I'm not that sad about, so I'm not sure what that says about our relationship. Just a few months ago, I had my whole life planned out, but now I'm not so sure it's what I want. And I'm in love with the boy next door, but I can't break up with my boyfriend because he's at college in New York and threatened to jump into the Hudson if I do."

"Shit," Lori says.

"But that's not why I'm here."

"It's not?"

"No," I say. "I want to fuck with the system."

Lori perks up. "That's what I like to hear. How do you want to start?"

"Have you ever noticed that there's a racist mural in the hallway?"

"I'm sorry, what?"

"Yeah, going up to the second floor. My friend Jamison pointed it out to me."

"I know Jamison. Is he the boy you're in love with?"

I nod. "That's the one. I want to get the mural taken down. Can you help me?"

She stands with intention. "First things first. I need to see this mural."

~

Lori sees the slave ship right away. And again, I find myself envious of that instant awareness. A list of profanities spills out of her mouth, mixed with shock and shame that she hadn't noticed the mural sooner. I'm quick to remind her that no one did. It's been in the school for years. Thousands of students and staff have walked by it, and no one said a word, until Jamison.

"That's symbolic, really," Lori says, shaking her head. "We're programmed to ignore what we don't want to see."

Jamison said almost the same thing.

"What should we do?" I ask.

"I think our first move is to inform the principal. It's his school, after all."

We make a plan for after school. When the first bell rings, I'm certain I did the right thing. I knew Lori would understand. And I know Jamison was nervous about saying anything, but the situation isn't so scary after all.

The day is the same as always, the forward march of education, fact stacking on fact as seniors try to appear engaged while texting under desks and counting down the minutes until the next bell, and the next party, and the eventual exit from high school so we can move on with our lives.

When it all happens in the hallway at the end of the day, the slow disintegration of what I thought would occur into what actually does, "Strawberry Fields Forever" plays in my head. The song is about a Salvation Army children's home next to John Lennon's childhood house. He would look over the fence at this place that everyone saw as sad and dreary and decrepit, but there was this beautiful wild garden in which he loved to play. Lennon never saw the home the way other people did. I read an interview online with Lennon and he said "Strawberry Fields Forever" was one of the few true songs he ever wrote. That he wrote it from his actual life and not an imagined situation or story. That the Salvation Army home Strawberry Fields represented how his whole life was—he saw the world differently than everyone he'd ever met. For a while he thought he was strange or crazy, because that's what the world does to people who see what we refuse to see—what we blind ourselves to. To make our own selves feel more comfortable, we negate the voices of others we simply don't want to hear.

I imagine the scene playing out. Of course our principal, Mr. O'Brien, will immediately get rid of a racist mural. He's a decent person. Sure, he dresses like it is still 1995 and makes pop-culture references from the same year. But those are his only flaws. And I wouldn't even call them flaws. Pearl Jam is a great band. Mr. O'Brien's flannels are a staple in the mountains, and let's be honest, everyone kind of wants to know what would have happened if Oasis hadn't broken up.

And Mr. O'Brien is gay. He's seen his fair share of oppression. He's in this fight like Sam is, right? But then there's Tucker. Sometimes people who are oppressed have to fight so hard for themselves, they're exhausted, and they don't have anything left to give to others.

Mr. O'Brien, Lori, Jamison, and I crowd around the mural. My heart beats rapidly. Change is on the horizon, and nerves always accompany a shift like that. But they're good nerves. I'm doing the right thing. I'm doing this for love.

But as soon as Mr. O'Brien speaks, the record starts playing in reverse. I go from thinking I know the next lyrics to hearing a completely different tune altogether. Life is backmasking me.

"I can't just go around covering up murals," he says, "when we have no idea if that is what you say it is. I'm not convinced it is. We don't actually know that the artist intended to paint a slave ship."

"Does it really matter what the artist intended," I ask him, "if Jamison feels the impact?"

"We can't just ignore that piece of our history, Amoris," Mr. O'Brien says. "That doesn't feel effective or educational."

"But this mural celebrates it," I counter. "There's a difference."

"To you. To others . . . maybe not. No one's noticed this for years. We can't just go around painting over these things because one student doesn't like how it makes him feel."

"How it makes a *Black* student feel," Jamison clarifies.

"I don't think it behooves us to draw racial lines," Mr. O'Brien says. "That only sets back progress."

135

"I didn't draw the lines," Jamison says. "But I'm forced to live within them. You can't just go around erasing realities when it benefits you, Mr. O'Brien."

This is the moment when it dawns on me, a truth I hadn't conceived of. I've rarely noticed the turning points in my life. They've been more like curves, gentle changes of direction that, only after time has passed, I look back and see as times of change. But this, right here—I feel the immediate shift. A pivot I was not expecting.

Mr. O'Brien is knotting his hands and clenching his jaw.

"If I may—" Lori attempts, but Mr. O'Brien cuts her off.

"It's not as simple as painting over a mural," he says in a professional tone that wasn't there before. "There's lengthy paperwork and procedure involved. I'd need to take this matter to the school board. That mural is technically school property. Defacing it is a crime. Even if I wanted to paint over it, I'm not sure I could. I'm sorry."

"That's bullshit," Jamison says.

"I'll ask you to watch your language, Mr. Rush."

"You're lying to save your own ass and avoid taking action," Jamison insists.

"That's your second warning."

"So, I'm supposed to walk past this mural every day," Jamison says, "just to keep everyone else in this school comfortable. So some unknown artist isn't hurt. So *you* don't have to fill out paperwork. What you're saying is—my pain means nothing."

"I did not say that," Mr. O'Brien enunciates. "Frankly, your insinuation that I don't care for each and every one of my students is insulting. I won't stand for it."

"This mural is insulting to me," Jamison counters. "But you think I should just put up with it."

"You're twisting my words."

"Or maybe you don't really know what you're saying," Jamison says. "Maybe you're not who you think you are."

136

Mr. O'Brien takes a step back. "I came here this afternoon with an open mind and heart, but you seem bent on attacking me when I've done nothing."

"*You're* feeling attacked?" Jamison scoffs. "That's so fucking typical."

"That's enough," Mr. O'Brien says. "I'll let your language slide today, but understand this, Jamison, I know you're new to this school, but I will not tolerate bullying on any level. I suggest you take a hard look at yourself and your actions. They will have consequences if you're not careful."

Mr. O'Brien storms down the hallway toward his office. Throughout it all, Lori and I haven't moved. I'm stuck in place, completely shocked.

Lori snaps back to the moment. "Shit. That did not go as I had hoped. But don't worry. You have my full support. Let me see what I can do." She leaves in a hurry.

Jamison paces back and forth, his hands clenched in fists.

"You shouldn't have yelled," I say.

His eyes are on fire when he turns to me. I've never seen him so angry.

"Were you listening at all?" he asks.

"Yes," I say. "But you flew off the handle, Jay. What did you expect?"

"Jesus Christ, Amoris! Are you serious right now? Were you listening?"

"I'm just pointing out that you could have handled the situation better. That's all. You didn't need to swear. You got too angry. If you would have just stayed calm, he would have responded better."

Jamison laughs. "This is a theme with you."

"What?"

"Protecting the guilty instead of the innocent."

"How can you say that?"

"Wake up, Amoris. I didn't do anything to Mr. O'Brien. He's the one refusing to address the mural. He's the one who gets to walk away when it's uncomfortable for him. But me?" Jamison gestures to the mural on the wall. "See what's still here? In broad daylight? I can't walk away. There is *no* walking away for me. Mr. O'Brien just made sure of that."

"But I told Lori about the mural for you. It's like you said. I'm standing up for you when you're too vulnerable to do it yourself."

"Don't twist my words against me," he says. "You didn't do this for *me*."

"How can you say that? I'm on your side, Jay. I want to help." Tears well up and spill down my cheeks. This is a disaster.

"Can't you see what you've done?" he asks. "What you've caused? I warned you. You're self-destructive, Amoris. And now, you've brought me down with you."

When he walks away, I holler at him. "Please, I'm sorry, Jay. Don't leave. I'll fix this."

"I need space right now," he says, not looking at me.

"For how long?"

"I don't know. I just can't be around you."

"But I didn't mean for this to happen," I plead. "I know you don't believe me, but it's true. I did this for you." I don't bother wiping the tears.

"The least you could do is be honest with yourself, Amoris." Jamison is stoic. Solid. Impenetrable. "You did this for you."

And there it is. The hidden message in reverse. I did this for me. I put Jamison in a vulnerable position for *me*. I wasn't showing love. I was trying to prove myself to him, prove that I'm a good person, worthy of his love. But needing to prove myself to him is inherently and positively selfish.

Ellis warned me. She said I like attention. She said I convince myself that what I'm doing is for the benefit of others, when it's really just for myself. I was too stubborn and arrogant to listen. I simply didn't want to spin the record in another direction and reveal a new message. Reveal the truth.

19

HOT CHOCOLATE AND MY OLD MAN

Jamison's voice, cold and coarse, echoes in my memory. *Can't you see what you've done?*

I wish it was a horrible nightmare I could wake up from, panting and sweating, only to realize I'm safe in my bed and my life isn't crumbling around me.

A light dusting of snow covers the ground. The garden that was overgrown and bursting with sustenance just months ago is now withered and dead. All that's left are the twinkle lights. Rayne leaves them up all year because they're friendly and warm, and in winter we need that most. Even the sun is dim this time of year, hanging low in the sky all day. That's exactly how I feel—weighted and drained. And it's all my fault.

School is officially on break. Christmas is in a few days. Sam is visiting his grandparents in Nebraska. In an odd turn of events, Matt planned a trip to Hawaii for himself and Ellis. She won't return to Alder Creek until after the New Year.

I offered to work extra shifts at the café during the school break. Not that it's much of a relief. It doesn't feel the same as it used to. I no longer look around and think of Grandma setting up shop, selling her first coffee, baking her first scone, hanging her first picture on the wall. Instead, I think about Jamison. The time he made me laugh with foam on his upper lip like a mustache. The hidden piece of paper under the cash register where Jamison and I play never-ending games of tic-tac-toe. The funny poem he wrote one day about the guy in town who walks his cats.

Now every shift with Jamison is a torture I didn't think possible. There's no laughing or goofing around. No secrets under the cash register. The silence leaves infinite room for the imagination to create whatever dialogue it wants. I've imagined so many conversations with Jamison since the mural incident, and not a single one ends the way I want it to. With forgiveness. With an erasure of what happened. I imagine apologizing profusely, only to hear Jamison say with finality—*You did this for you.*

He's right. The power of hindsight is the ability to see the disoriented building blocks that eventually led to the crumbling. How each step I took stacked incongruently on top of the other, forming a weak structure, until it all came tumbling down.

I've replayed the conversation between Jamison and Mr. O'Brien over and over in my head. And Jamison is right. Mr. O'Brien got what he wanted, and Jamison has to live with the consequences. The guilty prevailed and the innocent suffers. I should have listened to Jamison when he said I was self-destructive. More than that, I should have simply *listened* to him. But I didn't. I didn't want to hear what he was saying. I didn't want to believe him.

That's the worst part. He tried to tell me, but it was more important to protect my own interest—getting Jamison to see what I wanted—than it was to listen to him. I negated his voice completely. I put myself in an echo chamber.

I believed in my own good intentions with no regard for the pain they might cause.

The only positive of the holiday break is that I don't have to see the mural every day. I can hide from my own shame, lock myself in my room, and play the guitar until my hands hurt as much as my heart. That's my current plan of action—complete avoidance. I only take breaks to check my Snapchat and text messages, though my phone offers no reprieve.

Zach is home. He got in last night and texted me early this morning. He wants me to call him.

I toss my phone on the bed, wishing Zach's text, the length of a small novel, would disappear in the messy sheets and never come back. I can't stop staring at Jamison's apartment next door, even though he's not home. The Rushes rented a cabin by one of the local ski resorts for the holiday. Victor and Talia flew in from Kansas City.

You'd think Jamison's absence would be a relief. It's the opposite. I've gotten used to him being nearby, and the fact that he's not has left this giant hole in my chest where all my mistakes echo. I have this ridiculous fear that he won't come back.

"Can I come in?" Chris pokes his head into my room, offering up a cup of hot chocolate.

I gesture him in but don't take the hot chocolate. We haven't spoken much since Thanksgiving. Chris walks around as if admiring an art exhibit. He eventually takes a seat on my bed, setting the hot chocolate on my nightstand. He picks up my guitar and touches the strings.

"Remember when I gave this to you?" Like I could forget. "It was so beat up. I never thought it would play."

"Then why did you buy it, if you thought it was useless?"

"I knew if there was one person who could get it to work, it was you. That's how you've always been. Someone brings you a problem. You work at it until it's solved. You're like your mom that way."

He knows I like it when he compares me to Rayne. But I turn my back on him, putting away the clean clothes Rayne delivered to my room earlier. "Some people call that being stubborn."

"Being stubborn isn't necessarily a bad thing," Chris says. "Depends on how you use it."

Well, I've used it all wrong. But I'm not about to admit that to Chris. If he's expecting a father-daughter bonding opportunity, he won't find it today.

He sets the guitar down and moves to the record crates, flipping through them. He stops Joni Mitchell's *Blue* on the player and replaces it with the Grateful Dead.

"I was listening to that," I snap.

"You've been listening to the same album for days, Amoris. It's depressing around here. Rayne burst into tears twice today."

"Joni Mitchell can have that effect on people," I say.

"It's time to liven things up!" he says cheerfully. He places the needle down and scratches the record. "Shit. Sorry."

My frustration boils over.

"Like you have any idea what it's like around here!" I yell.

"Hey, what's that supposed to mean?"

"Forget it." I go back to organizing my clothes.

"No, Amoris. Talk to your old man."

I throw a shirt to the floor. It feels so good to release some anger. "Why would I talk to you about my problems? You haven't earned the right to know about them. You moved out. You come and go as you please, smoking weed all the time. You don't want to be a dad, so stop pretending. You said so yourself. You're an alien. Sometimes I wish you would just go back to whatever planet you came from. It would be easier."

But as I speak, I realize I've had it all wrong for months. I keep thinking my life has changed, but the truth is *nothing* has changed. It's the same as it always was. Chris isn't any different than he was five months ago. *I'm* the one who's changed. *I'm* seeing things differently. It's no wonder he stands there all statuesque, shocked as I rage.

"Is that what you think?" he asks. "That I don't want to be a dad?"

"Do you?"

Chris sits back down on my bed. "You know what I wanted when I was your age? For my parents to leave me the hell alone." He runs his hands through his curly blond hair. It's salted with streaks of white, the only differentiator between my color and his. "To be honest, I still want that."

I keep my distance, unwilling to give in easily.

"Were Grandma and Grandpa Westmore really *that* bad?"

Chris eyes me. "Is poison really *that* deadly?" He chuckles. "I know I'm not conventional. Far from it. I guess I'm trying to be the parent *I* wanted. I would have given anything for my dad to be out of the house more."

His confession still doesn't solve the problem. And I'm exhausted from holding my own life together. I can't do this for Chris. He's not a worn-out guitar that needs to be fixed. This is our family. Chris is not mine to remedy. He has to figure this out himself.

"What do you need from me, Amoris?" he asks.

I'm not sure I'm the one who needs mending most. And I'm done meddling.

When I can't offer Chris an answer, he says, "Well . . . I'm here if you need me."

But for how long?

"Thanks for the hot chocolate, Dad."

"Anytime, kiddo."

After he leaves, I check on the damage Chris did to my record. It's not completely ruined, but it won't play like it used to. I place it gently back in its sleeve and into its proper alphabetical order in the crate. I'll keep it, unable to let one of Grandma's records go, but I know I won't play it again.

As the day drifts on, the mug of hot chocolate goes cold, untouched. It seems cruel to keep avoiding Zach's text. And with so much damage around me, it's about time I fix something I should have long ago.

20

R-E-S-P-E-C-T

The first time Zach and I had sex was completely unplanned. Of course I had thought about it. I'd even planned how it might happen, in the common delusions-of-grandeur way so many high school girls imagine losing their virginity. It wasn't so much rose petals on the bed, but more like incense and Eric Clapton's "Wonderful Tonight" playing softly as a backdrop to the scene.

When it actually happened, I was surprised by the spontaneity. One minute I was half-asleep in Zach's bed, the television humming lightly in the background, and the next, we were having sex. All because Zach said I love you.

I would have given anything not to hear those words. Instead of feeling excited, I felt guilty. Zach felt more for me than I felt for him. Even back then, if I'm honest with myself, I knew I couldn't love Zach. No matter what he did, I always compared him to Jamison. It didn't matter how many years had gone by since I'd seen Jamison. He was constantly present in my mind, matched against Zach. And in that battle, Zach always lost.

That night, we found what I thought was a good compromise. Zach wanted to move our relationship forward, and I did that the only way I knew how. With sex instead of love.

As I stand in the doorway of his bedroom now, staring at the bed where it happened, I feel guilty all over again. Nothing has changed. Photos of us sit on his desk. The bed is neatly made. Zach is a stickler for that.

He holds a gift in his hands. My birthday is tomorrow.

But when he sees me standing stoically, unable to muster any enthusiasm, Zach looks as if the earth just fell out from under his feet. The present slips from his grasp and falls to the ground.

"We need to talk," I say.

~

Zach doesn't get mad that I don't want to be with him. He doesn't beg me to love him or reconsider. He just asks me why. Why did I lie to him? Why didn't I just tell him the truth months ago? Why string him along?

All my excuses feel like just that—excuses.

When I say I was worried he might hurt himself, he scoffs and tells me it was all hyperbole. And I knew that.

Because it felt easier to tell you a pretty lie, I reason in my head but don't say out loud. Things felt good until they didn't. Because lies, no matter how pretty, are just that. And cowards always look for the easy way out.

"I guess what hurts," he says, "isn't that you don't want to be with me, but that you thought I was so pathetic you needed to lie."

"I don't think you're pathetic."

"But that's what lying does. It makes me into a fool for believing you."

"I've just . . . changed."

"So you've said." Zach puts more distance between us. "I didn't need you to love me, Amoris. But I hoped you would respect me." Zach hands over the gift. "It's a snow globe of New York City. I think it broke when I dropped it."

"What are you going to do about Columbia?" I ask.

"Quite frankly, Amoris, now it's none of your business. Close the door on your way out."

I open the present when I get home. The box is full of water and tiny shards of glass. I throw it away, knowing it's not salvageable. Then I contemplate texting Ellis or Sam or Tucker, but instead I return to my room, put *Blue* back on the record player, and cry into my pillow until I fall asleep.

21

UNSAFE

I'm not sure what the stages of grief are, or what order they come in, but I know anger is one of them, and I think it comes *after* the "crying your eyes out" stage.

On my eighteenth birthday, I get angry. I don't know if it's because all of my friends are away. I don't know if it's the lingering echo of Zach's final words. Or that the apartment next door is eerily quiet. But a switch flips, and all the crying I've done becomes pathetic. The puffy eyes, the moping, the wishes that I could reverse time—it all seems so desperate and useless. Anger is much more helpful.

I call Marnie and beg to pick up an extra shift. I can't be in my room any longer. I need a distraction. I offer to do anything—run the register, bake, clean toilets—anything to keep my mind off my life. Marnie says she won't allow me to clean a toilet on my birthday, but she can always use the extra help. She's taking pity on me. I can hear it in her voice, even through the phone.

A stack of cards sits on the kitchen table. Rayne sets a plate of fresh chocolate chip pancakes down next to them. She examines my overalls, my hair held back by a bandana.

"You're working on your birthday?" she says.

"I offered."

"Well, you're officially an adult, so I can't stop you," she says.

"Does this mean we can vote River out?"

"Ha ha." River plops himself in the seat next to me, his blond hair dangling in his face. I can smell the slight tang of booze on his breath.

Even Chris shows up for breakfast. He kisses Rayne on the cheek before refilling his mug with black coffee. On the surface we appear to be a regular family, but underneath we're still a mess.

It's like all the birthday mornings that came before it. There's a card from Chris's parents. Inside is a check for $118. Last year, they sent $117.

"Ah, the gift of money," Chris says. "How capitalistic of them. At least they're consistent."

"I'm happy to take their money," River says, unsuccessfully attempting to snatch the check out of my hands. The quick movement clearly makes his head ache, and he backs off, grabbing his forehead and wincing.

River regifts me a $25 Amazon gift card he got for Christmas last year.

"There's ten dollars left on it," he says. "Don't spend it all in one place."

Chris then tells me that he and Rayne decided they wanted to gift me a special piece that Chris has been working on. "It's not ready yet, but we want you to have it for next year. Are you OK waiting a bit longer for your present?"

I shrug. Seeing as I have no idea what the future holds anyway, all I care about right now is getting out of this house.

~

Work is only slightly better. I leave my phone in my purse, but I can't avoid the clock on the wall. It torments me.

Head down. Don't look up. Let the day pass like any other. But it isn't just any other day. There are thousands of people born every day. But most people never actually meet someone born on the same day, at the same time. Let alone spend time with that person. Daydream about that person. It's fate to actually know Jamison. To know a soul mate.

The clock ticks on through the morning and afternoon. I watch the minutes pass. I can't seem to help it. When the clock finally reaches 3:29, I rummage through my purse, find my phone, and check my messages.

None. I wait the entire minute, watching my phone. Second by second. When it switches to 3:30 without a single message, I put it back in my purse, my stomach rotten with disappointment.

Jamison didn't text me, but I know he saw the time. And that knowing is what kills me.

Here's the thing with anger—it likes company, and blame is always willing to join. Later in the afternoon, as I'm cleaning the baking supplies in the back, it appears.

Wendy Betterman walks into the café. I've kept my rage tamped down all day, but as I start to make her drink, it suddenly feels uncontrollable. Blaming someone else would feel good right now.

Before I can think any better of it, I snap at her. "What did you mean when you said Jamison was well-spoken?"

Wendy is aghast.

"What has gotten into you, Amoris?"

I say it again, slower, holding back her coconut latte like it's for ransom. "What did you mean when you said Jamison was well-spoken?"

"Jamison?" And then Wendy seems to put two and two together. "The new employee. I just meant that he's well-mannered and intelligent—"

"For a Black guy," I finish. "You mean he's well-mannered and intelligent for a Black guy."

"That has nothing to do with it," she counters.

"Have you ever called a White person 'well-spoken'?"

"This is ridiculous. Give me my drink." Wendy reaches for it and I hand it to her, though she has to tug it from my grasp. "I don't know what you're getting at, but I don't like it."

"Just because you don't like it doesn't mean it isn't true," I say. "Trust me. I know from experience."

"I was giving that young man a compliment," Wendy insists. "Have we become so sensitive as a society that I can't even do that? Maybe I should just keep my mouth shut."

"Maybe you should. Maybe we all should!" I throw my hands in the air, exasperated.

"I'm going to tell Marnie about this," Wendy says.

"Good. I'm going to tell Marnie about what you said to Jamison. She should know one of her customers is harassing an employee."

"Harassing!" Wendy scoffs. "I said nothing wrong to that boy. It was a compliment. If he didn't like it, that's *his* problem."

Wendy storms out of the café, and the relief I feel from confronting her dwindles quickly. I finish my shift, but before I leave, I confess everything to Marnie, recounting the original scene with Jamison and my subsequent argument with Wendy.

"I won't tolerate that kind of behavior," Marnie says after I finish.

I shove my hands in my pockets, eyes on my dirty overalls. "I'm sorry. I shouldn't have yelled at a customer."

"Amoris," Marnie says, touching my arm. "I mean that behavior from Wendy. No one is allowed to make my employees feel unsafe."

Unsafe. I hadn't really thought about it that way.

Marnie thanks me for telling her and says she'll talk to Jamison. She gives me a batch of chocolate muffins, the one in the middle topped with a birthday candle.

"You have to make a wish before you leave." She lights the candle, and she and Louisa sing a horribly off-key version of "Happy Birthday." I blow out the candle.

"What did you wish for?" Louisa asks.

"She can't tell!" Marnie interjects.

"Well, whatever it is," Louisa says, "I hope it comes true."

"Me, too," I say.

It's highly unlikely, though. Jamison is done with me. But I had to try. One last time.

22

YOU DON'T KNOW ME

Two days after Christmas, someone breaks into the apartment next door. I sit up in bed at the noise. The Rushes are gone until the New Year, but a light is on in the apartment, and the door is cracked open.

I slip on my winter boots, phone clutched in one hand, a baseball bat in the other. I don't want to alarm Rayne, and since Chris left for yet another art show and River is out with friends doing God knows what, this falls to me.

I tiptoe across the bridge and inch my way to the open door. Keeping my back to the house, I yell, "I know you're in there. I'm giving you ten seconds to leave or I'm calling the police!"

A commotion follows, and I back away from the door, baseball bat primed.

Jamison emerges, panicked and yelling, "Don't call the police!"

I stand in front of him, bat raised high. "What are you doing here?"

"What are *you* doing with a baseball bat? Were you seriously going to fight off an intruder with that?"

"So?"

"*So*, you're basically a munchkin. Next time just call 9-1-1."

"You just told me *not* to call the cops."

"Because I'm not an intruder," Jamison says. "I live here."

"Why didn't you tell me you were coming back?" I ask. This could have been bad. I could have hurt him. Our house could be surrounded by police cars.

"I wasn't aware I needed to do that."

"Well, you do." I cross my arms over my chest, still holding the bat.

"Now I have to clear my schedule with you?"

"You're not supposed to be here. You're supposed to be gone for another week."

"Well, I took the bus and came back early. Surprise. Now put the bat down."

"Don't boss me around." I turn on my heel and storm away from the apartment. I make it halfway across the bridge before I change my mind. I spin around, only to find Jamison following me. "Where's Kaydene? Why isn't she here?"

"She stayed behind." Jamison raises his hands like I'm arresting him. "Whatever you do, please don't use your bat."

I groan and stomp away, but I only make it a few steps before I throw down the bat and confront him again.

"Why didn't you text me on our birthday? I waited."

"I waited, too," he says. "Why didn't you text *me?*"

"Because I'm stubborn, and you know it."

"That's not my fault. Any other questions, Officer? Or can I go to bed now?"

So much fire courses through my veins, I might combust. If I wanted to stop my mouth now, it would be impossible. I'm a volcano of words and emotion. I've had too much time to think, here all alone with no distractions. One thing *is* his fault, and I finally want an answer. "You know what? I *do* have another question. Why, Jay? Why did you kiss her?"

"What?" he asks, surprised.

My voice cracks, but I spit it out, because it can't stay locked in me any longer. "I saw you. Behind the garage. You could have kissed anyone. Why did you choose her?"

Jamison runs his hand over his forehead, slowly understanding. "First of all, I didn't kiss Ellis. She kissed me."

"You expect me to believe that."

"It's the truth," he says fiercely. "She pulled me back there. Said she wanted to help me hide. That she knew a good spot. I had no idea she had ulterior motives."

"But you kissed her back."

"Yeah, I kissed her back!" Jamison yells. "But not for the reasons you think."

"Why then? Because it sure looked like you enjoyed it."

"Because I didn't trust her, Amoris."

"What?"

"My mom warned me about situations like those. Piss the wrong White girl off, and you're guilty, no proof needed. I knew Ellis wasn't a girl to be messed with. I figured if I kissed her back, she'd be cool. We were leaving the next day. I never thought I'd see her again."

"Why didn't you tell me?" I ask.

"You didn't give me the chance. You cut me out of your life."

"I just . . ." But words fall short. And I'm so sick of falling short. "But what was so wrong with me, Jay?"

The anger that's kept me going for weeks, maybe years, completely deflates. I'm exhausted from trying to hold myself together.

"Nothing," Jamison says. "Nothing is wrong with you." He moves toward me, but I hold out my hand to stop him. He's inches away. So close. But there *is* something wrong with me. I've been awful to him. He may have caused me pain, but I've done the same to him.

"Don't," I say. I can't handle him being this close.

Jamison steps back. "If that's really what you want."

"I don't deserve what I want, Jay. I've messed up too badly."

"You made a mistake, Amoris. Do you really think I'd give up on you that easily?"

"I don't know," I say.

"Then you don't know me at all."

Jamison turns his back on me. I can't stand the sight of him leaving. I can't stand the distance. I can't stand letting him go, or letting him down again. I can't let it happen.

I grab him like I should have years ago, pulling him to me, pressing myself against him.

"I'm sorry." I say it over and over and over again. I'll say it until he feels it to his core. "For everything. I won't do it again. I know I'm self-destructive. I've been stupid and stubborn, but I'm changing. I broke up with Zach. I yelled at Wendy Betterman. I won't hurt you again. Please, you have to forgive me, Jay. *Please.*"

Jamison pulls away, and I think this is it. This is as close as I'll ever get again. This is when he lets me go.

But then his lips fall onto mine. We stand in the middle of the bridge, and my body responds before my mind can comprehend what's happening.

Jamison's hands tangle in my hair, pressing my lips even closer to his. Before I can think straight, we're in his apartment. We stumble to the couch, falling ungracefully, neither of us willing to let go. The pressure of Jamison on top of me is euphoric. My hips grind into his, begging for more, his breath on my cheek, on my ear, on my lips.

I can't stop and think. That would mean slowing down. Not now, when I finally have what I want.

I reach down for the bottom of his shirt and begin to pull it off, but Jamison halts. His lips leave mine. Everything stops.

He looks down at me. A thin stream of doubt winds its way into my mind. My brain catches up with my body, which is never a good thing when you desperately want to avoid reality.

"You yelled at a customer?" Jamison asks.

"She deserved it."

A delectable smile grows on Jamison's face.

"I'm sorry I didn't text," he says.

"Me, too."

"Happy eighteenth birthday, Amoris."

"Happy eighteenth birthday, Jay."

Another second. A heartbeat. A hesitation.

"Jay . . . are we doomed?"

His eyes convey only honesty, merciless honesty. "Amoris . . . I truly don't know."

23

TAKE IT SLOW

G o fish," Jamison says.

We sit on opposite sides of the table. It's one in the morning. I pick up a three of diamonds from the pile between us and place it next to the other card that's a three in my hand.

"Do you have any queens?" he asks.

"Go fish."

Jamison reaches for a card. The memory of his fingers tangling in my hair invades my senses. The smell of his clean clothes. The taste of his tongue on mine. The sound of our labored breathing.

"Earth to Amoris," Jamison says. "Your turn."

Jamison is right, I tell myself. We need to take this slowly. We can't mess this up. Better to be cautious.

So we decided to play cards. This might be our fortieth round of Go Fish.

"Do you have any tens?" I ask with a yawn. Jamison hands me the ten of spades. I add it to my hand.

"You're tired," he says. "Why don't you go home? Get some sleep."

But I just got him back. I'm not about to leave. He's handling this whole "let's take it slow" situation much better than I am. It's like Jamison flipped a switch. He's sitting across from me as if, just a few hours ago, we weren't on top of each other.

"No," I say. "I just need music. It's too quiet in here."

I connect my phone to the Bluetooth speaker in the kitchen and find a playlist, upbeat but not too sexy. One overly suggestive song and I'll lose my patience. As the music plays, I dance to the fridge for a soda. When I turn back toward Jamison, he's staring at me.

"What?"

He clears his throat, collecting the cards on the table. "Nothing."

"We weren't done with the game," I say.

"Time for a new game. Do you know how to play gin rummy?"

"No."

Jamison smiles. "Sit down. I'll teach you."

~

The soda is long gone. The playlist is on its second shuffle. The clock reads three in the morning. If my parents weren't as free-spirited as they are, my being out late might be a problem. But then again, I'm officially eighteen. An adult. The law says I can make my own decisions, and tonight's is the best one I've made in eighteen years.

I slouch in my seat, my fatigue growing, but I'm unwilling to leave and end the night, especially since Jamison doesn't appear to be tired at all.

"Another round?" He collects the cards again.

"Sure."

But my body betrays me, and I yawn. I jump out of my seat, declaring that we need another playlist. This one is officially overplayed. I scan my options and settle on "Songs to sing in the shower." I turn it up, hoping the beats will revive me. With every hip shake and shoulder sway, I perk up a bit.

"Come on, dance!" I attempt to yank Jamison from his seat, but he won't budge. I give up and just dance, until my heart is pumping and my breath is short.

The music suddenly stops. Jamison holds my phone.

"I can't do it," he says.

He's changed his mind. That's why he wanted to take it slow. He regrets kissing me.

"Can't do what?"

He drops the phone and grabs me, fingers in my hair, lips on mine, kissing me as hungrily as he did the first time.

"I thought you said . . . we need . . . to take it slow," I say between breaths and lips and hands.

"Fuck what I said," Jamison whispers, his mouth warm on my ear. "I was wrong."

~

It's been two days since we first kissed, and while we haven't taken it slow, we haven't taken it exceedingly fast either. Jamison and I are on the couch again. I'm watching a show on my phone, and Jamison is typing manically on his laptop. The deadline for his college application is bearing down on him, and in his words, he "can't mess around." He needs to focus. I'm trying to oblige his request.

He swears I'm not a distraction, but I'm not convinced. He keeps glancing in my direction every few minutes. He sits on the end of the couch closest to the wall outlet. His laptop battery has gotten so bad that it has to be plugged in constantly.

"That computer is a piece of junk," I say.

"Shhh." Jamison hugs his laptop close to him. "She can hear you."

I chuckle. "You need to start dating a new laptop."

159

"I told you, I'm a faithful man," Jamison says. "Till death do us part. Though I do hate when she shuts down on me without warning. And the E key has been missing for two years. But every relationship has its bumps. We've made it this far." He turns the laptop toward me so I can see the missing key. Instead I peek at what he's written, but he's too quick and turns the screen back toward himself.

"Can I read it?" I ask.

"No."

"Why not?"

"It's not done."

"I don't care."

"*I* care."

"Will you let me read it when it *is* done?" I ask.

"Maybe."

I groan and look at my phone again. "You suck."

Every few minutes, Jamison resituates himself on the couch, like he's uncomfortable, and I can tell he's deleting something.

"What if you don't get into the creative writing program at Western?" I ask.

"I'll go to one of my backup schools, I guess. Probably KU."

University of Kansas is a long way from Alder Creek.

"It's gonna happen, Jay," I say.

"How do you know? You haven't read my story."

"I don't have to read it to know it's amazing. You've been obsessed with books your whole life."

"I'm glad *you're* confident." He sits back on the couch, massaging his neck. If he'd let me get close to him, I'd do that for him, but he's put up an invisible wall between us.

"What is it?" I ask.

"What if it's all . . . for nothing? Changing schools. Living here. My mom changed her damn job for this. She left my dad and sister. They've sacrificed so much for me."

All for nothing? That stings a bit. What about this? Us?

"Kaydene and Victor wouldn't have done this if they weren't confident that you'll get in," I say.

"I hope you're right."

"I *am* right. And when you're a famous writer, you can buy yourself whatever laptop you want."

"No, I'm done with these. I want an old-fashioned typewriter. Something that doesn't need a plug. That can't die on me."

"Watch out. She might hear you."

Jamison apologizes to the laptop. It's so dorky and adorable for a person so incredibly attractive, so focused and caring. I want to jump his bones even more.

"Are you cold?" he asks me.

"A little."

Jamison grabs a blanket and spreads it across my legs, leaning down to tuck it in around me, touching me for the first time today. I resist grabbing ahold of him, and he takes a seat back on the other end of the couch, eyes glued to his laptop.

I go back to my phone, but the show I'm watching is nothing compared to the reality I'm living in with Jamison. We finally kissed. We're finally together. And now the only girl he's paying attention to is his laptop.

I stand up quickly. "Popcorn?"

Jamison nods, focused on the screen. "There's the microwave kind in the pantry."

I hide in the kitchen as it pops, trying to get control of myself. I need to respect his wishes, or he'll kick me out. When the popcorn is done, I add tiny marshmallows and chocolate chips and mix everything together. I set the bowl between us on the couch.

Jamison takes a handful, noticing what I've added. Kaydene always made popcorn this way. *A little salty and a little sweet,* she'd say. I'd end up eating all the marshmallows and chocolate, leaving Jamison the popcorn. He'd get so annoyed.

"You always went for the good stuff first," he says with a handful of popcorn.

"Why wait when I know what I want most?"

"Patience is a virtue, they say."

"I've never been a very patient person." I reach into the bowl for a marshmallow and pop it in my mouth.

"No, you haven't." Jamison's voice is strained.

I go back to the show, but when I reach my hand into the bowl at the same time Jamison does, our fingers meet. I have to bite the inside of my cheek. The simplest touch has my heart pounding.

"I need to work," Jamison says.

"You do."

"This is important, Amoris. It's my future."

"Yes. Very. You should concentrate."

"I can't get distracted."

"No, that would be bad," I say.

"Very bad."

"Epically bad."

"Right." Jamison nods. "Back to work."

He starts typing again. I throw a piece of popcorn at him. It hits him in the nose, and I giggle. He picks up the popcorn and eats it casually. A few seconds pass. I throw a marshmallow this time, hitting him in the temple. He brushes it away, ignoring me. I hit his cheek with a chocolate chip. Then his shoulder with another piece of popcorn. And his chin with another marshmallow.

Jamison calmly sets his laptop on the table. "What are you doing?"

"Nothing." I toss a chocolate chip in my mouth.

"Stop throwing food at me, Amoris."

"OK," I answer sweetly. But the moment he resumes typing, I hit his cheek with another marshmallow.

"That's it." He lunges at me. I yelp, and he's on top of me in a heartbeat.

He looks at me as I laugh, his body on mine, but I can tell he is holding back. Keeping his distance. Maybe it's the stress of college. Dreams can feel lofty, but they carry a lot of weight. Or maybe it's something else. I've thought about what he said—about why he kissed Ellis. That he was afraid of what she would do if he didn't kiss her back. I saw the same look in his eyes in the hallway that day with Mr. O'Brien. Jamison was protecting himself. Like he did with Ellis. And he was right to be worried. But he doesn't need to be worried with me. If it takes a lifetime of work, I'll show him.

When I softly touch his cheek, Jamison leans into the caress.

"If you don't get into Western, would this all really be for nothing?" I whisper.

Jamison shakes his head.

"Why do you want to write books so badly, Jay?"

"So people will see me."

We kiss, and I promise I'll never close my eyes to him again.

24

MAYBE

It's January second. The snow has melted. The sun is out. The cold wind whips at my face as I run home from my shift at the café. It all feels so good—the winter wind, the sun, my skin. A new year.

I don't care that school starts again tomorrow. If I get home quickly, Jamison and I can spend the next few hours together before Kaydene returns from vacation. She expects him to be done with his college admission material. That was the deal they struck.

"I blame you for all of this distraction," I said to Jamison last night.

"Me? How do you figure?"

"You really need to get your looks under control."

Jamison chuckled. "I blame *you*. I made that deal with Kaydene under false pretenses. You still had a Mack problem. I didn't know what I was coming home to."

Breaking up with Zach feels like it happened in another lifetime. Life is weird that way. The moment we think we know what's ahead of us is the moment it all turns upside down.

"Fine. We're both guilty," I said. "What's our punishment? Hanging? Death by firing squad? Burned at the stake?"

Jamison thought and said, "Solitary confinement."

"You wouldn't," I said seriously.

"For one afternoon. Or Kaydene might actually kill me."

I agreed, but only to save Jamison's life. He promised to make it up to me. It's the potential of that promise that has me skidding into my driveway, completely distracted, thinking of crashing my lips into Jamison's in T minus two minutes. I'm on my way to break down his door and almost miss the lump slouched on one of the garden chairs. A very tan lump with long dark-brown hair.

Ellis stands, looking oddly disheveled. She starts shouting before I can even think to speak. "Where the hell have you been? I've been texting you, like, all day. What the hell?"

Admittedly, I'd been ignoring those texts. My apron was abuzz all afternoon, and every time I checked and saw Ellis's name instead of Jamison's, I put my phone back in the pocket and made another cappuccino.

"I'm sorry." I try to sound compassionate. "It was busy at the café."

Ellis backs off with the third degree and collapses into the chair, sobbing. She's shivering, her shoulders doing that uncontrollable shaking thing that verges on convulsions. I can't just leave her here. Yet again, she's interrupting my time with Jamison. But there's a small voice in the back of my head reminding me that Ellis would never leave me sitting outside to cry by myself. She might be brutally honest and self-absorbed at times, but the last thing she would do is abandon me. Because she knows that feeling all too well.

I help Ellis out of the chair and bring her to my room. If I can calm her down quickly and send her home, there might still be time to see Jamison before Kaydene arrives.

Ellis falls on my bed dramatically, pulling her knees into her chest. "Shoes," she says. I pull them from her feet. "I need music."

"Any requests?"

"You know what I like."

Judging by Ellis's state, Carly Simon is appropriate.

"Was she the one married to James Taylor, or was that Carole King?" she asks, and then hiccups from crying. "I get those two confused."

"Carly Simon was married to James Taylor, but they got divorced."

Ellis groans. "Marriage is a fucking stupid institution that perpetuates archaic traditional feminine roles and squashes women's independence, making them utterly reliant on their husband's money. And it always ends in disaster. When will adults learn?"

None of this makes sense. Just yesterday, she was sending Snapchats of herself smiling on the beach, and now she's a tearful mess on my bed. I struggle to muster an ounce of caring, but nothing comes. She kissed Jamison. I've replayed it so many times in my head, trying to give Ellis the benefit of the doubt. She must not have known I liked him. But my gut says that's a lie. She was living in my room. She saw me preening myself daily. Fretting over what to wear, how my hair looked, whether my breath smelled. I don't know many fourteen-year-olds who hide crushes very well. I wasn't unique.

She must have known. Maybe. It's all so confusing.

Ellis lets out another wail. Now is not the time to bring it up. I don't want to relive the past when the present is so good. I just want to get Ellis out of my room so I can go see Jamison. I can already feel the time slipping away from us. It might only be January, but all too soon we're going to graduate, and he'll go to college. It's a gift to have him next door right now, and I just want to hold on to this time we have together. Last night, when we were lying in Jamison's bed, it all hit me. My head rested on his chest. I could hear his heart beating. This thud, thud, thud, right in my ear. Like a bassline, holding a song together. The reason for the song. Without it, the song feels wrong, it falls apart. I grabbed Jamison tighter, holding him like he might dissolve in my arms and leave me lying in the bed alone, desperately lonely.

When Jamison asked what was wrong, I deflected the question and asked him to read to me.

"You know the end, Amoris. Good wins. Voldemort dies. It all ends up OK."

"I know. But there's a lot of sadness along the way."

"Every story needs sadness," Jamison said.

That didn't make me feel any better. He must have understood, because he turned off the light and pulled me to him. I kissed his chest, right where his heart beat in my ear, and then I moved higher. His neck. His throat. His cheek. His mouth.

When Jamison pulled back, I could tell what he was thinking. *Slow down. Take it one step at a time. Guard yourself. Don't give too much, because someone can take it all away.*

"Does your story have a happy ending, at least?" I asked.

"It has a realistic ending."

"Meaning?"

"It ends the way it should," Jamison said. "But not necessarily the way you want."

"That doesn't sound too good."

"If I told the story any other way, I'd be lying," he said.

I didn't want to talk about it anymore. This wasn't the end of our story. No matter what the future holds for Jamison and me, we have a long story ahead of us. It's only just beginning. I have to believe that.

"Hello? *Amoris!*" Ellis barks, snapping me back to attention. "I'm losing my shit over here, and you're in fucking la-la land. I'm trying to tell you about my vacation from hell, and you're ignoring me."

"I'm not ignoring you. I'm just tired. I didn't sleep much last night."

Ellis makes a sound like she couldn't care less, and I just want her out of my bedroom. But the only way to accomplish that is to appease her.

I sit down on the bed. "Tell me what happened."

She looks at me with this dead expression. "My dad is getting remarried. That's what fucking happened."

Matt Osmond's surprise trip to Hawaii wasn't just a father-daughter bonding trip. He figured he would bribe his daughter with fruity umbrella drinks, sunshine, a new bikini, a pretty lie of family happiness, only to drop the marriage bomb on the final night.

"We went out to this really nice restaurant, and I was wearing this really cute dress . . ." Ellis wipes tears from her cheeks. "He ordered me a glass of wine, too. But it was all just a big fat fucking bribe."

Matt started into how much he loved Ellis's mom, and how no one would ever compare to her, but he still had a lot of years left, and he wanted to share those years with a woman.

"'And you're leaving for college next year. I'll be all alone,'" Ellis says mockingly. "That's what he said to me. Like this is all my fault. Like he's getting married because *I'm* leaving him. Fucking asshole."

"But Elle, you *are* leaving." She has been dead set on going to school in California for years. That's always been the plan.

"That's not the point."

Everything Ellis describes, all the reasons her dad wants to get remarried, makes sense to me. So I attempt a different tactic. "What's her name?"

"Darcy. They met at that yoga retreat in Mexico. Apparently she's a yoga instructor in Vail. How typical. Of course she's a skinny, bendy, blond yoga teacher. Fucking gold digger."

"How old is she?"

"Thirty-five. And *Darcy* is really smart and nice and loves kids and can't wait to meet me."

"She doesn't sound so bad."

Ellis flops back onto the bed. "I hate her. What if she wants to have kids? I'll have a fucking sibling. If my dad thinks I'm going to play house and call Darcy 'Mom,' he's got another think coming."

"You don't know her, Elle. She might be great."

"I don't need to know her," Ellis says. "She's not my mom."

There it is. The unsolvable problem that hangs over Ellis like an unpredictable storm.

"Darcy isn't trying to replace your mom," I say. "No one could ever do that."

My phone buzzes in my pocket. I sneak a peek at the message from Jamison.

Solitary confinement over. Application sent.

I'm typing back a response when Ellis says, "So I'm not important enough to text back all day, but whoever *that* is deserves your undivided attention."

I stop and set the phone down. "I told you, I'm sorry. It was busy at work. In my defense, you made it seem like you were having a great time on vacation. I had no idea."

Ellis stands up and shakes her hair out like she's ridding herself of bad energy. "I was, until last night." And then she turns to me with tears in her eyes, but not the same angry tears this time. They're big and swollen, the kind that fill your eyes slowly and only come crashing down your cheeks when they've exceeded your capacity to hold them back. The saddest of tears. "I miss my mom every damned day, Amoris. Every. Damned. Day. Why doesn't he?"

Ellis falls on the bed again. And while my heart is telling me to hug her, I don't move.

"I'm sure Matt misses your mom as much as you do. He just doesn't want to be lonely anymore. Can you blame him?"

"Yes," Ellis says. "No . . . I don't know." She curls up into a ball.

"When are they getting married?" I ask.

"Beginning of summer. She wants me to be a bridesmaid." Ellis makes a gagging face.

"That doesn't sound too bad. You have a few months to get to know her. You might be surprised."

"I already know she's a ho. What else is there?"

"Well . . . you get to wear a fancy dress to the wedding. You love fancy dresses. And you'll get your makeup and hair done. Maybe Darcy has a hot younger brother in college? And weddings are usually open bar."

Ellis sits up on her elbows. "And my dad can't get mad at me when I get completely lit, because it's all his fault," she says. "I *knew* coming here was the right thing to do. I just feel better when I'm at your house. Let's get fat on ice cream and candy and binge-watch *Friends* tonight. I'll find pajamas. You get the candy and ice cream. Rayne keeps a secret stash of Skittles in the cabinet above the fridge."

"Elle . . . I actually have plans tonight."

"What?" Ellis's mouth barely moves when she says the word. I swear she glances toward the window that looks out to Jamison's apartment. But she casually closes my dresser drawer. "I should probably go see Beckett anyway. He's been all desperate to see me. I'm sure he's about to explode. Just what every girl loves, a quickie."

"We can do the candy and ice cream thing this weekend," I offer. "You, me, Ross, Rachel, Monica, Chandler, Joey, and Phoebe. Sam and Tucker can come, too. I'm sure they're dying to see each other."

"Sure. Whatever." Ellis ties her shoes quickly. Before she leaves, she says, "I didn't even ask. Did you have a good break?"

"Yeah."

"Good." Ellis smiles, but it feels forced. Or maybe I'm just imagining that. "Better enjoy life while it's good, right? Who knows what might happen next?"

25

I DON'T TRUST YOU

I'd like to say I sit in my room, guilt-ridden for sending Ellis away when she's distraught, but I don't. I don't know if it's too many years of putting her first, of being bossed around and spoken down to, of focusing on making Ellis feel better at my own expense, or if it's simply residual anger from her kissing Jamison. I should have been more careful. I should have kept an eye on Ellis, but I was solely focused on Jamison.

The problem with tunnel vision is you can't see what's brewing all around you, from multiple sides, from deep emotional spaces, places you thought were long healed or at least patched. History. But history is ever present.

I brush my teeth, wash my face, change out of my coffee-smelling clothes, and dash over to Jamison's without checking my phone.

Kaydene opens the apartment door. "Hey, Amoris. What are you doing here?"

My heart flies up to my throat. "You're home."

"Just got here." She blocks the door with her body, and I know she's aware of what's going on. Moms are magic that way. Rayne has the same ability. I can walk into the kitchen and she'll start making hot chocolate before I've said a word about my horrible day.

"Seems like Jamison survived all on his own," Kaydene says. "Though he looks a little tired. Nothing a good night's sleep won't cure." Her eyes pierce mine, and it takes all my strength not to back away. "Why don't you come in and sit with me for a while? We haven't spent much time together this year."

"Jamison isn't here?"

"He's at the store. We were low on a few groceries."

She opens the door to let me in. I sit down on the couch, in the same spot I've occupied for a week. Kaydene sits in Jamison's usual position, and the room takes on a new tension.

"How was your trip?" I ask.

"It was a new experience," Kaydene says. "I think Talia would have preferred to stay home with her friends over snowshoeing with her parents. She doesn't like the snow."

An awkward silence falls between us, which is extremely odd. I've known Kaydene my entire life. The summers I spent in Kansas City, she became like a second mom—disciplining me when I deserved it, making sure I ate lunch and drank enough water, bandaging scraped knees and elbows. The summer I got my period, I told Rayne *and* Kaydene. Kaydene went to the store to buy me supplies.

"Do you know why I wanted to be a teacher, Amoris?" she asks. "Because none of my teachers looked like me. They were all White. That's not to say they weren't kind, or good teachers. Most were. But they had no idea what it felt like to be me. And kids need that. The secret to a good education has nothing to do with reading or multiplication, or facts. A good education is about belonging. It's about being seen. Learning you're important to the world. I wanted to make sure that kids like me knew I was seeing them."

"Jamison says the same thing about why he writes."

Kaydene smiles. "He's always been good about listening to his mom. Talia . . . now she's another story. That child was born to disobey me."

I chuckle. "River's the same way."

The light moment dies quickly. "I'm going to be honest with you, Amoris. And it's gonna hurt, but I want you to remember that honesty is the greatest respect we can give each other." And then she says, "I don't trust you."

I suck in a breath that I'm not sure I will ever exhale.

Why does she not trust me? What did I do to her? She's known me my whole life. I want to sputter so many words that won't come out. "But . . . why?" I manage.

"Years of experience." She doesn't expound. She stands up, stretches, and says, "Well, school starts tomorrow. You need a good night's sleep for optimal learning."

I won't see Jamison tonight. Whatever fantasy we were living for the past week evaporates in an instant.

"I know you love him, Amoris," Kaydene says. "On some cosmic level, I've known you two were destined for each other from the beginning, as much as that scared me. And he loves you, too. But love doesn't exempt you from reality. It only demands that you work harder in the face of it. I hope you're up for that."

26

TRY AND TRY AGAIN

I schedule another session with Lori.

"I'm glad you emailed," she says when I arrive. She shuffles the folders and papers on her desk. "I can't stop thinking about what happened with Mr. O'Brien. I feel guilty for how it all went down with the mural. But I don't think it's over. I think there's—"

"No," I stop her.

"Why not? We can't just give up."

I can't think about that day without a rotten feeling in my stomach. Jamison and I are finally in a good place. I can't ask him to relive that. What if it blows up and gets worse? Plus, we have more pressing issues right now.

"How do you know if you're in love?" I ask.

Lori sits back in her seat, eyebrows raised.

"I mean, like *real* love," I add. "Not bullshit love."

"Bullshit love?" she asks.

"Like Disney bullshit love."

"Is this about sex? Because I have a few brochures on STIs that you should read before you take the plunge." Lori rummages around on her cluttered desk. Then she holds out a fishbowl full of condoms. "Take some."

I do, to appease her, stuffing a few in my purse. "Been there. Done sex," I assure her. "And I'm on the pill. But this has nothing to do with sex. We haven't gotten there yet. Not that I don't want to have sex with him. I do. It's all I can think about sometimes."

"So what *is* this about?"

"If love is a verb, what's the *right* action?" I ask. I'm worried no matter what I do, no matter how much I care about Jamison, I'm going to hurt him.

"Is this about the mural? Like I said, I think I have a—"

"It's more than that."

Long after Kaydene closed the door behind me, her words echo in my mind. *I don't trust you. I don't trust you. I don't trust you.* I wanted to march back over there, bang on the door, and scream at Kaydene that she was wrong. How could she not trust me? She's known me since I was a baby. I've never done anything to her. In fact, I've only ever loved her family. Admired them. Hell, I wanted to be one of them. She's making this about race, and I don't deserve that. She knows how Jamison and I feel about each other. She said so herself. How did I become the villain? I'm *in love*. It didn't make any sense.

But then it hit me, and the truth stole my breath. I was doing it again. I was angry that Kaydene didn't trust me, just like I was when Jamison didn't trust me. A dirty-laundry list of moments from this past year came rushing back with a vengeance. I ignored the pain Jamison felt from Wendy's words at the café. I pushed him into confronting Mr. O'Brien about the mural, with no regard to how it might hurt him. Again and again I focused on myself, and not Jamison. Even when I thought I was helping—I was hurting him.

Why *should* Kaydene trust me?

I tell Lori all of this. She listens intently, nodding every so often.

"OK . . ." Lori sits up. "The way I see it, you only have one option."

"OK. What is it?"

Lori sits forward, leaning her elbows on the desk. "Try."

"Try? *Try?* That's your sage advice?"

"Yes. If it's worth it to you, then you need to try not to fuck up. Simple as that."

"But how do I know?" I plead. "I didn't think I was messing up before and I was. You saw what happened with the mural. It was a disaster."

"True," Lori concedes. "And you need to learn from your mistakes. But you know what's worse than messing up? Inaction. I'm not sure I can tell you what it means to be in love. I'm not married. I don't have kids. Hell, I'm a total runner when it comes to relationships. The second a person wants to get serious is the second I want to bolt. But I can tell you what love *isn't*, Amoris. Being in love doesn't mean being ignorant. It doesn't mean the world gets more beautiful. In fact, I'm pretty sure most people who fall in love are scared. All of a sudden, you care a lot more about what happens. It isn't just you anymore. You have to deal with someone else's pain, which, let's be honest, isn't easy. But someone else's pain shouldn't have to be suitable, or palatable, or convenient, or even make sense, for us to deal with it. Pain is pain. It isn't up for debate. It just *is*. Stop thinking this is about you. If this is about you, and proving *you're* not a bad person, then you don't really love him. You're using him to make *you* feel better about you. To prove Kaydene is wrong about *you*. If you continue to look at it like that, you're right. You are going to hurt him. So I ask you, is this about you or Jamison?"

"It's about the both of us."

"It doesn't sound that way."

"What?" I ask, frustrated.

"Are you mad that Jamison's mom said she didn't trust you? Or are you mad that she might be right not to trust you?"

I fumble for a response. "I just want her to trust me. I'm a good person."

"Not trusting you is not the same as saying you're a bad person. This isn't about you."

"It feels like it's about me. If I was Black, she wouldn't have said that."

"You're doing it *again*, Amoris," Lori says, with a huff I've never heard before. She's usually so calm, so even, so nonjudgmental. "You're prioritizing pain. You're trying to tell someone else how to feel. It doesn't matter that you think what Kaydene said is unfair. It's how she feels, and she's entitled to that. Negating her emotions won't solve the problem."

"Well, how do I prove her wrong?"

"Amoris, listen to me. It's not about proving her wrong. She's not your enemy." Lori sits forward and points at my heart. "It's about getting that in order. It's about taking a good look at yourself and being honest. I think the real reason you're frustrated isn't because Kaydene said she didn't trust you. It's that you know she's right to be concerned."

When someone says exactly what you're struggling to avoid, but desperately need to hear, there's this rush of calm. Like finally, someone understands how I feel. And then, after the calm, you realize what just happened—you've been outed. And you can't go back.

"I think you have some work to do," Lori says.

My instinct is to fight against Lori's advice. I've done the work. I want to make this all go away. I want to reverse time, wipe my mind clean of what it finally sees fully. But I can't.

I thought Jamison and I could just move on. I thought we could forget all that's happened. I thought that "I'm sorry" was enough.

But I was wrong. Love isn't about erasing the past. It's about dealing with it.

"Do you know where to start?" Lori says softly.

I do, I think to myself. And it's going to break my heart.

27

INTO THE DARKNESS

There's a moment of anticipation, right before Jamison kisses me, where the air between us gets hot and electric, and I wonder, just for a second, whether I'll survive. I think that my heart might not be able to take the intensity. That it will stop instantly, overwhelmed. And yet I know I'd do *anything*, risk death, to have a taste of that feeling, again and again.

I never felt that way with Zach. Kissing him was nice. Not bad. Not extraordinary. Just nice. He was a good kisser, not overly aggressive or sensitive. Not too much tongue, but not too little. Sometimes Zach would hold my face between his hands, like guys do in the movies when they kiss a girl, and my stomach would flip, and I'd think this is how it feels to really like someone. It was pretty and gentle and fine.

But Jamison makes my whole body flip. He turns me inside out. I didn't think I could want anything as much as I want him.

After I kissed Jamison for the first time, and felt that intense anticipation, I thought this was what love is. Hot. Electric. Passion. But I was naïve. I'd forgotten.

Love is a verb, an action, even when that action hurts.

"I don't understand," Jamison says. We're standing in the kitchen at the café, hidden from view of the customers, and if I look at him, cute and sexy in his apron, I might not go through with this. So I keep my eyes down.

"I just need space."

"Space," he repeats. "What the hell does that mean?"

It means I need to trust myself with you. It means I need to stop trying to prove I can be trusted and actually show that I can be.

"For how long?" he asks.

"I don't know," I say, still looking down. "I just know I need to get my head on straight."

Jamison brings his hand to my cheek, brushing his fingers lightly on my skin. "I like the way your head is right now."

Every urge in my body wants to crumble and tell him what Kaydene said to me. Tell him that *she* planted the seed of doubt. *She* made me do this. But that's just another lie. And it's exactly what's wrong with this whole situation. What I perceive as right and what is true aren't matching up. Kaydene didn't do anything. She is simply protecting her son, and why shouldn't she? What have I done to show her I can be trusted? To show her I won't cause pain? I've been blind, unable to see the world Jamison lives in. And until I can see it for what it truly is, my good intentions are a threat to him.

Jamison lifts my chin, so I'm forced to look at him. My knees might give out.

"I just think we should take it down a notch," I say, stepping back from his touch. "It's all happening so quickly. I don't want to mess this up. I just think it's better if we go back to being . . . friends. For a little while."

"Friends." The word comes out of Jamison with a disgusted edge. I hate it as much as he does. "This doesn't make any sense, Amoris."

I know, I think. This makes no sense at all, except . . . it makes complete sense. I dove in without thinking because it's what *I* wanted. Just like everything else. But I need to stop doing what I want and start doing what needs to be done. And I know this hurts Jamison, but in the long run, he'll thank me.

I give him the only excuse I can muster. "You're going to college next year, and I have no idea what I'm going to do. Long distance never works. I just think it's best if we think about this logically so we both don't end up hurt."

"That's bullshit." He's right. It is. Complete and utter bullshit. "Just tell me the truth," Jamison says flatly. "What do you really want?"

You. All of you. Every moment with you. For infinity.

"I need time," I say.

"So, eighteen years wasn't enough?"

Jamison is so close I can smell him, warm and inviting and swirling with memories that pull me closer to him. I need Rayne to break me of this habit. To massage the memories clean from my system. Maybe then this would be easier.

The knot in my throat tightens. Tears well in my eyes. I'm about to break. All I want is to pull Jamison to me, feel the press of his chest on mine, hold on tight and never let go.

But Kaydene echoes in my mind. *I don't trust you.* And until I feel confident that Jamison can trust me, that I can trust myself with him, I need to do this.

I'm choking on my silence. If I say anything else, I'll crumble and take it all back. But in the end, Jamison lets me go.

"Fine," he says. "We'll be friends."

He walks out of the kitchen. The moment he's gone, my knees give out and I crumble to the floor in a weeping mess.

∿

When I get home, it's late. I'm so tired I'm not even sure sleep will help.

The smell of food makes my stomach roll. River sits at the kitchen table, his face over a heaping plate, his hair dirty and his clothes smelling like a gymnasium. Chris is still traveling. He's supposed to come home next week.

"I saved you a plate," Rayne says from the sink, her hands in soapy water.

But my limbs feel too tired to move. My heart too heavy.

I stare at River. He shovels food in his mouth, smacks his lips, and chews with his mouth open, without a care for anyone else in the room. It's all about him and what he needs. His arrogance boils my blood.

"What are you looking at?" he scoffs at me.

I get right in River's face, my finger practically touching his nose. "Don't you ever call my friend Sam a faggot again."

River sputters, completely shocked, and for once I'm glad it isn't me who can't find the right words.

I disappear into my room, into the quiet where I can't hear Rayne bring the wrath down on River. I don't turn on the record player. Music won't help. I simply turn off the light and lie still in the darkness.

28

KEROUAC AND CARHENGE

I delete all the college applications from my computer. Throw out the brochures. College isn't for me. I know this now. I google Alaska and Boston and Detroit and Rocky Mountain National Park. I make a list of all the places that interest me. Historical music sites. Graceland. The Grand Ole Opry. Carnegie Hall. Anything that might inspire me.

Then I can't stand my house anymore, so I go to the only place that might help me feel better. When Terry finds me in the book section of Black and Read, he practically has a heart attack.

"Whoa. Am I having a psychedelic flashback?" he asks. "Did someone slip peyote in my matcha?"

I sift through the "H" section. "Did you know a person in Nebraska made a replica of Stonehenge, out of cars? Guess what it's called?"

"Shit. You're talking," Terry says. "My hallucinations rarely talk. Who are you and what have you done with Amoris?"

"You're not imagining this. It's me. And it's called Carhenge."

"Prove it," Terry says. "Prove you're who you say you are."

"Pink Floyd's *Dark Side of the Moon* lines up perfectly with *The Wizard of Oz*."

"But only if . . ."

"You start the album after the third MGM lion's roar," I say.

Terry gasps. "It *is* you. But you don't do books. You do music." Terry points toward the front of the store.

"I need a change," I tell him. "It's not right to spend your whole life in one section of a store when there's a whole other world so close by."

"What kind of change are we talking? Ziggy Stardust to Aladdin Sane?"

"More like Cat Stevens to Yusuf Islam."

Terry nods understandingly. "A spiritual shift."

"Something like that."

"So, what do you need?"

"That's the problem. I don't know. I just know . . . I can't stay there." I point to the front of the store. "I'm just listening to the same damn albums, you know. Playing the same damn songs by the same damn artists with the same damn lyrics. And they're the same songs my mom listened to, and my grandma. I've always considered it a legacy, a good thing, but maybe it's not. Because it just goes on and on, everyone in my family listening to the same music, generation after generation hearing the same message. It's like I've memorized my life by listening to the same damn thing over and over. I'm just on repeat."

"Damn. That's profound."

"It's sad, really. I want to know the world as it truly is, not just play along to someone else's song, someone else's vision."

"It sounds like you need some Kerouac." Terry disappears into the back of the store that doubles as his living quarters. When he comes back a few minutes later, he's carrying a beat-up copy of *On the Road*, its spine held together with duct tape. The cover is faded and crinkled, and the pages have obvious water damage. Terry hands me the book. "It's my personal copy. Take it."

"I can't," I say. A used book is precious. Jamison's copy of *Harry Potter and the Sorcerer's Stone* is in similar condition.

But Terry presses the book into my hands, the wrinkles on his face almost disappearing, and I can see the young man he once was, the one who believed peace was possible if you protested hard enough, and love could end wars.

"Books are like hearts," he says. "They should be shared with the people we trust."

"Wow, Terry. That's poetic."

"I have my coherent flashes."

I take the book. "It's in good hands."

But I can't leave without saying what's been eating at me for months now. Something I should have noticed. A moment I should have rectified, instead of ignored. I saw it happen, and I let it stand. Because I let my love for Terry blind me. I let hope blanket truth. We put people in pretty boxes with pretty labels, so they can't disappoint us. But that's how we get pretty lies. We even do it to ourselves.

"Terry, I need to talk to you about something," I say.

"Uh-oh, this sounds serious."

"You know the guy you saw me with a few months back," I say. Terry looks confused. "The Black guy."

"Yeah . . . what about him?"

"He's my friend. Has been for my whole life." And then I ramble a bit, because the thought of Jamison turns me inside out. "A best friend really, but more than that. He actually might be everything to me. My . . . everything. I should have told you that when you met him. But that's not the point." I take a breath. "The point is . . . he was in here that day looking for a book. Jamison loves books. He could give you a diatribe on how he loves the smell and feel of the pages, how the anticipation of reading a new story is the best feeling in the world, how words are the most powerful weapon humans have, and how we should use them wisely." And then I repeat what Jamison told me. "How books make us feel *seen*."

"And you said I'm poetic?" Terry jokes.

But the hard part of this conversation is upon me, and I promise myself I won't back down. Like Kaydene said, honesty is the greatest respect we can give another person.

"That day," I continue, "you assumed Jamison was here for rap music, and then you thought he was stealing a book. *Because* he's Black." Terry starts to protest, but I stop him. "I was there, Terry. I saw it happen. You shouldn't have done that, and I should have said something. We both need to do better."

"But—"

"Don't say anything, Terry. Just think about it. *Really* think about it."

I thank him for the book and promise I'll return it. Then I leave, no lighter than when I walked in, but more aware of the person I want to be, and the world I believe in.

29

WHEN THINGS GET INTERESTING

Ellis, Sam, and I sit at the table in Nicky's Diner, sharing a plate of cheese fries. It's crowded, like every Saturday night after a varsity basketball game. Not that Alder Creek is celebrating a victory, although River did play a good game.

Chris was there tonight. He came home a day early just to go to the game. I was shocked to see the old Airstream roll up the driveway. Chris is never home early. And the Airstream was practically unrecognizable, with new tires and the crack in the windshield repaired. It was even washed and waxed. I've never seen it so sparkly.

I couldn't tell if River was happy or embarrassed to see Chris at the game. It's the great conundrum of being a teenager—you crave your parents' attention, but you're not so sure you want them around.

River left the game with his friends and never acknowledged Chris. If my dad was hurt by the slight, he didn't show it. I have a feeling it will take more than one game to satisfy River.

Most of the students from the game are now waiting at Nicky's to hear where the postgame party will be. We're in a teenage purgatory of greasy food and soda before everyone levels up to alcohol and weed.

Ellis is finishing up a rant about her dad's wedding. His fiancée, Darcy, is in full planning mode—flowers, dresses, rings, location—and Ellis does not like her choices. I have a feeling no matter what Darcy did, Ellis would hate it out of spite. I'm listening just enough that if Ellis quizzed me, I could deliver a SparkNotes answer. That's been the status of our friendship lately—abbreviated with little depth.

"I swear this wedding might make me an alcoholic," she says. "It's the only way I'm going to survive the next five months." She checks her phone for the millionth time.

"Another thing you can blame on your dad," I say into my soda so Ellis can't hear.

She groans. "Beckett needs to text me, like, now. I can't eat any more fries or I won't fit into my prom dress. Paisley's being such a bitch about this party. Everyone knows it's at her house. If she didn't want tons of people to come, she shouldn't have a party."

Apparently Paisley is being selective on who gets an invite and who doesn't. Sam sits next to me, sketching in his notebook, his brow pulled tight. He's been edgy for a few weeks now.

"Speaking of prom," Ellis says, "when are we shopping?"

"It's not even February yet," I say.

"It practically is, and May will be here before we know it," she counters. I don't want the reminder.

"I might not go," Sam says.

That gets Ellis's attention. "What? Why not?"

"I can't take my boyfriend, Elle. What's the point? I'll just be miserable all night."

"Like that's any different from right now," Ellis says. "You're always miserable lately."

Sam sets his sketchbook and pencil down. He looks exhausted. Tucker's at an Eaton Falls party tonight, "playing hetero," as Sam calls it.

"He's probably got his hands on some boobs right now. I can't think about it."

"You can put your hands on my boobs if you want, Sammy," Ellis offers. "I'll do anything to make you feel better."

"Tempting, but I haven't been in the mood for boobs since freshman year. I'll let you know if that changes, Elle."

She sticks her chest out. "They're here for you when you need them."

"Tucker wouldn't do that," I say, touching Sam's hand lightly.

"I don't know if I'm so sure about that. Fear does strange things to people." Sam waves off his own concern. "It's . . . whatever. I get it. It's just . . . sometimes I find myself wishing Tucker was stronger. Like, fuck all those homophobes in his shitty little town. But that's messed up, too, because it's not Tucker's fault that he isn't safe in Eaton Falls."

"I'm so sick of Tucker playing the victim," Ellis counters. "He can't blame the whole damn town when he refuses to speak up for himself. He isn't giving them the chance to change. Some victims just like to be victims, Sammy. If you want my opinion, you should dump Tucker. I'm sick of him dicking you around. There are lots of gay fish in the sea. It's time to put your hook in another guy's mouth."

"Nice innuendo, Elle," Sam says. "And spoken like a true White cis hetero. He is the victim, and you're shaming him for it. The sacrifice always seems worth the cost when you're not the one sacrificing."

"Like women haven't sacrificed," Ellis says. "We've been burned, raped, sold, and murdered for millennia. By men."

"Some women more than others," Sam contests. "So based on your theory, women chose to be burned, raped, sold, and murdered?"

"I didn't say that," Ellis says. "I just think Tucker needs to work harder if he wants Eaton Falls to change."

"Interesting," Sam says. "So women weren't working hard enough for thousands of years? They deserved what they got."

"Of course not."

"But you said some victims just like to be victims."

"Whatever." Ellis stands. "This conversation is depressing. Keep dating Tucker. I don't care. I need a drink. I'm calling Beckett. We're getting out of this grease pit. I want to have fun tonight."

Ellis walks out of the diner, phone pressed to her ear.

"God, that's just like Ellis," Sam says. "Victim blaming. Remind me why we're friends with her?"

Lately I've been wondering the same thing. "She throws a good party?"

"Even that's getting old."

Fighting with Ellis feels pointless when we're all scattering next year. "Don't worry. You won't have to deal with her soon enough."

"I wish. The world is full of Ellises." Sam picks at a fry. "And I hate to admit it, but she might be right about one thing. Me and Tucker . . . maybe it's better if it ended. I mean, who am I kidding? College isn't going to make our lives any easier."

"Could you walk away from him? Just like that?"

"No," Sam says quickly. "Even if Tucker is touching some girl's lady bits tonight, there isn't love there. That's just playing a part, for survival. Gay men have been doing it since the beginning of time. I see the truth in his eyes when he kisses me."

But is that enough? I think to myself.

"Speaking of denying feelings . . ." Sam picks up a fry. "Look who just walked in the door."

Jamison stands at the counter, almost instantly surrounded by people from school.

"What happened with you two?" Sam asks.

"Nothing." I slump down in my seat, wishing I could bury myself. "Liar."

I don't have the energy to tell Sam everything. It's a swirl of madness and complete clarity. How can the world all of a sudden come into focus and also be a mess at the same time?

Jamison leans on the counter, talking with Michelle Hernández. They smile. Laugh. It's easy. She touches his arm. Is she flirting with him? Of course she is. Who wouldn't? I decide that I hate Michelle.

"Jamison!" Sam hollers. "Over here!"

I swear I see a moment of hesitation before Jamison walks over to us. You'd think after countless shifts at work that I'd be used to the gut-wrenching awkwardness, but it never goes away.

"I just closed the café," Jamison says, too quickly. "I'm picking up dinner after my shift." He seems eager to leave.

"That's nice," I say, attempting to sound casual. "The burgers are good here."

"Jamison, I'm glad we ran into you," Sam says. "I need your help. What are you doing tonight?"

Jamison holds up his takeout bag. "You're looking at it."

"Good." Sam shows Jamison his sketchbook. "I have one more piece to do to complete my application to USC. I'm in desperate need of models."

"I'm no model," Jamison says. "Better to ask Amoris."

"What?" I gasp. "I'm not a model. Models are tall. I'm short. Too short."

"First of all, I draw eyes," Sam says. "That has nothing to do with height. And second of all, I actually need you both." He shimmies out of the booth as Ellis walks back into the diner. She acknowledges Jamison with a cordial greeting and a smile.

"Let's go," Ellis says. "Beckett's waiting outside. We are officially on the list for Paisley's party. Jamison, you can come, too."

"Tempting, Elle, but I pass," Sam says.

"What?" she snaps. "It's Saturday night. Don't be lame."

"That's a derogatory word, by the way," Sam says.

Ellis groans. "Stop being so sensitive."

"I pass, too," I say. "I'm not in the mood for a party."

190

Ellis is aghast. She turns to Jamison. "Please tell me you're not joining these losers."

Jamison holds up his takeout. "I'm just here for the food."

"Fine," Ellis says. "Do whatever you want, losers. I'm going with Beckett."

We watch her go, though none of us is disappointed.

"Do you guys hear that?" Sam asks. "I hear munchkins. Singing. Something about a dead witch." He smiles wickedly. "Come on. Let's go."

"Where?" I ask.

"Do you think your dad would mind if we used his art studio?"

~

I rarely go in Chris's studio. Not that I'm forbidden, but it feels like Chris's home. And not mine. Like I'm trespassing. I always assumed Chris moved out to get away from us, which meant he didn't want us in his studio. He quartered himself next door by choice.

It's strange to be here now, seeing the familiar objects that inhabited my house years ago. Chair, table, bed, French press, an old stereo. Chris's coffee cup with the permanent brown stain at the bottom. But lately, his toothbrush has been in Rayne's bathroom, and the bed in the studio is still made from the last time he left on a trip.

Sam moves around the studio, rearranging the furniture, like it's his own. The studio feels untouched. Each paint brush is clean, organized by size in mason jars on Chris's desk. Completed artwork is stacked against a wall. I didn't realize how hard Chris has been working lately. I thumb through the paintings, all new, all work I've never seen before. All landscapes of Alder Creek.

"I may have my issues with this town," Jamison says from behind me, his chest practically touching my back, "but no one can deny it's beautiful. This place is worthy of art. Chris has captured it perfectly."

I look at Jamison. His heat collides with mine. We haven't been this close in weeks. It feels better than good. It feels like we could heal each other simply by being this near.

"OK," Sam says. "I need you both to sit here."

Two seats are positioned next to each other, Chris's easel facing them, Sam's sketchbook propped there. Jamison and I take our seats. Sam stands back, examining us.

"Jamison, turn toward Amoris. And, Amoris, do the same."

I can smell the scent I was struggling to re-create in Rayne's studio. I've missed it so much. My heart aches at the smell of it now. Sam walks around us, exploring the angles of light. He adjusts Jamison's position slightly.

"Sam, what are we supposed to be doing?" I ask.

"Just look at each other," he says.

I don't know how often two people stare at each other for more than a few seconds, but it's awkward. At first, it's only slight, but the longer Jamison and I are locked in a gaze, the more I want to cry. I feel empty without him. I'm just going through the motions every day. I had a taste of what life could be like with Jamison, together. And as he sits in front of me now, he looks at me as if he can read my mind, as if he's trying to figure out why I'm doing this to us.

Why, Amoris?

Why did I push him away?

I can't do this. I stand up and break the moment. Sam stops drawing. I pace.

"My foot fell asleep," I lie.

"I need to check on Tucker anyway," Sam says. He disappears into the back room as I walk around, attempting to breathe evenly. I can do this. I said "friends," so we need to be just that, and I need to start acting like it.

"I guess I can take model off my list of possible future professions," I say, attempting to lighten the mood. "Good thing I have a fallback."

"What's that?" Jamison asks.

"Professional basketball player."

"Really."

"You've seen me on the court."

He chuckles, and some of the tension eases. "You still owe me a rematch."

"Anytime you're in the mood for losing."

"So, it's like that?"

"Like what?" I ask. "You're not . . . scared, are you?"

Jamison gives me a warning look. "You better watch what you say, Amoris. You might be eating those words."

"I'll take my chances."

Jamison picks up the garbage can from the corner and sets it in the middle of the room. He balls up a piece of scrap paper. Then he steps back and shoots. The paper ball glides easily into the can. Jamison gestures to where he's standing. "Your shot."

I accept the challenge and aim, sending the paper ball straight into the basket.

"Child's play," I say.

Jamison's second and third shots land in the can as effortlessly as the first. I, on the other hand, am not so lucky.

"You've been practicing," I say.

"Maybe . . ."

"I better step up my game."

Jamison stands close to me as I prepare to shoot. As I'm about to launch the paper ball, he leans down and gently blows in my ear. The ball misses completely.

"Cheater!" I shove him playfully in the chest. He laughs and grabs me by the wrists, spins me around, and pins me to him. And before I know it, we're in a full-fledged wrestling match. Jamison picks me up and carries me to the couch.

"Put me down!" I scream, kicking and laughing.

"If that's what you want," Jamison says. He lifts me high and drops me on the couch like a pro wrestler. I can't stop laughing. He's over me immediately, tickling my ribs.

"Not there!" I barely manage to get the word out. "Not there!"

The weight of his body on mine, his fingers crawling over my skin, it's ecstasy. A dream. This is the best I've felt since I uttered that awful word. The more Jamison presses into me, the more I want to melt into this couch and forget about "friends." Forget about drawing boundaries. Forget it all. This feels too good.

Sam clears his throat, and we stop moving. "Sorry to interrupt. I can go if you want."

Jamison is up in an instant. "No. Stay."

I sit up, fixing my chaotic hair. "We were just—"

"No explanation needed," Sam says, moving back behind the easel.

Jamison sits back in his seat. "How's Tucker?"

"He didn't pick up," Sam says, trying not to sound bothered.

"I'm sorry," I say. "I'm sure he's fine."

Sam lets out a long breath. "I can't think about it. I need a distraction. Let's try this again, shall we?"

This time Jamison and I are better at holding still. Goofing around eased the tension, and for the first time in weeks, I'm not in complete agony this close to him.

"Good," Sam says. "That's better."

If my eyes could say one thing to Jamison right now, it would be that I'm sorry. *I'm sorry. I'm sorry. I'm sorry.* I'm sorry I put space between us by uttering the dreaded "friend" word, but I swear it's for us.

As if he can hear my mind, Jamison reaches for my face, his fingers hesitant, and brushes my hair from my forehead. It's the kindest of gestures, and I don't deserve it. As his hand skims down my cheek, I turn into his touch, willing him to know how badly I want this, how good it feels.

"There," Sam says seriously. "Don't move an inch."

Jamison softly touches my face, and I don't turn away. Before I couldn't look at him longer than a few seconds, and now I'm desperate for time to stop, right here, just the two of us, locked in touch.

As we're holding the pose, it dawns on me that it's nearly February. Sam already applied to art school. His portfolio is complete. He did this on purpose. I wonder if Jamison knew. Was he hoping this would happen? Either way, I don't care.

The silence is broken when a phone rings, startling us all.

"Tucker." Sam sounds relieved as he grabs his phone, but it's not his that's ringing.

There are moments in life when we know that what's coming is bad. An intuition springs, like a little gift from the universe, preparing us before the fall. I feel it drop in my stomach.

I scavenge my cell from the bottom of my bag and answer it. "River?"

"Amoris?" His voice is frantic. "Please. I need you."

30

WINNERS AND LOSERS

The lights on top of the police car are off. At least there's that. The entire neighborhood isn't witnessing this. River made me promise on the phone that I wouldn't involve Rayne and Chris. I wanted to scream at him, but I was too panicked to resist. As we pull up in Sam's car, River leaning against the police cruiser, intoxicated, I regret it now.

A uniformed officer stands next to River.

"I'll stay here," Jamison says.

The smell of sour vomit edged with alcohol hits my nose as I approach the police car, alone.

River attempts to stand. "Thank God you came. You're the best sister in the world."

River looks sallow and pathetic. He's so drunk, his eyes are sagging.

"What the hell happened?" I ask.

The police officer, whose badge says Monroe, tells me he was driving by, his shift at an end, when he saw River puking on the side of the road. He pulled over to help. That's when he smelled the alcohol.

"Do you know anything about a party tonight?" Officer Monroe asks me.

"No," I lie.

"Look," he says. "I remember being in high school. Sometimes you just have a little too much fun. Get a little carried away. I'm not sure your brother needs to be arrested for that. But he needs a safe ride home and a good night's sleep."

"I can do that," I say.

"Good." Officer Monroe seems satisfied. River thanks him over and over for not arresting him. "Just promise me you'll be safe the next time. Mind your intake and always have a designated driver."

"Yes, sir," River says, holding on to the car for stability.

"We'll forget this happened," the officer says. "Now, get this boy home."

I take River around the waist to keep him steady. He's been behaving all year as if he's above the law, and tonight just proves that he is. He should be marinating in a jail cell, paying the consequences for his mistakes. Instead, I'm dragging his drunk ass home, and now I'm responsible. An accomplice.

River flops into the back seat next to Jamison. The officer leaves. I just want to get home and get River out of my sight.

"You're a real shithead, River," I say as I fasten my seat belt. "You know that?"

He blows out a deep breath, and I have to roll down the window. "It's fine," he says. "No big deal. I'll be more careful next time. I was just having a little fun."

"Next time? How is this *fun*, River? You're lucky you weren't arrested."

"He wasn't going to arrest me."

Now that River is safe in the car, his panic is replaced with arrogance.

"You heard what the good officer said," River continues. "I got a little carried away. It was an innocent mistake."

"I should have let you rot on the side of the road," I say.

"Too late."

Jamison speaks now, his voice stern. "I need to get out of the car. Sam, pull over."

The car isn't even stopped fully when Jamison opens the door and gets out. River flops over in the back seat.

"I'm gonna take a nap," he mumbles. "Wake me up tomorrow."

I can't stand the sight of him. The arrogance.

"I'll stay," Sam says.

Jamison is halfway down the street when I catch up to him, hollering his name.

He turns on me, a fire in his eyes I haven't seen in months, like he wants to break something. "This is fucking bullshit!" he yells.

"I'm sorry I dragged you into this. River's an idiot. I'm done helping him."

"It's not just River, Amoris. It's everything. Some days, I can't breathe in this damn town. Do you think that officer would have been so kind if it had been me puking on the side of the road? Do you think he would have chalked it up to good-old teenage innocence? Or would I be handcuffed in the back of a squad car."

"You're right. This whole situation is messed up. If you can't breathe here, let's leave," I say, pleading with him. Anything to make this better. Anything to take the pain away. "Wherever you want to go."

Jamison starts pacing, rubbing the back of his neck. "It doesn't matter. It's the same everywhere."

"Just tell me what you want, Jay. Whatever you want."

He pauses, then pulls me to him, his hands tight around my arms. All the air leaves my lungs. His lips hover over mine. *Just do it,* I beg silently. If Jamison kissed me, I wouldn't be able to resist anymore. I'd give in. This forced distance would all be over.

He sets me down, as quickly as he grabbed me, and my knees give out slightly.

"I can't do it anymore," he says, more to himself than to me. "I'm sick of pretending shit doesn't bother me. I'm sick of my opinion meaning nothing. I'm sick of other people telling me what I can and cannot have."

"Jay—"

"I want it gone. Painted over. I can't look at that mural anymore."

I don't expect *that*. I thought this fight was over and lost. "Are you sure you want to do this? Last time—"

"Yes, Amoris," he says. "It's my decision. I want that fucking thing gone."

31

A MEETING COMES TO ORDER

Lori is confident this is going to work. She said so herself when Jamison and I met with her last week. She'd thought about it, and it boils down to a numbers game. The more people, the more pressure. That's what we need. And power—power helps. I said I know someone with a lot of power. Jamison was against the idea, but there is no student at school who has as much power as Ellis. He eventually conceded, and we made a plan. Having Ellis on our side should have increased our confidence in the mission.

But when we walked out of Lori's office that day, Jamison said, almost to himself, "Why is it always like this? Why do I have to risk so much just to do what's right?"

And that's when it appeared—anxiety that something was coming. Something I couldn't predict. Something unseen.

Ellis and I stand in front of the mural now, and I should feel relieved. But the whole scene feels odd.

Ellis examines the painting with a critical eye. "Holy shit," she says. "That's totally a slave ship. I can't believe I never noticed."

"I know. I had the same reaction."

"Jay's right. This definitely needs to come down."

"You're sure?" I say.

"Like there's a debate? It's an ugly fucking mural anyway. Who cares if it's painted over?"

Ellis doing the right thing should make my anxiety evaporate, but for some reason, it only makes the situation feel wrong . . . off. Because in the midst of all of this, what really bothers me is the way she casually just called him Jay. I feel nauseous.

I swallow it down and thank her for her help. Ellis agrees to bring up the issue at the next Senior Senate meeting, which is two days from now. And then she says, "*But . . .*"

I knew there would be a catch. A hook. A tentacle. I try to remain calm. "What?"

"My dad is making me go to dinner with stupid Darcy this weekend. I was going to bring Beckett, but we broke up." Ellis groans, more annoyed than heartbroken. "Will you come with me? *Please.* I can't do it alone."

The cost for my favor feels too small. Too easy. But maybe I have Ellis all wrong. Maybe I haven't given her enough credit. Maybe, just maybe, she's helping because it's the right thing to do, and Ellis wants to be on the right side. I've just painted her poorly, but I didn't used to do that. There was a time not so recently when I trusted Ellis wholeheartedly.

I agree to go to dinner. It's one night. I owe her that. I've spent too much time trying to make Ellis into what she might not be. Into the villain.

"You think this will work?" I ask her. "You think you can convince the Senate?"

"Please," she says with a callous eye roll. Then Ellis hugs me to her, like a best friend comforting her closest girlfriend. "Don't worry, Amoris. I got this."

～

Every year, the incoming senior class votes in twenty students to be on the Senior Senate, the governing body of representatives for our final year of high school. The students that are voted in host the best parties, get good grades while still getting completely plastered on the weekends, are the good-looking people with nice cars and wealthy parents. The kids who come into the café and pay for lattes with credit cards for which they'll never see a bill. It's a teen cliché, but one that's alive and well. And one I didn't give much thought to. Until now.

Of the twenty students, eighteen are White.

This is who Jamison has to put his faith in. It's no wonder he stayed quiet for so long.

When Ellis begins the meeting, I might throw up from nerves.

"Listen up, people," she says. "We have a big fucking problem in this school. And we're going to do something about it."

32

PAID IN FULL

We used to hold hands when we slept. Somehow in the middle of the night, in the darkness, my fingers would find Jamison's and hold on tight. That's all I keep thinking as he stands next to me in a room that suddenly feels filled with strangers. That's what racial situations do—make even the people we think we know completely unpredictable.

I should hold Jamison's hand. It used to be so easy. So why does it feel so hard to touch him now? When he needs me. It's amazing how freely we tangled with each other in our youth, and how complicated it feels now.

Hold his hand, Amoris. My own voice echoes in my head.

"I understand what you're saying, Ellis, but this mural *does* depict history," Paisley Phillips says, her wavy brown hair hanging down her back. "I'm not sure it's right to just erase America's dirty past. I say we leave it up as a reminder of how corrupt this country is. I mean, we are literally standing on stolen land. If you ask me, that's a bigger issue. Maybe we should start a petition to give *that* back."

Hold his hand, Amoris. It's right there, inches away.

"Let's not go down the indigenous rabbit hole, Paisley," Ellis says.

"Real sensitive, Ellis," Paisley counters.

"Just stick to the topic at hand," Ellis says.

Nash Ogden pipes up. "I disagree with Paisley. This painting clearly *celebrates* America's past. Slavery shouldn't be celebrated. That's fucked up. I say take it down."

Michelle Hernández, who's one of two kids of color in the Senate, speaks next. "While I also understand what everyone is saying, we're missing a huge point."

"And that is?" Ellis asks, annoyed.

Hold his hand, Amoris.

"This is still a piece of art," Michelle says. "We need to take that into account. Shakespeare may have been a raging racist, but we don't go around burning his books."

"Shakespeare was a racist?" Sam says. He's been hanging in the back, more observant than vocal, but he wanted to be here today. Insisted on it. To support Jamison.

"Haven't you ever read *Othello*?" Michelle chides.

"Is it on Netflix?" Sam's joke doesn't work on her.

She turns to Ellis. "Why is he here? He's not on Senate."

"Don't get off topic," Ellis says. "And I think we can all agree this isn't Shakespeare. I've seen graffiti better than this."

"Are you saying graffiti *isn't* art?" Jamison says, his first words since the meeting began. This startles everyone into silence. Now is the time to take his hand, with everyone looking in our direction. Make a statement, show everyone how I feel.

I reach out, my fingers about to find Jamison's, when Ellis gently touches his arm.

"Of course not," she says. "I shouldn't have said that, Jay. I'm sorry."

My hand falls back to my side. What is wrong with me? Ellis is making all the right moves, saying the right things, being supportive, and I'm just stuck.

"I don't see it," Tice Jennings says. "That just looks like a regular ship to me."

"You need glasses, Tice," Maeve Higgins says, pointing at the painting. "Those are totally Black people on that ship."

"But if none of us has ever noticed this before," Tice says, "is it that big a deal?"

"The *bigger* problem is that no one has noticed it," Nash says. "What does that say about us?"

"And just because *you've* never noticed doesn't mean it isn't wrong," Paisley says. "Would you think it wasn't a big deal if you were Black?"

"I don't know," Tice says. "I'm not Black."

"Real sensitive, Tice," Paisley says, eyeing Jamison.

Tice throws his hands up. "Whatever. Take it down. I don't care."

"See, that's a problem, too," Paisley continues. "If it doesn't get them more Instagram followers, people don't care. That's the state of America. You just have to look like you support a cause. You don't actually have to do anything about it."

"Taking this mural down isn't going to solve racism," Michelle says. "You have to deconstruct the whole system. And I doubt we'll see that in our lifetime."

"But it's a start," Sam chimes in. "People said the same thing about gay marriage. Imagine if everyone just gave up? Or gave in? If we allow this mural to remain hanging in our school, we're essentially saying it's OK to represent Black people this way."

"What, accurately?" Beckett says. "Let's be for real, a lot of Black people were slaves."

Sam rolls his eyes. "You've always been small-minded, Becks."

"What's small-minded about the truth?" Beckett counters.

"First of all, call them enslaved *people*," Sam says harshly. "Second of all, generalizing and treating Black people as a collective is a huge problem. That *is* racism. We don't do that to White people."

"If we're going to argue proper historical representation," Paisley says, "we should start with the fact that this land's history goes back a lot further than colonization."

"I'm just saying, I don't see what the problem is," Beckett says. "It's a picture. Who cares?" He turns to Jamison. "Sorry, bro."

I can't take it anymore.

"He's not your *bro*," I snap at Beckett. "And he never will be. Using a condescending term of endearment to minimize the fact that you just said *you don't care* about his feelings? *That* is exactly the problem. You think you can dismiss someone's pain and then casually pat him on the back, like you're friends, which only demonstrates what an inconsiderate, narcissistic asshole you really are."

People snicker. Beckett turns a bright shade of red. I've singlehandedly brought this meeting to a standstill.

"OK," Lori says. "Let's stay on topic. One thing at a time. This is about the mural."

The Senate continues arguing, and Jamison walks away, hands balled into fits. I follow him, and soon we're alone in the hallway. Jamison paces in long strides, his gaze on the floor.

"Jay . . ." I start to say, but I stop when Jamison punches a locker, startling me.

"This is bullshit!"

"I'm sorry," I say. "I shouldn't have spoken for you. I was just so mad. And Beckett is such a dick, and it all came out before I could think any better of it."

Jamison gestures to where we came from. "They don't get it, Amoris. They just don't get it."

And he's right. Most of the people in that room just want to hear themselves talk. They don't understand the privilege they have, to debate another person's humanity. But what other choice do we have? If we want this mural taken down, this is our only option. And that only solidifies the truth of Jamison's reality.

He shakes out his hand, cringing.

"Does it hurt?" I ask.

"A little."

"Let me look at it." And finally, I take his hand in mine. I turn it over, running my fingers gently along his knuckles. "You're gonna have a bruise, but I don't think it's broken. You should ice it."

"Anything else you recommend, Doctor?"

Jamison's frustration has eased. He's staring down at me. My knees go weak, along with my resolve.

"What you said to Beckett . . ." Jamison says.

"I'm sorry. I shouldn't have spoken for you."

Jamison presses a finger to my lips. "It's the hottest thing you've ever said."

That might be my undoing. "You know, my mom always says a kiss makes the pain go away, though I'm not sure that's medically proven."

"We should probably test the theory."

I pause, to savor the moment. "Only if it's OK with the patient."

"I think I can handle it."

As I bring Jamison's hand toward my lips, my anxiety disappears. My lips barely touch his skin when Ellis comes running down the hallway.

"Jay! I need you!"

Jamison steps back, and our hands fall to our sides.

"What?" he asks.

"The Senate voted, and everyone wants the mural painted over. Lori suggested we draft a letter to Mr. O'Brien. All the Senate members agreed to sign, but I need your help with the letter. You're a way better writer than I am."

"Beckett agreed?" Jamison asks.

"Believe me, he's all bark and no bite. I should know. Now, come on. I want to get started on the letter. The sooner we get it done, the sooner that hideous thing disappears." She pulls on Jamison's arm, leading him away from me.

"Just give me a sec," he says. He turns back to me, and the anxiety is back and worse than ever.

"This is good," I say, forcing a smile. "This is what we wanted."

"It is." But he doesn't sound convinced.

"Go." I nudge him toward her.

"Jay, come *on*," Ellis urges. She wraps her arm around his as they leave.

And then it hits me. I was so naïve to think Ellis's favor wouldn't have a cost. A string attached. I just didn't realize what that string might be. Who it might be tied to. But as they walk away together, I see it clearly now.

The string is attached to Jamison.

33

THIS TOWN IS CRAZY

The café is closed for the night. Shades pulled, chairs stacked on tables. All except one table for two, which is set for an intimate meal, complete with a candle at the center and a bag of food from Nicky's Diner.

Tomorrow is Valentine's Day, and Marnie has the windows decorated in hearts and cupids. Tonight it's Friday the thirteenth, though that doesn't seem to be affecting the warm mood in the café. The smell of greasy takeout is starting to override the smell of coffee.

Marnie gave me permission to use the café after hours, and Sam has promised he'll clean everything up. Presently, he's commandeering the stereo system.

"I don't understand why you hate country music so much," Tucker says.

"It's not the music. It's what it stands for. Beer, guns, misogyny, hillbillies, and homophobes."

"Is that what you think I am? A hillbilly?" Tucker shoves his hands in his jean pockets and rolls back on the heel of his boots. He's even wearing a flannel, tucked in tonight.

Sam waves off the question. "That's just a costume."

"No, it ain't," Tucker says. "This is me."

"Get with the stereotype, Tuck," Sam says. "Gays are into Betty Who, not Dierks Bentley."

Tucker walks right up to him, their faces inches away from each other. They couldn't be more opposite—Tucker with his scruffy hair and bulky athletic body, Sam thin and delicate—and yet they make perfect sense.

"Not this gay," Tucker says. "You should know better than to judge people by how they look." He swipes Sam's phone to change the music. Sam grabs for it, but Tucker is taller and stronger, a fact he's relishing. Country music fills the café as I flip the new sign Marnie bought. One side says "Closed, Come Back Soon!" and the other says "Welcome, All Sizes, All Colors, All Cultures, All Sexes, All Beliefs, All Religions, All Ages, All Types, All People." She said she got it as a reminder to customers.

"My ears!" Sam yells. "They can't handle all this toxic masculinity! Turn it off!"

Tucker sings along, even louder. When the song ends, he says, "Serves you right, Sam. I can like whatever music I want."

Sam swipes his phone back. "Why shouldn't I judge? Hillbillies judge me."

"If no one is ever the bigger person, we all remain small-minded," Tucker says.

"What if I'm sick of being the bigger person?"

Tucker runs his hand over Sam's cheek, which instantly calms Sam. The gesture is so intimate, I turn away, wanting to give them privacy. "Then that makes me sad," Tucker says.

"Don't I deserve a break?"

"Heroes don't get breaks."

"I'm not a hero, Tuck. I'm a labelless kid who wants to love whoever he chooses."

"You're my hero," Tucker says.

"Stop trying to butter me up," Sam says, "because . . . it's working."

I turn just in time to see them kiss. Two bodies pressed closely, hands on faces, a beautiful intimacy. I can't help but watch, though it makes my chest ache, knowing I won't have that kind of intimacy tonight or tomorrow or anytime soon. But I can't forget how it feels to dissolve into another person. Nothing can satiate the desire. Close isn't enough.

I take a bus bin full of dirty dishes into the kitchen. I run my hands under the tap and then splash myself. But nothing helps when Jamison is on my mind.

Against my better judgment, I check my phone. No new texts. Jamison didn't tell me if he had plans tonight, and I didn't ask. I haven't heard from Ellis either. She's been quieter lately. Content. That should be a good sign, but I prefer vocal Ellis. Then at least I know where she stands. Silence has a way of eating at a person until madness takes over. And I'm teetering on the verge.

Dishes, I think to myself. Focus on the task. At least I know what Ellis is doing tomorrow night. I can keep an eye on her. Matt and Darcy are away on a romantic ski weekend in Utah, so Ellis is throwing an Anti-Valentine's Day party. She came up with the idea earlier this week, when she was feeling extra annoyed at Beckett and their current breakup.

"No couples allowed," she said. "It's a hook-up only party. I want to take full advantage of my newly single status. Spread the word. I don't care if the whole school comes. More people to choose from."

I said I'd make sure Jamison knew about the party.

"Oh, I already told Jay," Ellis said. "He's the one who came up with the idea for the tents."

"Tents?"

"I'm going to set up 'hook-up tents' all over the property. It's brilliant."

"Jay came up with that?" I asked.

"Why do you sound so surprised? He's a guy, not a saint. Jay wants to have a good time just as badly as everyone else."

"I didn't say he was a saint."

"No, you just treat him like one."

"What does that mean?" I asked.

"It means you hold Jay to an impossible standard, Amoris. You idolize him. Like he's some demigod from your childhood who can do no wrong. That's a lot of pressure. Turns out, he's human."

"Did he say that?"

Ellis didn't answer. She detoured back to the plans for the weekend, but her comment still eats at me. It's none of my business what Jamison talks to Ellis about. I let him go. I'm not allowed to be upset.

But every day, I feel as if I'm hovering one inch above a blade that's pointed right at my heart. One wrong move . . .

I scrub the dishes harder, my hands raw from the scalding water. I'm so focused that I don't notice Tucker until he hops up on the counter next to me.

"I'm almost done," I say, picking at dried food on a plate. "Then you'll have the place to yourself."

"You can stay if you want. There's plenty of food."

I'm not so pathetic that I need to crash Sam and Tucker's date. "Three's a crowd."

Tucker swings his legs playfully as he watches me wash dishes.

"What?" I ask.

"Nothing." But a wide smile grows on his face. I don't know if I've ever seen him so happy, and that in itself should make me feel the same.

I throw the dish towel over my shoulder and lean back on the counter to face him. "What?"

"I was just thinking about how we could have kissed at homecoming."

I roll my eyes. "You didn't want to kiss me."

"You didn't want to kiss me either. But I wouldn't have objected. It's hard to constantly look at the person you want and know you can't have them. It can make a person crazy. Crazy enough to kiss a girl when you're in love with her best friend."

I know Tucker's talking about Sam, but I can't help but think about Jamison and Ellis, kissing behind the garage. How would our lives be different today if I had just told him how I felt back then?

"I thought about ending our relationship, you know," Tucker continues, his confession surprising me. "It's not fair, what I'm putting Sam through. Most days I think he'd be better off without me."

"Tucker . . ."

"I know it's selfish. Not letting him go. But . . . I love Sam. And in this messed-up, shitty world where I have to deny my own being, shouldn't I at least get to hold on to love?"

"Yes." Of course yes.

Tucker slides off the counter. "Then why are you pushing it away?"

"What?"

Tucker gives me a sidelong glance. "Don't play dumb with me. I may not live in this town, but I know what's going on."

I go back to the dishes. "It's not the same."

"It isn't?"

"It's complicated with Jamison and me."

"Life is complicated."

"It's better this way."

"You call this better?" he asks.

"Better for some is worse for others."

"Jamison isn't better without you," Tucker insists.

"You don't know that. You don't know what I've done. I can't hurt him again."

"Like you're not hurting him now?" Tucker takes my hands. "He wants to be with you, Amoris."

"He doesn't know what he wants."

"Don't do that," Tucker says. "Stop making decisions for him. It might be a risk for me to be with Sam, but it's a risk I'm willing to take. Sam isn't allowed to rob me of that choice. Not when we're deprived of so much else."

He makes it sound so easy. And maybe it is. Maybe I've complicated this. Maybe being with Jamison is the least complicated act there is. And maybe there's a part of me that's afraid of what that means. Afraid to give in to the simplicity and utter complexity of love.

"If you're waiting for the world to be perfect before you let yourself have him, you'll die alone," Tucker says.

"I don't deserve him, Tuck," I say.

"When did love become something a person deserves? Love is a human right, not a reward for good behavior."

"But I can't be trusted. What if I hurt him again?"

"Removing yourself from the situation doesn't prove that you can be trusted, Amoris. In fact, it only reinforces that you can't. You quit when it got tough. I understand needing to take a step back, but you've done that. Do you want to spend the rest of your life punishing yourself? Who does that serve?"

"I just want to protect him," I say.

"And how's that going?" Tucker asks.

"Honestly . . ." I say. "Terribly."

"And whose fault is that?" Tucker pulls me into a hug. "You and Jamison are meant to be together. I can see it. Sam can see it. You know it. Jamison knows it. The only thing preventing it is you."

"But what if—"

Tucker stops me. "Life is unpredictable. But some risks are worth the potential fall. All you need to ask yourself is, Is Jamison worth it?"

And when I say yes, it's the most honest word I've ever uttered.

"Then what are you waiting for? Go kiss the boy you *want* to kiss instead of standing here in a dirty kitchen with some hillbilly in cowboy boots."

"You're not a hillbilly."

"So what if I am," Tucker says, "I still deserve love."

I hug him tightly. And when we pull back, I kiss him on the lips, sweet and gentle.

"Thank you," I say.

The dishes are done, and my decision is solidified. I need to see Jamison. I need to apologize. I need to tell him what an idiot I've been.

I'm almost home to Shangri-La when my phone chimes. I expect to see a text but instead find an email from Mr. O'Brien. The subject line is startling. I read the entire email. Then I run the rest of the way home. Now I need to see Jamison even more.

When I get there, his apartment is dark. I knock on the door relentlessly, hoping someone is home, but no one answers. I text Jamison.

Where r u? Need to talk.

Three dots pop up right away. But too soon they disappear. No text comes through, but I know he saw mine. Where could he be? What is he doing?

I stop myself from texting Ellis, knowing the torture of finding out they're together would be too much. I can't do it. I don't want to involve her. I just need to wait for Jamison to get home.

But as I'm on my way to my room, I halt at the sound of female voices in the kitchen. Rayne and Kaydene are talking about the email. It must have gone out to parents, too. The whole town might know about the mural by tomorrow.

"You don't look relieved," Rayne says.

"I am," Kaydene responds.

"But . . ."

"In my experience, removing something from sight doesn't fix the problem."

"Would you rather they keep it up?" Rayne asks.

"No," Kaydene says with certainty.

"You should be proud of him, Kay," Rayne says gently. "Jamison has grown into such an impressive young man."

There's a pause before Rayne speaks again.

"What is it?" she asks. I imagine her reaching across the table, putting her hand on Kaydene's.

"I was just thinking how much our lives have mirrored each other's. We had babies on the same day, at the same time no less. We're both married with two kids each. Both parents work. Middle class. And yet, your daughter was raised knowing she could be whoever she wants to be. And my son was raised knowing he'd have to prove he wasn't what other people think he is."

There's silence after that. I lean back against the wall and check my phone again. Jamison still hasn't responded. Where is he?

The back door opens, as if answering my question. *Jamison* is my first thought. But it's River.

I've hardly seen him since the police incident. He's been hiding in his room when he's home, or avoiding home altogether, going to school early to lift weights or run in the gym. I don't want to talk to him right now.

River yells after me as I walk away. "Wait, Amoris!"

"I'm done saving you, River. I don't want to listen to your whining. Go complain to someone else. You're probably drunk anyway."

"I'm not drunk. I haven't touched the stuff since that night. *Please.*"

I don't want to interrupt Kaydene and Rayne, so I pull River outside, into the backyard.

"What is it?" I ask curtly.

"Look, I just wanted to say I'm sorry."

"For what?"

"For dragging you into that situation with the cops."

"Situation? It was a little more than a situation, River. You could have been arrested. Kicked off the basketball team. Suspended from school. Or worse. I get that you're pissed at Dad, but ruining your life won't fix the problem. How could you put Rayne through that? She doesn't deserve it."

"I know," he says.

"Do you? Really? Or are you just mad you got caught?"

"No, really. I *am* sorry. For everything. For that night, and for what I said about Sam."

"Why the sudden change?" I ask, hugging my arms around my torso to stay warm. "What do you want?"

"I don't want anything."

"That's bullshit, River. Everything you do is for yourself."

"No, it's true. I just want to apologize."

"Why should I trust you? You've been a dick all year."

"I know," he says. "I just got wrapped up in it all. The parties. The drinking. The popularity."

"Oh, boo hoo. Am I supposed to feel sorry for you?"

"No. I'm just trying to explain."

"Well, sorry if I don't want to hear your shitty excuses. I don't feel bad for you, River. You have everything. You're practically high school royalty."

I start to walk away again, but River blurts out, "I was jealous!" I stop at the declaration. "You want the truth. There it is. I'm jealous."

"Of what?"

"Of what you have with Sam and Ellis and Jamison. And Mom and Dad. You fit in, Amoris. I . . . don't."

"What are you talking about? You seem to fit in pretty damn well at school."

"You and I both know that's fake bullshit. I mean *real* fitting in. Not the fake, surface shit that exists between guys. You have no idea what it feels like to be an outsider in your own family. You, Mom, Dad . . . you're so much alike. You listen to the same music. You see the world in the same way. Sometimes it feels like you speak a different language I don't even know."

"That's not true."

"It isn't? Mom didn't give me crates of albums when I was born. She didn't make me sit there and listen to song after song."

"Don't blame Mom for this."

"I'm not," River amends. "But even Dad gave you your first guitar."

"So?"

"They saw something in you, Amoris. They just put up with me. Dad's never given me anything like that."

"What about the basketball hoop?" I counter.

"I asked Mom for that," River says. "And Dad has never played with me. The best he gave me was a lock for my door when I hit puberty."

My first instinct is to say that's untrue, but when I think about it, River might be right. "Maybe that's because you don't ask Dad to play." But as the argument comes out, I know it's weightless. Chris wouldn't play even if asked.

"He just sees me as a stupid jock," River says. "I figured if that's the way my own father sees me, I'll just be the stereotype. It was better than feeling . . . alone."

"You're not alone, River."

He doesn't look at me. "Dad is ashamed of me, Amoris. That's why he doesn't come to any of my games."

"He's not ashamed of you," I say.

"How do you know?"

"Because . . . Dad loves you."

"He has an odd way of showing it."

I sit down in the garden, twinkle lights overhead, digesting what River has said. "This is all very Neil Young 'Old Man,'" I say.

"What?"

"The song 'Old Man' by Neil Young."

"See. There's that secret language." River sits next to me. "I don't know that song."

"It's really good. You should listen to it sometime."

"Even you, Amoris . . . you have your records and your guitar. But you never ask me to listen with you."

"You don't like my music."

"It's not about the music. It's about being asked. You play basketball with Jamison, but you never play with me."

I want to refute him, but it's true. I've never thought about River being an outsider because he's such an insider at school. But we're all a little bit lost.

I get the basketball and head toward the hoop at the front of the house. "Come on," I say to River. "H-O-R-S-E."

"Don't do me any favors, Amoris. I know this is just a pity move."

I toss the ball at River. He catches it with skill.

"Are you scared I'll beat you?"

"That's impossible," River says.

"Prove it."

With every shot we take, River loosens up. A smile returns to his face, and the angst he's been carrying around slowly disappears as we play basketball. We stay outside so long, I lose track of time. The game finally ends when I miss from the free-throw line.

"That's an E for me," I say.

River seems disappointed. "I saw the email from Mr. O'Brien. About the mural. That's crazy."

"There's a lot of crazy shit in this town."

A beat passes between us. "You're gonna leave, aren't you, Amoris?"

I can't bring myself to answer. He saves me from having to by tossing me the ball.

"Rematch?" River asks.

"You're on."

We play two more rounds before heading inside for the night. I don't let River see the disappointment on my face. It isn't his fault. It's been years since River and I have had this much fun together.

But Jamison still isn't home, and it's eating me alive.

34

TIME'S UP

I regret offering to work the double on Valentine's Day. Any moment I might have had to talk to Jamison is gobbled up with work. The café is busier than usual.

Louisa, Marnie, and I work tirelessly all morning, only to be slammed again later as customers need an afternoon pick-me-up. A lull finally comes as the sun sets, but due to the heavy flow of customers earlier, there are still hours of cleanup and prep for tomorrow.

By the time Marnie flips the sign to "Closed," it's nearing eight. Ellis's Anti-Valentine's Day party is underway. I check my phone. Jamison still hasn't texted. My mind instantly plays tricks on me. Terrible tricks. Torturous tricks. It takes all my might to push the doubts away and focus.

In the bathroom, I change out of my work clothes and into a fresh outfit I brought specifically for the party—tight black jeans, a cropped white T-shirt, and sneakers. I wash my face and pull my hair into a high ponytail. Louisa offers to give me a ride to the party, and I take her up on it, wanting to get there as quickly as possible.

When we pull up to Ellis's house, the large yard littered with tents, Louisa says, "This looks like Bonnaroo."

"The underage, illegal version."

"Don't do anything stupid. And call me if you need anything."

"I will. Thanks for the ride."

Louisa is right. Ellis's house looks like a camping music festival, complete with alcohol and drugs, but less music. There's something different about this party. Almost too careless. Like Ellis is no longer testing her boundaries but jumping directly over them.

Inside, the party is crawling with people. Music plays loudly from speakers hidden all around the house. Michelle, Beckett, Paisley, and a handful of other people play flip cup on the dining room table. That's nothing new, but beer puddles are leaving marks on the wood, and no one is cleaning it up.

It's stifling hot in here. Too many bodies are smashed into one place. A cloud of weed smoke lingers. At past parties, anyone smoking inside would have been kicked out. But tonight, Ellis is either too busy or too drunk to notice.

I head to the kitchen and fill a glass with water and take a deep breath. My head is cloudy. My long day is coming back to bite me, blurring my eyes with fatigue.

Someone grabs my arm, and I turn, hoping it's Jamison.

"This is insane," Sam says. When someone bumps into him, he steadies himself on the counter.

"Apparently, everyone hates Valentine's Day," Tucker adds, "and they're taking it out on Ellis's house."

Sam giggles. "Ellis has never had so many friends."

There are stains on the carpet, food scattered everywhere.

"If this is friendship, count me out," I say. "Matt is going to kill Ellis."

"I think that's the point," Tucker says.

Her dad doesn't deserve this. All for falling in love. I thought Ellis was doing OK. All her actions pointed to that, until tonight. Ellis always does this when she's mad. She's destructive. Breaks everything around her, hoping someone will notice, but she never cleans up her own messes. She leaves that to everyone else.

As if by instinct, I start dealing with the mess in the kitchen. Not for Ellis, but for Matt. He shouldn't have to deal with Ellis's juvenile antics and a ruined house just because he wants to remarry. Tucker nailed it—love is a human right, not a reward for good behavior.

Sam follows me, holding a garbage bag as I collect the empty cups that have accumulated on the counter. I wipe down the large center island and hide a few breakable items in the cabinets. Where is Ellis?

I refill my water glass and lean back against the counter. It's just so hot in here.

"So . . ." Tucker says quietly. "I can barely stand the suspense. Did you talk to Jamison?"

I take a sip of water, trying to clear my head. Yesterday feels so far away already.

"I got distracted," I say.

"Well, now's your chance." Tucker nudges me and discreetly points at Jamison, who's just walked into the kitchen, a red plastic cup in his hands. A flood of adrenaline washes over me.

I stand up straight, heart in my throat.

But when he looks at me, I can't read his expression. Is he surprised, relieved, disappointed?

Jamison approaches us, but before he can get a word out, I blurt, "You didn't text me back!"

Those aren't the words I was hoping to say. I wanted to say, *Forgive me. Can we start again? I've been an idiot. Kiss me.* But instead, an accusation.

"Amoris, we need to—" But before Jamison can get the rest of the sentence out, Ellis appears, draping herself on his arm.

"You're here!" Ellis says, looking at me, her words slurring. "Just in time! Jay and I were just celebrating!"

"Celebrating what?" I ask.

"The mural, silly. We're the perfect team." Ellis clinks her plastic cup on Jamison's. "Cheers to our victory!" She drinks a long gulp. "Come on, Jay. You have to drink after a toast. That's the rule."

He sets his cup down, releasing himself from Ellis's grasp. "I need some air," he says, and disappears into the crowd again.

Ellis wobbles on her feet. "What's his problem? There's always one pooper at the party. You'd think he'd be a little more grateful after what I did."

"What *you* did?" I ask.

Ellis looks at me with drunken, vacant eyes. "Whatever." She stumbles away, pushing herself through the crowd, but her footing is sloppy, and she trips, falling to the hardwood floor. She goes down with a thud, hitting her elbow and then her head. And yet with a house full of "friends," no one comes to her aid. They just stare as she whines in pain.

Sam, Tucker, and I push people out of the way, pick up Ellis, and set her down on a chair in the kitchen. I inspect her head for blood. It's clean, though a bump has already formed.

"We need ice," I say to Sam.

As he races around the kitchen searching for a dish towel, I check Ellis for any other damage. She sits limply in the chair, her dark-brown hair hanging long over her face and shoulders.

"Why is it always me who gets hurt?" she says, seriously. Her drunken slur is gone. "Dead mom. Nonexistent dad. Why can't it be *you* for once? With your perfect house and your perfect family."

I can't believe what I'm hearing. It must be the booze talking. Ellis closes her eyes, her body going loose again.

Sam and Tucker get her to bed. Tucker fills a glass of water and sets it on her nightstand, next to her lavender oil. I stand back, struggling to muster an ounce of caring.

"What if she has a concussion?" Sam asks. "Or pukes in her sleep?"

"Why don't we stay and watch her for a while." Tucker climbs into bed next to Ellis. He pats the seat next to him. Before I leave, I remind them that the bedroom door locks. At least some love will be celebrated tonight.

But me—I need to get out of this house.

Outside, the air is cool, a refreshing change from the oppressive heat inside. I take a breath, clearing my lungs, and start walking around the yard. I want to go home, crawl into bed, and erase this night from my memory, but one thing keeps me here—Jamison. If he's around, I want to find him.

Voices come from the tents, giggles and rustling. The longer I look, the more I worry that Jamison left already. Why does it feel like he's avoiding me? What just happened in there? The way Ellis hung herself on him—the casual nature of it—it was like she was laying a claim. A desperate feeling settles in my stomach. And the longer I search, the more I lose hope.

I decide to circle the property one last time. My feet hurt, and I can't shake the cloudiness in my head. The long day has worn me out. I'm about to give up and call Louisa for a ride, convinced my mission is useless, when I see him.

Jamison wanders aimlessly around the yard. I can tell by his expression that he's deep in thought.

Here's the problem with Ellis. It dawns on me as I watch Jamison. She believes she needs to stake a claim to what she deserves because life has been unfair to her. But Jamison isn't a possession to be won or lost. Power over another just proves how scared and desperate a person is. That's Ellis. And that's pathetic.

I close the distance between me and Jamison, and before he can protest, before I let another word pass between us, I press myself against him, my lips finding his in the darkness. My arms circle his neck, pulling him down to me. *I need you,* is all I can think. *I need you like I need air.* Why have I been so stupid?

Jamison pulls back. "Amoris, what are you—"

But I'm done talking. Words won't suffice. Action will. Love is a verb.

I bury Jamison's words with my lips, parting his mouth so I can taste him. I actually feel his body release the tension he's carrying. His arms reach around me, hugging me tightly, his hands grasping at my back. No more letting go.

But we're too exposed out here. Even in the dark of night, I don't want to risk anyone interrupting us. I pull Jamison toward a nearby tent, listening for the sound of people inside, but it's empty.

"In here," I say, unzipping the tent while not letting go of Jamison's hand. The air is slightly warmer inside. I pull Jamison to me again, gently finding the ground beneath us, the floor covered in blankets. Lips meet lips. Hands grasp. I peel my shirt off. Jamison does the same. For a moment, I think I smell a hint of lavender on his clothes, but then it's gone. My pause is brief, and then skin meets skin. Bare chest to bare chest.

All the questions that have overwhelmed me for months disappear. Jamison's hips press into mine. I can't get close enough. And I can't stop. Not when this feels so good.

"We don't have to do this," Jamison says.

"I *want* to do this."

"It's not safe. I don't have anything." He puts space between us. "It's too risky. We need to stop."

I remember the gift Lori unknowingly gave me weeks ago, during one of our sessions, and take one of the condoms out of my purse.

Our clothes fall in a pile on the ground. I feel untouchable, removed from the world outside. I didn't know I could feel this way, completely euphoric and yet wholly grounded. Familiar and yet unknown.

Jamison's lips stay on my skin. He covers me like a safe shelter. Our frenzy slows, the minutes growing longer, more intense. I don't want this to end. This night, this moment, this feeling. How quickly everything can change.

When it does inevitably end, Jamison and I lie curled into each other, wrapped in blankets.

"Amoris," he whispers.

I prop myself up to look at him. "Yeah?"

"You know I love you, right?"

My heart might flutter right out of my chest. "Yeah. I know."

"Good." He rolls over, pinning me beneath him. "Don't ever forget it."

It would take a catastrophe, I think.

His lips meet mine, and it begins again.

35

ROOM FOR TWO

Terry is behind the counter at Black and Read when I show up to return his copy of *On the Road.*

"Done already?" he asks. "Did you find what you were looking for?" His long gray hair hangs in two braids over his shoulders. He wears a multicolored tie-dye T-shirt that might be forty years old. Terry looks like he always does, and yet today, everything feels completely different.

"Turns out, I don't want to read about someone else's adventure," I say.

Terry comes out from behind the counter as I aimlessly wander the aisles of records, dragging my hands across the tops of the bins.

"Heading into the listening booth?" Terry asks.

"No need." I'm not looking to escape today. It feels too good to be me.

Terry leans on a bin of records. "So . . . what happens now?"

"I'm just going to let my life be for a while."

"Let it be. Wisest words Paul McCartney ever wrote," Terry says. "Well, the booth is here for you when you need it."

"Thanks, Terry." I don't tell him that I think I've outgrown the booth. I need to find a new way of dealing with my problems. My life is changing, and I might not be in Alder Creek for much longer. But I don't want to alarm Terry. I still have a few months of high school left.

Back at Shangri-La, Chris is in the driveway, cleaning the Airstream, music blasting from its speakers. Canvases and paints and brushes litter the lawn, and the van is barely recognizable. The inside has been totally redone. The old burners in the minikitchen have been replaced with new ones, and it no longer smells like a backed-up toilet. Chris has even replaced the upholstery on the chairs. Now he's vacuuming inside, his head bobbing along to the song.

"Leaving for an art show?" I ask.

He turns the music down and the vacuum off. "I'm taking a short trip to Denver in a few days. Meeting with a guy. I won't be gone long. Where were you?"

"Black and Read."

"Terry's going to miss you next year."

"Who said I'm going anywhere?"

Chris looks at me knowingly. "You're one of the only people in this town who speaks Terry's language," he says.

"You know . . ." I lean on the hood of the van. "Maybe it's time to teach River how to speak music."

"Do you think he'd like that?" Chris asks. "He's never seemed interested before."

"I think River might surprise you."

Chris shrugs but considers the idea. "If you say so."

"I do." A bucket of soapy water sits next to the car, and there's still time to burn before Jamison gets home from the café, so I grab the bucket. "Need some help?"

Chris turns the music back up, and he and I continue to clean the Airstream. The unusually warm day makes the air feel light and hopeful.

It's amazing what a little heat does for the psyche. I clean to the beat, running the sponge in rhythmic waves and circles.

When the Airstream is polished, and the inside more organized than I've ever seen, Chris leaves to help Rayne with dinner.

I lie in the bed at the back of the van, the sun pouring through the polished windows, the radio now on low, a satisfied feeling settled in my chest. It's been years since I've been in this van. Lying here now, the memories of so many trips to Kansas City practically come alive. The anticipation of driving hours across multiple states, the games we played to occupy the time, the cooler Rayne would pack full of food, the excitement of just knowing I would see Jamison for an entire month.

"Room in here for two?" Jamison sticks his head in, as if on cue. I scoot over on the bed, smelling the sweetness of the café on his clothes. "This is more comfortable than I thought," he says, though his legs can't stretch out completely.

"It's a good size for two people," I say.

Jamison edges closer to me. "Two people who really like each other."

"It's a good thing I like you, Jay."

"Is that all?"

I haven't said the words yet. I don't know how to explain to him that I'm worried I don't deserve it. I don't deserve to love him. Tucker said love isn't something a person deserves, it's a human right, but actually believing that, for myself, is hard.

Jamison kisses me. And as the day turns to night, and darkness falls on the Airstream, hiding us from the world, that kiss grows into more, just as I'd hoped. There's time to say the words. We're together now, and that's all that matters.

36

A FRESH COAT OF PAINT

Ellis is absent on Monday, but that's not the first thing I notice when I walk into school. It's the smell of paint. Jamison notices it at the same time.

The mural is gone. The wall freshly painted in white. We haven't talked about the email Mr. O'Brien sent, about how Jamison feels, about Ellis and her part in all of this. The past two days have been like a dream, but reality has come knocking.

"He made himself look like a hero," Jamison says. Without him saying it, I know he's talking about Mr. O'Brien. And Jamison is right. The email was as hopeful as it was discouraging.

> In instances like this, one mustn't wait for others to do what's right, one must act. And for that reason, I made the executive decision to remove the mural without waiting for the approval of the school board. It felt like the right thing to do. I accept the consequences of my actions should the school board decide that any are necessary.

I'm so proud of our Senior Senate for rallying behind this cause, making their voices heard, and demanding a safer environment for all students at Alder Creek High. They are the true great leaders of tomorrow.

As principal of this school, I value Alder Creek's diversity, celebrate its many colors, and commit to serving all who walk through our doors.

The letter was a pretty lie. Like a con artist finally telling the truth, Mr. O'Brien congratulated the efforts of the student body while simultaneously negating any resistance he had to the mural coming down in the first place. The letter felt false, contrived, a load of bullshit fed to the school community so we'll keep believing we're better people than we actually are.

Jamison examines the painted wall.

"I wonder what they'll put in its place," I say.

"The Senior Senate is in charge of coming up with a plan," he says. "But they seem more concerned with prom. I have a feeling the wall will stay blank for a while."

"Does that bother you?"

"What bothers me more is that I'm not surprised everyone at school has moved on to easier topics, like prom."

I take Jamison's hand in mine. "At least the mural's gone."

He looks at me earnestly. "Do you think whatever is painted next will make a bit of difference?"

And I don't have an answer.

~

By Wednesday I still haven't heard from Ellis. A creeping fear has trailed me since the party. I've managed to push it away, but the longer I don't hear from her, the more worried I get.

I ask Sam if he's had any contact with her, but he hasn't either.

If Ellis needs space, I can give her that. Everyone needs room to breathe.

That's what I've told myself for the past few days, but I had forgotten. Forgotten . . . or didn't want to remember. Ellis doesn't like "space." She doesn't like time to herself. If she did, she wouldn't have spent so many nights in eighth grade sneaking out of my house, meeting boys who were too old for her, boys who didn't care about taking advantage of her. Ellis just wanted human touch, to be held, noticed, seen.

When she moved into my room, I offered to sleep on the floor so she could have the whole bed, thinking she might want to cry without me next to her. But Ellis said no.

"Don't leave me, Amoris. I'll be swallowed up by all this space." What she meant was she would be swallowed up by all that grief. So I climbed in and slept next to her, night after night.

It takes four days, but Ellis finally emerges. I was naïve to think she was resting, recovering, recuperating. That's not Ellis. Even her silence is active. It means something. Silence wants to be seen, too.

Jamison and I are standing in the hallway by his locker when Lori approaches us. I think nothing of it. I've spent so much time in her office this year, I assume she's bringing me another brochure or wants to talk about the mural. But the expression on her face gives me pause. More than pause. It bottoms out my stomach.

Then she turns to Jamison next to me, his hand in mine, and that panic rises in my throat.

"Mr. O'Brien needs to see you, Jamison." Lori sounds different. Formal.

"Why?"

"I think it's better if we don't discuss this in the hallway."

"I'm coming," I say.

"This is a private matter, Amoris." Again, Lori sounds too serious.

"She's coming," Jamison insists.

Lori acquiesces, giving us both a small sad grin, and we follow her down the hallway. I won't let go of Jamison's hand. No matter what happens. I've learned my lesson.

I've never actually been in Mr. O'Brien's office. It's different than I imagined. He has hundreds of pictures of students collaged on one of the walls, like a timeline of his career, from twenty years back when he was a teacher all the way until now. His multiple degrees are framed and hung, too. It's the office of a person who loves his job. He even has a "World's Best Teacher" mug on his desk next to a picture of him and his husband.

Mr. O'Brien gestures to the chair across from his desk. "Jamison, please take a seat."

"I'd rather stand if that's all right with you."

"Suit yourself." Mr. O'Brien sits behind his desk.

I try to relax. Maybe Mr. O'Brien wants to apologize. But then why is Lori here? Her presence makes me uncomfortable. It's so . . . official.

"Jamison, a student has filed a report against you," Mr. O'Brien says. "And we've opened an investigation into the allegations."

I'm slow to process what this means.

"What are the allegations?" Jamison asks, his voice steady.

"I've been in contact with your former high school," Mr. O'Brien replies. "Is there anything you'd like to tell me about your time there?"

"What are the allegations?" Jamison asks again.

"Now isn't the time to keep secrets, Jamison. If there is anything we should know, I suggest you reveal it. Did you have many girlfriends?"

"What does that have to do with anything?" Jamison replies.

"Maybe an arrest record we should know about?"

This is absurd. I glare at Lori, but she looks as helpless as I feel. "That's ridiculous," I manage to utter. "Jay has never been arrested."

"Are you sure about that, Amoris?" Mr. O'Brien asks. "How well do you really know him?"

"That's none of your business," Jamison interjects.

Mr. O'Brien's eyes drift down to our interlaced hands. "Where were you on Saturday night, Jamison?"

"Again, none of your business." Jamison holds his back straight. I can feel his tension radiating through his palm.

"When it affects the students in my school, it *is* my business."

"You still haven't told me what the allegations are," Jamison says.

"Would you say you have a history of violence?" Mr. O'Brien asks.

"What?" I snap.

"You seem prone to outbursts, Jamison. Is that something you have a hard time controlling?"

"This is crazy!" I turn toward Lori. "Can't you fix this?"

But Lori seems caught, restrained by some invisible, bureaucratic rope.

Mr. O'Brien continues evenly. "A student reported that you punched a locker."

Jamison and I glance at the fading bruises on his knuckles. Someone must have been eavesdropping on us in the hallway during the Senior Senate meeting.

"I can explain that," I say.

"Amoris, have you considered that this boy isn't who you think he is?" I hate the sound of my name coming out of his mouth. Mr. O'Brien stands up from his chair but stays behind the desk, as if to protect himself. "I've seen your temper firsthand, Jamison. If you're willing to act violently toward authority, there's no telling what you'll do to a person your own age. This is a serious matter. It's your senior year. You're courting colleges, and they won't want to admit someone who's potentially a threat to other students."

"I didn't do anything to anyone," Jamison says, his voice still calm.

"I saw the bruises on her arm." Mr. O'Brien acts like he's commenting on the weather, not ruining Jamison's life in a sentence.

"Her," Jamison says.

Mr. O'Brien's confidence seems to weaken for the first time. He sits back down and gestures toward Lori. "As mandatory reporters, Ms. Collins and I are obligated to take this issue to the police," he says. "And though you are eighteen and technically an adult, we have informed your mother of the situation."

Words keep falling out of the principal's mouth, but they all run together into a mumbled mess. All I keep hearing is the word *her*.

Her. Her. Her.

Ellis.

We're ushered out of Mr. O'Brien's office, still clutching each other's hand. Are the police on the way to the high school right now? Why is Jamison guilty until proven innocent? Isn't this what he has been trying to tell me all year? This is his reality. To the world, he's a thief before a customer, a thug before a scholar, a criminal before a person.

"Listen to me," Lori says. "Don't panic. The best thing you can do is hold tight and lie low. Don't make any rash decisions. We'll figure this out."

Does that mean she's on our side? What authority does she really have? Compared to the police? She walks off, too quickly, and Jamison and I are left alone.

"It's over," Jamison says, more to himself than to me. "I'll never get into Western now. You heard what he said. I bet he already contacted the university. My chances are ruined. He's had it out for me ever since that day with the mural."

"Ellis did this," I say. "We can't let this happen. We can't let her win."

"It's over," he says again.

"It's not over. This is bullshit! We can fight it, Jay."

Jamison doesn't speak. He's still. Barely flickering.

"We can't stay silent. This isn't fair," I plead. "You didn't do anything."

Jamison refuses to speak, and a new possibility begins to dawn on me. Maybe I've been naïve, seeing only what I wanted to see. I've been known to do that. I think of the text message I sent him. His nonresponse. The feeling like he was avoiding me. The smell of lavender on his clothes. I thought it was my imagination.

His hand falls from mine. I don't know who lets go first.

"Did something happen?" I ask.

"I didn't hurt her, if that's what you're asking."

But it's not. I know Jamison didn't hurt her. I saw her fall like a ragdoll at the party. I saw her bash her elbow on the ground. I saw her hit her head.

"You never texted me back, Jay."

"I was busy . . . thinking. It slipped my mind."

"Busy. With who?"

"No one," he says.

But I don't feel like he's telling me the truth. I can see it in his face. There's only one reason Ellis would lower herself to this level of vengeance. "Did you . . ." I can't get the words out of my mouth.

Jamison doesn't deny it. I think I might be sick. I stumble back, the ground unsteady beneath me. Jamison catches me, his words coming quickly.

"It happened so fast. One minute we were in her room, drinking, talking about the mural coming down, and the next minute Ellis is kissing me."

"Did you kiss her back?"

When Jamison fumbles, I get my answer. Images from our night together come back to me, this time in a new light.

"But we . . ." I can barely say it. "You were with her, before you were with me?"

"It wasn't like that," Jamison says. "It was only for a second. One delusional second. I was confused and frustrated. You broke it off with us, Amoris. For all I knew, we were never going to be together. I had no idea you'd changed your mind."

"But you kissed *Ellis*."

"It could have been anyone! I was just sick of being alone. But then I came to my senses and pushed her away. There is nothing about Ellis that I want."

"Why didn't you tell me?"

"You didn't give me a chance."

"So, this is all my fault?" I ask.

"No," Jamison says quickly. "I just didn't want to ruin . . . us. Over a kiss that means absolutely nothing."

My whole body feels like sinking to the floor, just collapsing right here. "What else aren't you telling me?"

Jamison looks at me. "What's that supposed to mean? Are you doubting me?"

I don't know what I mean. All I know is that I'm confused and hurt. Nothing makes sense, not Mr. O'Brien, not Jamison, not even Lori. It feels like lies swirl all around me. I'm not thinking clearly. I can't decipher what I know is true and what is a figment of my imagination.

"I can't believe this . . ." Jamison starts to walk away.

"Wait. Don't leave." I attempt to grab his arm.

"Why? It's over. There's nothing left for me here."

I slump against the wall, worried that my legs might give out. That the world might crumble around me. I try to breathe evenly, try to calm my heart. But I'm all alone, standing in the hallway, frozen in place, the pervasive smell of fresh paint around me.

37

LOVE HAS LIMBS

I cut class immediately. I couldn't care less about any potential punishment. When I get home, Chris is packing groceries into the Airstream for his trip to Denver. I ask if I can go with him. Lori's advice was to stay calm and lie low. What better way than to get out of Alder Creek for a few days? I can get my head together. Chris must be able to see the desperation in my eyes, because he says yes without any questions. I suggest we take River, too. He needs a break as much as I do.

As I pack a quick bag, throwing clothes and toiletries together without care, I can't stop thinking about Jamison kissing Ellis. This is eighth grade all over again. I thought we were past this, but all the sadness, all the hurt, all the loneliness from that defining moment are back with a vengeance. It feels like I'm trapped. I just want to get out of town.

We pick River up from basketball practice.

"The Denver Nuggets are at home this week," Chris says. "I thought we might catch a game."

"You know who the Denver Nuggets are?" River seems skeptical.

"Sure," Chris says. "They won the Super Bowl last year."

We cross the Alder Creek town line, River in the front seat, Chris listening intently as River explains the rules of basketball, and me lying in the bed in the back. I watch as Alder Creek fades from sight, but the smell of Jamison is locked in the sheets I lie on. He is everywhere I go. I can run. I can hide. I can ignore. But he will always come back to me.

I roll over and close my eyes. I wish this all would go away, but I know that's impossible. That's not how problems work. You have to dig to the center, pull the problem out by its root, and plant a new beginning.

But what happens if there's nothing left to plant after you've destroyed it all?

~

We go to Red Rocks, shop at REI, ride bikes along the Cherry Creek Trail. River hasn't looked this happy in years. Chris hasn't gone this long without weed in years. And me . . . I haven't been this miserable in years. None of what we do distracts me like I need. The ghost of my unfinished conversation with Jamison follows me.

River sleeps next to me at night, squeezing me up against the side of the Airstream uncomfortably. Chris takes the floor, on a camping mattress. Three days into the road trip and I miss my bed. Why was I so hasty to leave? Why is my instinct *always* to run? I should have stayed. Banged on Jamison's door until he had to talk to me.

But what would I say? Did he like kissing Ellis? Was it different from that last time? Was he thinking about her while we were hooking up? If it could have been anyone, why not Michelle or Paisley or some no-name junior with a nice smile? Why *Ellis*?

My stomach turns sour at the thought of her. How could she do this? And not just the kiss, but to be so vengeful as to report Jamison for a crime he didn't commit. That is truly fucked up. She has harmed him in a life-altering way. Jamison must be in so much pain right now, and I'm in a van with two smelly guys when I should be with him. Why did I think this was a good idea? We can't fix anything from miles apart.

But I'm stuck here for one more day. Chris has a meeting in the city, and then he's taking River to a basketball game, leaving me to my own devices.

I can't take the claustrophobia any longer. I crawl out of the Airstream for some fresh air. The night is cold and clear. I lean back against the van, pulling in deep breaths. I've been in and out of sleep all night.

I've written numerous texts to Jamison but erased them all. What is the right thing to say? I left when he needed me, but he walked away, too. He lied, but I lied, too, when I said I wanted just to be friends.

The Airstream door opens, and River crawls out quietly.

"Hey," he whispers, wrapping his arms around his torso.

"It's cold. Go back inside."

"I can handle it." River's body has morphed so much over the past few years. A short, skinny kid has grown into the strong, tall teenager before me now. His muscles pull his T-shirt tight. I watched enough of his football games to know the strength locked in his body. River could knock a person over with a simple push. "What's going on, Amoris?"

"Nothing."

"Don't lie. We might not spend time together like we used to, but I still know when something's wrong."

The past few days have been exhausting, holding myself together. As I tell River all that's happened with Jamison and Mr. O'Brien and Ellis, tears roll down my cheeks in uncontrolled streams.

"That's complete bullshit," River says. "Jamison wouldn't hurt a fly. He's a . . . nerd."

Leave it to River to draw that conclusion. "Nerds can hurt people, too." I hiccup and attempt to stifle the crying.

"I just mean . . . Jay is smart," River clarifies. "He's calculated. Goal oriented. He always has been. Everything he does serves a purpose. He wouldn't do anything to jeopardize his future."

I slump back on the car. I've never seen anyone want anything as badly as Jamison wants to go to Western University. He upended his whole life for the chance to go to that school. It was his first concern when we left Mr. O'Brien's office. To work so hard, and to suddenly feel threatened that it might be taken away? It's heartbreaking. And I should be with him right now to help mend it.

"Do you want to go home?" River asks.

It was stupid to run away. Just when I think I'm strong, I lose my grip and I'm self-destructive, falling again.

But this trip isn't just about me. We can't leave. Chris has his meeting, and he and River have their basketball game. I can't steal that from them when I see how much this trip has repaired their relationship. They're both trying so hard.

It's just one more night. And then I'll be home.

"Let's go back to bed," I say.

"You know what Mom would say."

"Nothing gets fixed in the dark," I answer knowingly. "Wait for the sun to rise. You'll see better then."

River and I climb back into the Airstream, and I try again to sleep. I'm done letting Jamison down, but one more night won't be the end of us. Jamison will be there when I get back. And then we'll make it right.

～

I roam the aisles of a local bookstore, coffee in hand, wasting time while River and Chris are at the Nuggets game. My hand runs over book after book. This would be Jamison's heaven. I can see him spending hours in here, pulling books from the shelf, reading quietly, telling me about the authors, his enthusiasm at a peak.

241

I wish he was here with me. Why didn't we do this together? Why did we stay locked in Alder Creek, like there wasn't a gigantic world out there for us to roam?

Just being around books, smelling them, touching them, makes me feel closer to Jamison. Love has limbs after all.

After the Tattered Cover, I pass an antique shop. Sitting in the window is an old-fashioned typewriter. I buy it, intending to give it to Jamison the moment I get back. Not as an apology—I owe him more than that—but as the simple extension of a love limb.

The drive back to Alder Creek is grueling. It seems to take longer getting home than it did getting to Denver. The minute you want something back, you realize just how far you've run from it.

Rayne waits in the driveway to welcome us. I leap out of the Airstream, racing toward Jamison's duplex, but she stops me.

"Someone's been waiting for you in your room," Rayne says knowingly.

It's Jamison. I know it. I rush up the stairs, hearing music playing from my bedroom, and fling open the door.

The smell of lavender greets me instead.

I become angrier than I've ever been before. "Get out, Ellis."

"Please, Amoris. I came to explain."

"I don't want your excuses, Ellis. I want you to leave."

"I told Mr. O'Brien the truth," she says. OK, now I'm listening. "The very same day. I couldn't live with myself."

"So it was about you and how *you* were feeling."

"It wasn't like that," she pleads. "I never intended to get Jamison in trouble."

"You want me to believe it happened by accident?"

"Just listen to me," she says. "I had gone to see Ms. Collins first."

"Lori? You don't even like her."

"I thought she could help me, like she's helped you. I was upset. I needed someone to talk to."

"Upset because Jamison rejected you."

"Upset because I was losing everything and everyone!"

"You're so selfish, Ellis. So because you were losing everything, you had to do the same to Jamison."

"Lori noticed the bruises. I didn't say anything!"

"Now you're blaming Lori?"

"No," Ellis amends. "She started asking me how I got them. I couldn't really remember. I told her I had thrown a party. Gotten pretty drunk. And the last thing I remember is Jamison pushing me."

"When you were kissing him," I state. "He pushed you away to make you stop."

Ellis squeezes her eyes closed. "Lori started asking me more questions. I told her I had a pretty bad bump on my head."

"That you got from falling over drunk."

"I don't remember that! All I remember is being alone in my room with Jamison, and the next thing I know I woke up with a nasty bruise on my arm and a bump on my head."

"So you decided to blame Jay?"

"You know how huge he is! Is it that big a stretch that he could hurt someone, even if it was unintentional?"

"He would never hurt you!" I yell. "Just because he's strong doesn't mean he's a monster! Do you think the same thing about River? He's stronger than Jamison and just as tall!" Ellis holds her head in her hands, but I have no sympathy for her. "No, you wouldn't."

Ellis keeps explaining herself frantically. "I ran into Sam later that day, and he told me what happened. He told me how I fell in the kitchen. I swear, I went straight to Mr. O'Brien and told him the truth." She steps closer to me, tears about to fall down her cheeks. "I didn't mean for any of this to happen. It was a mistake. A misunderstanding. But I've made it right. I told the truth, and they dropped the allegations against Jay."

"Stop calling him that." I move away from her, but my room feels claustrophobic. How did I live in this small space for so long? And with Ellis here, too?

"Please, Amoris. I want to fix this." Ellis's tone is desperate. Pleading. Pathetic.

"Get out."

"What?"

"Get out of my room. You're not welcome here."

"You can't be serious," Ellis says. "We can work this out. We've been best friends forever. Isn't our friendship more important than a simple mistake?"

"No. Because it's not a simple mistake." It's her. Ellis. She is the cancer. She needs to be pulled out of my life by the roots, or else she'll continue to wheedle her way into everything, infecting all of us with her poison.

"I can't lose you. I can't lose this." Ellis frantically looks around the room as if it's her own. "You're my only family."

"No, we're not. You have your own family. Stop using mine."

"I can't believe you're saying this," she says.

How many times have I said exactly that this year? Maybe it's time we all start to believe it. We're lying *to* ourselves, *about* ourselves. And it's high time we take action.

"I said get out."

Ellis leaves slowly, as if I might change my mind. But I don't.

"Please," she whimpers. "I'm so sorry."

But apologies only go so far. It's our actions that truly speak for us. I let her leave. I let her go. And when all that's left of her in my room is the smell of lavender, I don't feel bad. She did this to herself.

It's the pretty lies, only the pretty lies, that destroy us the most.

38

HOPE ISN'T THE ANSWER

Jamison is gone.

I stand at the open door, looking into the empty apartment. Not a pillow or a picture or a book remains. Rayne told me, but I had to see it for myself. Kaydene and Jamison went back to Kansas City two days ago. In one afternoon, they packed everything and started the long drive home. I couldn't understand what Rayne was telling me. Jamison just up and left? What about school? It's only February. But she said Kaydene was going to enroll him in the online school she works for.

"Why didn't you warn me they were leaving? I would have come home."

Rayne was apologetic. "Kaydene asked me not to. It only would have made their decision harder. I had to honor that. For my friend."

Having been betrayed by a friend, I couldn't get mad at Rayne. She loves Kaydene.

"He's not coming back."

"No," Rayne answered in a whisper.

I walk into the apartment now, hoping Jamison has left me a clue. A crumb to follow. A piece of hope that tells me this isn't the end.

But I find nothing. Not a bag of popcorn, a T-shirt, a picture. I had hoped he'd left his copy of *Harry Potter*, as a sign that it's not over. But it's not here.

I sit on the couch and pull my knees to my chest, no blanket to keep me warm. The apartment is cold, but I refuse to turn on the heat. I rely on my memories for warmth. I can see Jamison across from me, laptop propped on his knees, typing while I watch.

You know I love you.

It almost doesn't feel real, the memory of my body pressed to Jamison's. My face hovering above his, the anticipation of lips on lips, skin on skin. It's as if I made it all up.

~

Weeks pass. I work, and when I'm not at the café, I'm locked in the listening booth at Black and Read. But unlike all the previous therapy sessions, no music plays. Instead, I sit in the silence and read all the books Jamison wrote about in his letters. Books I should have read years ago when he asked me to. New stories. New perspectives. I imagine Jamison sitting next to me, pointing at the words on the page.

See, Amoris? This is what I've been telling you.

I make Terry order more copies. These are books that Jamison would want in the store.

For eighteen years, I've told myself the same story, played my life to a single soundtrack instead of seeking out the hidden tunes, the suppressed melodies, the ignored truths.

Ellis attempts to rectify our friendship, but I shoot her down. Even Sam rejects her after he finds out what she did. Even after so many years of friendship, I don't feel her absence. I only feel the loss of Jamison.

"I miss him," Sam says. We're sitting outside the café and drinking lattes. Spring is in full bloom. I don't ask if he's heard from Jamison, if they text or talk on the phone. If Sam said yes, it would break my heart. If he said no, guilt might eat me alive.

I thought about calling Jamison. At first I told myself to give him time. A week or two. Maybe a month. But I was waiting for a reason. A moment that would bring us back together, that would heal us. I knew what it was. I just needed to be patient. I watched the mail every day for letters addressed to Jamison or Kaydene, their legal residence still in Alder Creek. And every day, hope grew a little more.

When it finally arrives, I don't care what laws I'm breaking as I open the letter.

Rayne finds me in the garden, where the tulips are just beginning to poke up through the ground. The letter sits limply on my lap.

"He didn't get in," I say.

Western University is sorry to inform Jamison that they cannot admit him to the Creative Writing College. The number of applicants has risen significantly in recent years, making the program highly competitive. The admissions committee takes many factors into account, including the writing sample, high school transcript, personal and extracurricular credentials, and recommendations.

Rayne sits next to me. "Kaydene told me a few days ago. Jamison got an email from the university."

My one last hope was that he'd get in, so at least his time in Alder Creek wouldn't have been a complete disaster. But Jamison predicted what would happen, standing in the hallway after he'd been accused of hurting Ellis. He said it was over. That Mr. O'Brien would see to it. Ever since their interaction about the mural, it felt like Mr. O'Brien didn't like Jamison. Or didn't like being challenged by him. Jamison was a threat to his power and intelligence because Jamison saw something Mr. O'Brien couldn't. Will Jamison ever know for sure that Mr. O'Brien is the reason he didn't get in? I wish life made people like Mr. O'Brien accountable, but the truth is that the system protects him.

"He must be so disappointed," I whisper. And I wasn't there for him. I couldn't hold his hand or kiss him to ease the pain. "What's he gonna do now, Mom?"

"Kaydene said he's going to KU in the fall. He still plans to major in English."

"His backup school," I say. But Jamison deserved better than that. He deserved his dream school.

The white wall, where the mural once was, remains empty. The Senior Senate meant to decide on what would replace it, but they became occupied with other important events. Senior Skip Day goes off without a hitch. Everyone meets down by the river in bathing suits, carrying coolers of booze stolen from parents' liquor cabinets. And the wall remains white. The Senior Prank takes weeks to orchestrate, but Beckett and his friends eventually collect as many chickens as they can and release them into the hallways during first period. And the wall remains white. And then, there's prom. Ellis picks the location, a fancy hotel tucked back in the mountains where the wealthy come to get married in the summer. And the wall remains white.

Sam and I go to prom together. It's a formality, really, checking a box. Everyone goes to their senior prom. But Sam and I are miserable, neither of us with the one we love. Tucker plans to meet us at Sam's house later. Sam has promised him a *Friday Night Lights* marathon.

I should bail and leave them alone, but the one bright spot in my life is seeing the two of them together. Tucker's finally starting to talk about coming out. He has a date picked and everything. September twenty-first. "The beginning of a new season," he said.

As Sam and I walk out of the hotel, an hour after arriving at the dance, Ellis chases after us. She's wearing a long black lacy dress. I wonder who she went shopping with. She's been spending a lot of time with Michelle.

"My dad is getting married in two weeks," Ellis says. "Right after graduation."

"Good for him." I start to walk away. I know perfectly well when Matt is getting married. We're all invited to the wedding. But I'll be gone by then.

"I've been thinking about my mom a lot lately." Ellis focuses on her feet, shifting her weight back and forth. "Would she be proud of me? Would she think I look like her? I've been thinking about that day, too. About the day she died. You were there, Amoris. You never left my side." She pauses to take a breath. "I guess what I'm trying to say is . . . I need you. I don't think I can get through my dad's wedding without you. Please. Don't make me do this on my own."

Ellis's pleas have a familiar ring. Her pain tugs at my heart, for the girl she was, for the mom she lost. A piece of Ellis died along with her mom. And for that, my heart will always hold sympathy for her.

But it isn't my job to hold her together, or fill that void, or pacify her bad behavior.

"You're on your own, Ellis."

She doesn't need me. She'll be just fine. The world loves people like Ellis. She was winning the moment she was born, though she'll never admit it. People like her never do.

~

When Zach shows up at my house a few days later, standing nervously at the front door, I'm caught off guard. I haven't heard from him since Christmas, and I've avoided his social media.

We sit in the backyard. The garden is blooming, the green returning to the trees. Twinkle lights tangle in the fresh branches.

Before he can speak, I say, "I'm sorry, Zach. For everything."

He looks different. Older. More mature. "Don't be," he says. "It all worked out in the end. I'm actually here to thank you. You dumping me was the best thing that could have happened." He tells me all about college. His classes. His friends. His girlfriend. "It's strange how some of the worst moments in life tend to be the most transformative. Sucks at the time, but in the end . . ."

"I'm glad everything worked out," I say.

"You OK?" he asks.

I don't know why it's Zach, of all people, that I finally crumble in front of, but I do. I unload the entire story while he listens intently, and by the time I'm done, some of the pressure in my chest has lifted.

"It's not over," Zach says, placing a comforting hand on my thigh.

"How can you say that? I ruined everything."

"Because I've been in his place," Zach says.

It's not fair that the hope I need right now comes from Zach, but I take it thankfully, knowing hope won't stick around forever. I better grab ahold while it's here. He asks if he'll see me around Alder Creek this summer, and when I don't respond, Zach smiles and says, "I thought so."

~

It's my last day of high school. Exams are done. My locker is empty. My time at Alder Creek is coming to a close.

Lori's office is cleaner than usual, her pamphlets and picture frames packed in boxes.

"You're leaving," I say as I take a seat in my usual chair.

"After what happened with Jamison . . . I can't work for a principal like that."

"So Mr. O'Brien wins?"

"I think we all lose in this case."

It feels that way, I think to myself.

"You still haven't heard from Jamison?" Lori asks.

"No." I slump back in the chair. "I keep thinking he went through all of that, and for what? Nothing came of it. Sure, the mural is gone, but now the wall is just . . . blank, like none of it ever happened. And nobody seems to care."

"I feel the same way some days." Lori picks up the last remaining picture from her desk and comes to sit in front of me. "Did I ever tell you that I used to work as a counselor at this summer camp in Michigan? It was a place for teenagers who felt . . . lost. The thing is, Amoris, what I've come to realize is that most of us are quick to lose hope. The world just seems so bad sometimes. Hope feels . . . impossible. But I've seen what can happen when people find it again."

"What happens?"

"The world changes," she says. "I'm not saying hope is an answer, I'm just saying it's a start." She puts the picture in a box and seals the box with packing tape. "Have you decided what you're going to do once you graduate?"

"I have."

Lori offers me a warm smile. "The world is waiting for you, Amoris Westmore. Get out of line, and don't waste its time."

~

That night I write Jamison a letter. The letter I should have written nearly four years ago.

It's a simple sentence—a subject, its object, and most importantly, the verb.

I love you.

The truth, finally, among all those pretty lies.

39

HOME SWEET HOME

The Airstream is packed and sitting in the driveway. It's mine now. All those months Chris was fixing it up, he was working on it for me. A belated birthday present, he and Rayne called it. He no longer needs the van to travel to art shows, since he's staying in Alder Creek and turning his studio into an art gallery. With our houses in a prime location on Main Street, he thinks it will do well. Apparently the meeting he had in Denver was with an investor interested in his work. A partner, really. Someone to run the business side of the gallery, giving Chris the freedom to create. He even moved back into Rayne's bedroom. He still works next door, where he's finishing a new collection of Alder Creek–inspired paintings, but he spends his nights eating dinner with us, and washing dishes, and giving Rayne the massages she deserves.

The smell of summer blows through my bedroom window as I carry the last crates of records into River's room.

"Are you sure you want to give these to me?" he asks.

"Just try not to scratch them."

"I can't promise anything." River flips through the records a little too vigorously. I slap his hand.

"Easy . . ." I say. But then I stop myself from dishing out a diatribe on the importance of these records. The legacy.

"Where should I start?" he asks.

"That's for you to figure out, River. Just remember, there's a lot of music out there. Don't get too caught up in these."

"It's gonna be so weird around here without you. And now that Dad lives in the house . . ."

Rayne sticks her head into River's room. Her usual earthy scent follows her. "You better get going if you're going to make it to Santa Fe tonight."

River and I hug. "Does this mean I can take over your room?" he asks.

I shove him away. "You're such an ass."

I take one final look through my bedroom, making sure I have everything I need. But the truth is, I can't take most of this stuff with me. It feels better to leave it behind.

Chris appears at my door, holding a large envelope in his hand. "Mail just came. This one's for you. Glad it got here before you left."

I recognize Jamison's handwriting instantly and grab the envelope from my dad.

"I'll leave you alone." Chris closes the bedroom door behind him.

I open it carefully, nervous. I unfold the pages, worry and hope tangling together, not knowing what I'll find. I sit down on the bed and just stare at what's in my hands.

The story. *His* story.

I take in each word slowly. I turn every page carefully, like a vinyl record I don't want to scratch. And when I'm done, and my tears have dried, I tuck his story neatly into my bag, leave my bedroom, and close the door behind me.

I don't know if Jamison can forgive me for running away when he needed me. I don't know what will happen to us, or if he'll wait for me. I don't expect him to. Jamison's life goes on. He won't give up on his dream. Of that, I'm sure.

This is just the beginning. I have a long journey ahead of me, and a lot to see of this world. But I think I know where it ends. As I drive away from Shangri-La—the Airstream packed, my guitar in the back—I grasp the steering wheel tightly. Next to me sits the typewriter. I don't know when I'll be back, or even if I'll return to Alder Creek.

But here's the simple truth—all this time, I've known where I belong. Turns out, it isn't the place I love most. It's a person.

With the windows rolled down, I can smell summer in Kansas City already.

AUTHOR'S NOTE

My editor first told me of the mural at his daughter's school, and the subsequent movement to have it removed, at a casual dinner in New Orleans the night before a book event. I had no idea then that this story would change my life. I should have known better. Storytelling has always had, and will always have, the power to incite change. But that night I returned to my hotel, belly full, and slept soundly.

It wasn't until months later that a residual question plagued me: *What character would I have played in the story?* Would I have been as brave as my editor's daughter, standing up to the principal of her school when he refused to address the issue? Would I have been the librarian who gathered the students together in thoughtful reflection that resulted in big action? Would I have been a parent who heard of the mural secondhand and gave it little thought? Would I have been the principal who refused to take it down, who threw up bureaucratic walls to hide his White fragility?

The answer was simply . . . I don't know.

I believe the best fiction touches on our deep, intrinsic, universal humanity. To create from that knowledge, I must be mercilessly honest, with myself and my characters. If I wanted to find my answer, I needed to dig deeper, search my soul, open my ears, shut my mouth, see through the eyes of others, and pull the truth out by its deep-seated roots. And then I needed to write about it.

The answer to my question is this book.

But important answers *must* lead to more questions. On the subject of racism, no single answer absolves us from constant and vigilant work. There is no typing THE END and walking away. There is no putting down the pen. There is no homework pass, or gold star, or A-plus grade that tells the world, "This person has mastered antiracism." There is only work.

This book is not a pardon from the role that I have played in perpetuating racism. It is, instead, a doorway. And now that I've stepped through, I cannot, will not, must not go back. This story is just one step forward in a lifetime of repeatedly asking myself, Who am I and what is my role in perpetuating or dismantling racism?

I must be mercilessly honest with myself. Every day. Every hour. Every minute.

We all must be.

To all my teen readers—you have the power to change the world. I know this because I was changed by one of you.

ACKNOWLEDGMENTS

First, I'd like to acknowledge all the writers, activists, artists, journalists, scholars, and others who have written and spoken out on the topic of racism and antiracism. They were (and are) my guides and teachers through this journey. Without their work, this book would not exist. Too often, they are overlooked or silenced when they should be supported, amplified, championed.

My agent, Renee Nyen, as always, I thank you for sticking by my side, picking up my phone calls, and listening to my sometimes harebrained ideas with enthusiasm.

My editor, Jason Kirk, as always, thank you for picking me out of a pile of manuscripts years ago—a moment that would change both our lives. It has been an honor creating art with you.

This book would not be nearly what it is without the feedback of readers who offered their honesty and intelligence. Jamal, Tyler, Maggie, Lashanna, Ami, Coco, Mitchell, Muriel, Kai, Chris—you are in the pages of this novel. I hope I've reflected you well.

A special thank-you to Brittany Russell, my publicist and feedback reader, whose narrative commentary on this book was editorial level. You are a gift.

To everyone at Skyscape who championed this novel, thank you for believing in my story, and for believing in me.

And to the reader, as always—I am your biggest fan. Thank you for joining me on this journey.

READING GROUP GUIDE

1. The book begins with Amoris describing her grandmother's legacy. We learn about her grandmother's café and the vinyl records she left behind. Why do you think the author chose to start the book with this theme of legacy? How does Amoris's perspective develop over the course of the book, and why?

2. Amoris's family life is a little unusual in that her artist father lives in the duplex next door and goes on long trips without the family. Meanwhile, her mother, a holistic body healer, seems at ease with the situation. How does Amoris rationalize and understand her parents' relationship, and how does that understanding evolve over time? How does River's point of view affect his own understanding? How is Jamison's family different from Amoris's? Why do you think the author chose this difference?

3. Amoris tells the reader how specific smells remind her of her family and friends, but Jamison "doesn't have a smell. His scent would be impossible to capture. What he is to me isn't easily replicated and bottled." Why do you think she feels this way?

4. The novel is set in Alder Creek, described as a place counterculture thrived before it became a tourist destination.

Why do you think the author chose this fictionalized town as the setting? When does Amoris first realize her hometown may not be as it seems?

5. How do Sam and Jamison relate to each other? What does Jamison find in their friendship that he doesn't have with Amoris?

6. How does race factor into Amoris and Jamison's budding romantic relationship? How does their childhood relationship influence their interactions as teenagers? Do you think it's possible for Jamison and Amoris to have an honest, true relationship after everything they've been through, and why?

7. In the wake of her mother dying, Ellis spends a lot of time with Amoris and her family. What responsibility does Amoris have in supporting Ellis through her grief? How does their friendship evolve during the novel? Does their relationship represent a greater societal conflict, and how so?

8. When Amoris first looks at the problematic mural, she doesn't see Jamison's issue. Why do you think the mural was ignored by the student body prior to Jamison's arrival? Why does it take Amoris a moment to see the slave ship?

9. Jamison is a voracious reader and loves to write. He moves to Alder Creek so he can apply for a competitive writing program. Why is writing so important to Jamison? What do the computer and typewriter symbolize to him?

10. Toward the end of the novel, Amoris stops going to Black and Read to listen to records in the music booth, and she begins reading instead. Why does she think of music differently now? What does Amoris's taste in music (or lack thereof) symbolize throughout the novel?

11. What do you think the author meant by the title *Only the Pretty Lies*? Why do pretty lies "destroy us the most"?

ABOUT THE AUTHOR

Photo © 2018 Kate Testerman Photography

Rebekah Crane is the author of several critically acclaimed young adult novels, including *Postcards for a Songbird*, *The Infinite Pieces of Us*, *The Upside of Falling Down*, *The Odds of Loving Grover Cleveland*, *Aspen*, and *Playing Nice*. A former high school English teacher, Crane now lives in the foothills of the Rocky Mountains, where the altitude only enhances the writing experience. For more information about the author and her works visit www.rebekahcrane.com.